DYING
FALL

PATRICIA HALL

St. Martin's Press
New York

PARK RIDGE
PUBLIC
LIBRARY

DYING FALL. Copyright © 1994 by Patricia Hall.
All rights reserved. Printed in the United States of
America. No part of this book may be used or
reproduced in any manner whatsoever without written
permission except in the case of brief quotations
embodied in critical articles or reviews.
For information, address St. Martin's Press,
175 Fifth Avenue, New York, N.Y. 10010.

Library of Congress Cataloging-in-Publication Data

Hall, Patricia.
Dying fall / Patricia Hall.
    p.   cm.
"A Thomas Dunne book."
ISBN 0-312-13477-0
1. Women journalists—England—Yorkshire—Fiction.
2. Police—England—Yorkshire—Fiction.
3. Yorkshire (England)—Fiction.   I. Title.
PR6058.A46D9   1995
823'.914—dc20   95-22686   CIP

First published in Great Britain by
Little, Brown and Company

First U.S. Edition: September 1995
10 9 8 7 6 5 4 3 2 1

Dying Fall

Dying Fall

ONE

'JACKO, THERE'S A PIG CAR on your left coming up Salter Street.' The black-clad figure on the roof spoke quietly but urgently into his mobile phone. In the broad street a hundred feet below Jacko slammed on the handbrake of the stolen Astra and expertly skidded the car round in a 180 degree arc. He accelerated hard away from the approaching police car with tyres smoking and engine screaming. His passenger, even smaller and slighter than Jacko himself, crowed with delight.

'Go on, Jacko,' the younger boy cried, eyes alight. 'They'll not catch us now!'

With a grunt of satisfaction muffled by his balaclava the man on the roof moved like a shadow to the other side of the building to watch the white Astra circle the block of flats, weaving between shifting knots of people on the street corners, their excited murmur clearly audible even at roof level. It was the third night of joy-riding he had organised around the Heights, the four massive blocks of flats which loomed on the western slopes above Bradfield town centre, and so far the reckless display of turbo-power had gone as smoothly as the others.

The stolen cars had attracted large crowds onto the streets and the walkways of the flats. The weather was hot and humid, thunder storms had been rumbling around the hills to the west for days, and whole families, some carrying fractious babes in arms, had spilled from their stifling living-rooms to watch the free entertainment.

Until now, the police had been slow to appear and when they did they were easily tracked from the flat roof of

1

Bronte House. A word of warning from above allowed the stolen cars to disappear at will into the maze of older streets that linked the Heights to the town centre in the valley below.

So far the joy-riders, audacious by conviction as much as necessity, had easily evaded their more cautious pursuers. Close encounters with crushed metal and mangled flesh had been too close and too frequent to allow the pursuing drivers to follow their reckless quarry with total dedication. There was no reason yet to suppose that tonight would be any different.

'Jacko, he's turned down Oldfield. You're in the clear now.'

Jacko's reply was no more than an unintelligible stutter through the distorting crackle of static, but the man on the roof saw the Astra turn again in response and head back up to the broad strip of road between the flats and some old people's bungalows where the main displays took place. As he watched he heard a faint clatter behind him and, scanning the darkly orange urban sky with a vaguely stirring anxiety, he spotted the flashing navigation lights of a helicopter thirty seconds before it switched on its searchlight and began sweeping the entire estate with a dazzling funnel of light.

With a muttered curse the man ducked into the deep shadow beneath the roof's low parapet and froze, knowing that the sharp eyes in the helicopter would be focused on the road below rather than the cluttered roof of the block as it was swept momentarily by the unforgiving beam.

The racket of the helicopter engine became deafening as it moved up fast and hovered directly overhead, sending clouds of dust and debris swirling around the roof and flapping curtains wildly at the open windows below. The light swung apparently at random before focusing and holding steady. Cautiously the man raised his head above the parapet to see the Astra fixed in the searchlight's harsh eye as it accelerated away again down the road beneath. The scream of its engine was drowned out now by the overwhelming clatter of the chopper's engine.

'Get out of there, Jacko,' the watcher shouted into his transmitter, feeling the first hint of alarm as events began to slip away from his control. This time there was no reply. Helplessly he watched as the white car swung round the corner of the flats, still gaining speed, into a side road where several patrol cars and a heavy police van, its windows covered with thick wire mesh, had quietly assembled under cover of the noisy diversion above.

In a panda car, parked unobtrusively behind the vans, PC Alan Davies, a green anorak over his uniform shirt indicating that he was, technically at least, off duty, sat hunched over the steering wheel as if in pain. He cursed virulently and monotonously under his breath as he watched three years' patient hard work destroyed.

In the Astra the boy driver, eyes dilated in concentration and fear, saw the approaching police vehicles too late. He attempted another handbrake turn, but the road was too narrow and he lost control, realising in that final moment of terror that he was not, after all, immortal.

The off-side wheels mounted the kerb at speed, flipping the car over into a series of crunching somersaults which hurled debris from lights, bumpers, doors and wings across the roadway. It ended abruptly when what remained of the car slammed engine first into the solid concrete doorway of Bronte House.

The searchlight was unmoving now, fixed like the eye of God on the wreckage-strewn street and the still spinning wheels of the upturned car as residents and police shook themselves out of shock and began to run in a light as harsh as a desert noon. There was little enough left that was recognisable as a car or of the two boys who had been in it. The wreckage enfolded crumpled forms like some bizarre man-trap of metal and glass, making it impossible for even the most willing hands to free the lifeless bodies.

'Fire brigade and ambulance!' said the police inspector who had taken charge of the abortive rescue sharply to the sergeant at his side. He eyed the gathering crowd of spectators warily. 'And get this lot back,' he said. 'In fact clear the street or we'll have a riot on our hands.'

3

As outstretched uniformed arms urged the murmuring spectators away a single shrill voice cried out in anguish.

'They were only kids, you bastards.' There was a low growl of agreement from the crowd but the spark needed to ignite their fury did not come, and gradually they allowed themselves to be shepherded from the scene.

The inspector, grim-faced, picked up the mobile telephone from where it lay in the gutter, smashed and sticky with blood, and caught his sergeant's eye across the wreckage in a moment of shared pity and anger.

'Blasted kids,' the sergeant muttered. 'Blasted stupid kids.' Behind him PC Alan Davies echoed the sentiment more obscenely and turned back to his panda car in disgust, his jacket collar turned up to conceal his face.

High above, the man in black watched, his eyes glittering behind the balaclava mask, as the crowd was chivvied away and police reinforcements and a fire tender arrived, blue lights flashing. Imperceptibly the helicopter gained height and began to edge away.

'Shit,' the watcher said viciously before slipping silently towards the door at the head of the lift shaft and disappearing from sight.

It was lunch-time the next day before Laura Ackroyd could get away from her office at the Bradfield Gazette to visit her grandmother who lived alone at the heart of the Heights. The newsroom had been frantic all morning as the paper had handled its biggest story for months. Ted Grant, the Gazette's irascible editor, had prowled between the desks, reading computer screens over people's shoulders, as piece by piece the events of the previous night had been put together and assembled into some sort of coherence for the readers of the first edition.

This was a bit different from the usual lowlights of an August newsroom, Laura thought wearily, pushing a damp strand of red hair away from her eyes as she sent her own contribution to the front page to be set in type by the computer system. The adrenalin high on which she had been carried along all morning ebbed away, leaving

4

her drained and irritable.

The paper's staple summer diet of exam results and the occasional holiday accident was normally dealt with easily enough by a depleted staff. A three-night orgy of car crime at the Heights, culminating in last night's tragedy, was something else, and Laura, diverted from her less hectic world of the feature pages, had been drafted in at eight o'clock that morning to augment the inexperienced team of young reporters who were all Grant had to call on that day.

Grant, with one eye on the clock, came towards her between the rows of work-stations. He was a heavy, grizzled figure, shirt-sleeves rolled up, belly slackly rolling over his belt, a cigarette as always drooping from one corner of his mouth, his colour high enough under stress to make his colleagues debate, some with more hope than concern, the state of his blood pressure. He'd risk a green eye-shade if he thought he could get away with it, Laura thought with momentary amusement, though without affection, as he approached.

She had, not without some spectacular battles, learned to live with Grant's one-man war against the incursions of the management accountants, computer experts and graduate trainees into the craft he had been apprenticed to as a sixteen-year-old copy boy. Grant was one of a dying breed and deeply resented it. He still bashed out his editorials on an arthritic typewriter which lived under a green dust-cover in the corner of his office, leaving it to subordinates to put his staccato prose into the computer system. He filed his used papers on a lethal spike and long and often regretted the passing of the noisy telex machines and the clatter and smell of hot metal.

For his part, he had learned to tolerate Laura better than he did most of his staff on the simple grounds that although she was female she had at least been born and bred in the borough and had chosen, unlike so many of her contemporaries, to remain there.

'I think that's as far as we can take it today,' he said. 'I've done my leader, so that about wraps it up.'

5

'Who've you blamed this time?' Laura asked, a touch sourly. 'The parents, the teachers or the police?'

'The whole bloody lot of them,' Ted said. 'They get not a scrap of discipline, these kids.'

'They should bring back National Service,' Laura said solemnly. 'That would get them off the streets.'

Grant looked at her for a moment with his pale watery blue eyes, well aware he was being sent up, but the explosion Laura half expected did not come. Instead he glanced down at the proof of the front page which lay across Laura's desk, his eyes on the blurred school photographs of the two teenagers who had died in the stolen car.

'It's a bloody tragic waste,' he said, and Laura felt herself more reproved than she would have been if she had succeeded in provoking his anger by her levity. She distractedly ran a hand through her hair and gave Grant a wan smile.

'It gets to you when it's kids,' she said quietly.

'Tomorrow,' Grant said aggressively, as if anxious to cover up his momentary lapse into sentiment. 'Brief Jane and Howard, will you? We'll want interviews with the families, anything else they can get up there this afternoon. See if you can find the headmaster of St Marks, though I expect he's staying in some bloody *gite* in the Dordogne. That's where the lads went to school, apparently.'

'If they every went,' Laura said. There were no jobs for school-leavers who bore the stigma of living on the Heights. At Wuthering, as the Heights had been irreverently dubbed by the locals, Laura knew the children were quickly demoralised and spun away, out of school and out of control, almost before they were tall enough to see over the steering wheels of the stolen cars which were their single passion in life.

'Aye, well, see what you can dig up,' Ted Grant said dismissively. 'I'm away to the Lamb. I need a jar. Are you coming?'

Laura shook her head. The court Ted Grant conducted

each lunch-time and early evening in the Gazette's local, the Lamb and Flag, was not one she had felt much like frequenting recently and this lunch-time she had other urgent business.

'I want to go and see my grandmother,' she said. 'I'll see what I can pick up while I'm up there.'

Grant nodded. He had spent most of his working life in Bradfield, apart from a brief and not very productive foray to Fleet Street in its fading days, and he knew Joyce Ackroyd, Laura's formidable grandmother, as a force to be reckoned with.

'You want to get her off that bloody estate,' Grant said grimly. 'At her age.'

'Fat chance,' Laura said. 'She'll come down from the Heights in a box, and not before.'

'Aye, well, you're an obstinate bloody family,' Grant said. 'Must be the red hair.'

'It won't be so bad if the council gets funds for this plan to renovate the flats,' Laura said placatingly. Wuthering's squat, 1960s blocks suffered all the woes that prefabricated concrete construction and inadequate insulation were heir to. Named, with literary insouciance, after the Yorkshire authors Bronte, Holtby, Priestley and Bentley, they threatened to collapse into complete dereliction.

'Last I heard, that had all fallen through,' Grant growled. 'That's not for public consumption yet,' he added hastily, and Laura wondered which councillor had let the indiscretion fall over a Scotch in Grant's second favourite haunt, the bar of the Clarendon Hotel. It had to be someone sufficiently influential to persuade Ted that his scoop was not for revealing yet.

She drove thoughtfully out of town and up the hill to the Heights, taking a detour around the blocks, which appeared deserted now apart from a few gangs of boys desultorily kicking balls about on the dusty grass surrounding them. It was another insufferably hot day, the sun hidden behind a bronze haze of high cloud, the temperature climbing into the eighties, as it had for weeks now. There was not a breath of wind to cut the almost

7

palpable humidity.

Down the narrow road at the side of the flats a couple of uniformed policemen loitered in the entrance to Bronte. The debris had been cleared overnight, and the only evidence of the fatal smash was the boarded-up glass panels in the doors and a smear of black rubber on the tarmac where the car had spun out of control. A large oily stain near the doors had been sprinkled with sand. But the dead boys had their memorial. Right at the policemen's feet a small pyramid of flowers was already growing on the spot where they had died. Wuthering, she knew, would not deny its own.

Laura drove her white Beetle slowly past the scene and turned left into the main thoroughfare. Here the tyre marks were more extensive, making a tarry track which swung in a tight semi-circle where the constant handbrake turns had excited the spectators for three hot and sticky nights, patterns of defiance indelibly marked on the roadway.

She parked outside the row of bungalows immediately facing Bronte and Holtby, tiny refuges for the elderly built in the hope of enabling grandparents to be close to their young families but in reality, more often than not, leaving the old stranded under the lowering shadow of the blocks from which their own children and grandchildren had long fled.

Joyce Ackroyd was standing at her door waiting as Laura locked the car and opened the wicket gate on its retaining strand of thick wire. She was a small, wiry woman, white-haired and neatly dressed in a blue and white spotted blouse and navy skirt, and leaning heavily on a stick. Laura kissed her on the cheek, aware of the papery thinness of the old woman's skin and the faint smell of scented soap. She took her arm as she turned back into the house.

'You've not got that awful walking-frame thing today,' Laura said as Joyce moved painfully slowly into her living-room.

'I thought I might try growing ivy up it in the back yard,'

Joyce said dryly. Laura grinned, knowing how hard Joyce was fighting the arthritis which was crippling her.

'Take it easy,' she said. The older woman sank thankfully into her favourite armchair and Laura noticed a new fragility around her eyes, the skin darker than it should be and slightly puffy.

'You had another bad night,' she said. Joyce nodded grimly.

'No one got much sleep,' she said. 'I've asked a couple of the lasses from Bronte to come over for a chat a bit later on. I think you should talk to them for the Gazette.'

Laura glanced at her watch. After her early start she reckoned she could get away with an extended lunch-hour, just so long as she took something of interest back to the office with her later.

'I wanted to ask you about something different,' she said, switching her mind to a preoccupation which had been thrust aside by the events at the Heights. She rooted in her capacious shoulder-bag and brought out a sheaf of cuttings from the Gazette.

'Do you remember this murder?' she asked, handing the cuttings to Joyce who quickly skimmed through them.

'Aye, well, no one up here's likely to forget it,' she said at length, her expression sombre. 'There's nowt upsets folk like a child being killed. It must have been just after I moved in here. All of ten years ago. What of it?'

'You know that television programme, "Case Re-opened"?'

Her grandmother nodded. She still took a keen interest in the world although it was the best part of that decade since she had had to retire from her beloved council.

'They rang me the other night from London,' Laura said. 'They want some local research done into the case. The mother of the lad who was convicted is still swearing blind that he's innocent. She contacted the programme because they're proposing to commit him to Broadmoor or somewhere because they reckon he's gone completely off his head. She reckons if that happens she'll never get him out.'

9

'I dare say she's right,' Joyce said grimly. 'If he's not mad already they'll soon make sure he is.' She flicked through the newspaper cuttings again. 'I thought he confessed,' she said.

'He seems to have confessed and then retracted it in court. But they found him guilty just the same. There was some other circumstantial evidence,' Laura said.

'Aye, I remember now. It was a nasty business.' Joyce glanced at the cuttings again, her eyes thoughtful. 'Little Tracy Miller,' she said softly. 'You can imagine the panic it caused up here, mothers not letting their youngsters out of their sight. And then they arrested her own brother.'

'Stepbrother,' Laura said. 'The boy was no relation, a child of a different partnership. The couple both had children from previous marriages.'

'They called him her brother, all the same,' Joyce said grimly. 'At the time it seemed just as bad as if he'd been a blood relation. There were a lot of folk over there who'd have killed him if they'd got their hands on him.' She nodded through her open window at the looming bulk of Bronte House. 'These TV people, they really think he might not have done it after all?'

Laura shrugged.

'I don't really know what they think,' she said. 'All they've asked me to do is have a preliminary talk to the girl's father and the boy's mother. They split up of course when Stephen was arrested. Do you remember the policeman on the case – Chief Inspector Huddleston?'

Joyce laughed delightedly, her face suddenly animated at the memory of old battles.

'Once met, never forgotten, is Harry Huddleston. You'll get short shrift from him if you go suggesting he made a mistake. He's retired now, of course.'

'Yes, I remember. Michael Thackeray's predecessor,' Laura said half to herself, and immediately felt irritated that she had so readily called to mind the name of a man she was trying to forget. She felt Joyce's interest quicken but refused to meet her eyes, a faint blush colouring her pale red-head's skin and momentarily blotting out her freckles. She let her hair fall forward for a moment to mask her face while she regained her composure.

'He won't have gone far, won't Inspector Huddleston,' Joyce said, restraining her intense curiosity. She knew better than to try to push Laura into confidences she was not prepared to offer willingly. 'He'll not stray from the county cricket grounds at this time of the year, if I remember Harry. Almost as fanatical as your father was, before the sun went to his head.' It was a source of never-to-be-forgotten resentment that Joyce's only son Jack, Laura's father, had sold out his local business interests and retired to Portugal well before the latest recession had begun to bite.

'There was a big splash when he retired, wasn't there?' Laura recalled. 'After that drugs case? We did a big profile of him on the leader page. The funny thing is I can't remember much about the Tracy Miller murder.' She glanced at the dates on the cuttings. 'It all happened the year I was abroad after university.'

'Thought he was God's gift to law and order, did Harry Huddleston,' her grandmother said. 'He'll not thank you for casting doubt on one of his greatest triumphs.'

'Well, he can stay on the back burner for a while. They don't want me to stir up the police unless there seems to be something in what the mother's saying. But if Harry Huddleston's triumphantly locked up the wrong person, he'll have to put up with it,' Laura said unsympathetically. 'It won't be the first time the police have got it wrong, will it? They were making quite a habit of it ten years ago.'

'It'll be the last straw up here,' Joyce said thoughtfully. 'There's no love lost now with the joy-riding, with one half saying the police did too little too late and the other half saying interfering at all last night was tantamount to murder.'

'Is that what they're saying?' Laura asked. 'I need to talk to people about last night. I need some reactions.'

As if on cue, the doorbell rang.

'That'll be Linda and Jackie,' Joyce said. 'You can talk to them for a start.'

11

Laura waved her grandmother back into her chair and went to answer the door herself. She let in two young women in brightly patterned shorts and baggy tee-shirts, followed by two straw-headed children in swimming costumes, their fair skin pink and blotchy from too much sun. When they were all packed into the bungalow's tiny sitting-room Joyce introduced Linda Smith, a plump, pregnant and pasty-faced woman in her mid-twenties, Laura guessed, although she could have been younger, and Jackie Sullivan, taller, thinner, and some years older, with a face prematurely aging. Jackie puffed incessantly on a cigarette as she talked, her hands shaking slightly and her eyes darting this way and that as she tried to control her children.

'Linda and Jackie are trying to set up some sort of action group amongst the tenants,' Joyce said by way of introduction across the children's noisy squabbling. 'My granddaughter works for the Gazette,' she explained. 'She can give you some useful publicity.'

The two women looked Laura over with a chilly, neutral gaze and Laura felt, not for the first time, the gulf that separated her from so many women her age or less. With these two and the sticky, fractious children, she was embarrassingly aware of her well-cut cotton suit, her clear skin and eyes, her tanned legs and her glossy hair. At thirty, she knew that she was blooming while these two younger women were already aging, worn down by a poverty which she might resent as much as they did, but could not alleviate.

'We're starting a campaign to get families with kids off Wuthering,' Jackie Sullivan said, stubbing out her cigarette without apology in one of Joyce's plant-pots and lighting another immediately. 'We've had it up to here – noise, filth, bits of kids on the game, drugs in the effing school playground, little lasses molested, squatters! And now this joy-riding—' She broke off in a fit of dry coughing, too overcome to continue.

'We've not had a wink of sleep for three nights,' Linda said, her voice cracked with tiredness. 'We're getting up a petition to t'town 'all. They're talking about renovating the flats. Well, sod that, we say. We want them bloody well pulled down.'

'Look at them two,' Jackie came back, jumping out of her chair to prevent the little girl, hardly more than a toddler, from pushing Joyce's pot-plants out of the open window. She slapped a bare arm and a leg and dumped both children unceremoniously onto the settee where they grizzled tiredly, rubbing grubby hands into bleary eyes. 'You watch Chrissie, Darren, can't you? You're old enough,' she said to the older child, a stocky boy of about six, who responded with a sulky glare.

'What sort of future is there here for them?' she asked bitterly, turning back to Laura and Joyce. 'They'll be careering round in stolen cars before they're out of primary school if summat isn't done about this place.'

Laura glanced at her grandmother, who was sitting bolt upright in her chair, hands clenched in her lap, her eyes filled with pain and frustration. Around the time Laura herself had been born, the Heights had been Joyce's other pride and joy, a monument to the brave new world she had hoped to build, a monument now collapsing in shoddy dilapidation and bitter recrimination.

Laura pulled her tape-recorder out of her bag.

'Tell me what you're planning to do, who you're planning to talk to,' she said quietly, defusing the tension. 'I'll write something for tomorrow's paper.'

TWO

'WHAT'S THE POINT OF COMMUNITY coppers if the community coppers don't know what the hell's going on?' Detective Chief Inspector Michael Thackeray asked the head of Bradfield CID irritably as they walked back to their offices. They had just sat impotently through a management meeting called to discuss what was already openly being described around the station as the previous night's major cock-up. Detective Superintendent Jack Longley shrugged wearily.

'Don't ask me, lad. Just thank your lucky stars crime prevention's not our brief, that's all. Those yobbos are running rings round us on Wuthering.' He opened the door of his office and nodded the younger man inside. Thackeray crossed the room and stood by the window, looking bleakly down at the dusty, littered pavements of the town hall square outside, where a good proportion of Bradfield's unemployed gathered regularly in strictly segregated ethnic groups. The modernistic fountain, which might have provided a little relief as the temperature climbed inexorably to a heavy, humid eighty degrees, had been turned off to save water.

There are times, Thackeray thought, when I would give my right arm for a drink. He was a tall man, with the build of a rugby forward, a role he had taken enthusiastically when younger, and without the paunchiness that many of his beer-swilling colleagues acquired as they approached middle age. Dark-haired and blue-eyed, he did not look like a Yorkshireman, although he had been born less than thirty miles from Bradfield. He was the son of a hill

14

farmer in a Pennine village close enough in distance but remote from the town in culture when he had roamed the moors as a boy.

'I don't envy the uniformed lads trying to keep the lid on that lot,' he said turning back to his boss with the faintest look of interrogation in his eyes. He did not think that he had been invited in simply to continue the inconclusive discussion of how to handle the outbreak of near-anarchy on the Heights which had begun in the divisional commander's office. Crime management was the name of the game these days and Bradfield division, for all its liaison meetings and strategic plans, was not currently managing it very well.

Longley waved Thackeray to a seat.

'Keep me closely informed about what young Mower turns up, will you?' he said. The fact that CID had a detective sergeant on the estate incognito, looking into allegations of child molestation, had led to some sharp exchanges between Longley and Chief Superintendent Dobson on the sharing of intelligence.

'He won't close his eyes to other things,' Thackeray said mildly. 'Far from it, knowing Mower. But I've told him his top priority is the kids. It won't help the situation generally if the mothers are up in arms about that, on top of everything else up there.'

'Aye, well, keep on top of the car-theft angle too. I don't believe those two lads went all the way to Harrogate to nick that Astra. It looks organised to me, in which case I want to know who by. A few tid-bits to throw in Les Dobson's direction won't come amiss, tell young Kevin.'

Thackeray nodded.

'I'll have a quiet chat with the community bobby too,' he suggested.

'Aye, well mind whose toes you're stepping on,' Longley said. The tension between CID and the uniformed branch would not ease while part of the town teetered on the edge of violent disintegration and scapegoats were being urgently sought. Longley took off his jacket, loosened his tie and nodded to Thackeray to do the same.

'If the bloody weather broke it'd help,' he said, subsiding heavily into his chair again, his almost bald head and heavily jowled face glistening. 'I'd not last ten minutes in a hot climate.'

Longley sat breathing heavily, looking at Thackeray speculatively, taking in the square-jawed face, with its dark shadows even early in the day, the sharp eyes and sombre mouth, slow to smile. They had not worked together long, and there was still a distance between them, made harder to bridge by a determined reticence on Thackeray's side. Longley knew the source of that, in so far as one could know anything from the bare bones of an officer's record and what he had gleaned on the grapevine from colleagues elsewhere in the county. The full implications he could only guess at, not being an imaginative man.

At last, apparently making up his mind, he opened a drawer and pulled out a file which he passed across the desk to Thackeray.

'I want you to have a look at that,' Longley said slowly. 'You probably won't remember it. It was a child murder up on the Heights ten years ago. A little girl, Tracy Miller. Caused a big stir at the time. No one likes those cases.'

Thackeray took the buff folder and looked down at it, avoiding Longley's gaze. Least of all me, he thought bitterly. He should bloody well know that.

'I was still in Arnedale then, sir,' he said carefully. 'I think I remember the case.' That was a lie, and Thackeray guessed that Longley, who was never less than well informed, knew it was likely to be. For him the year in question had begun in tragedy and gone downhill. It was a time he flinched from thinking about, still less discussing. Longley recognised the frozen look on the younger man's face and went on quickly.

'Harry Huddleston wrapped it all up pretty fast. Just as well – there was a lot of aggro on the estate – another hot summer, as I recall. A good result, it looked like. The girl's brother, stepbrother in fact, was sent down for life.'

'And?' Thackeray asked, knowing there had to be more.

16

'A little bird tells me that television programme, "Case Re-opened", is looking at it — seems to think it's another miscarriage of justice,' Longley said, suppressed anger causing his colour to rise.

'And was it?' Thackeray persisted, knowing he was living dangerously. Longley took a deep breath before answering, and what he said was evidently not what he had first thought of saying.

'I worked with Harry Huddleston for twenty years,' he said. 'There may be coppers who've got cases badly wrong in that time, made mistakes, fitted people up even, for all sorts of reasons, but not here, not in this division, and not Harry Huddleston. No chance.'

Thackeray shrugged almost imperceptibly. In his book it could happen anywhere, in any division, with any officer. Given the intense pressure there would be to make an arrest in a case of child murder it did not particularly surprise him that a mistake, deliberate or otherwise, might have been made. But that was not a view he intended to share with Longley in his present mood.

'If there are serious doubts raised they'll send someone in from another force to look at it,' he said quietly. 'So what do you want me to do?'

Longley gritted his teeth in impotent fury.

'Read the file. There's a summary there of all the evidence. Then go and have a quiet word with Harry Huddleston. Off the record. Just between ourselves. Him, and his sergeant, a man called Jim Redding. He's retired now and runs a pub somewhere up the dales. It'll be in the files. Just see if you can pick any holes in it, to set my mind at rest, will you? I'll not see Harry's reputation ruined by some pinko telly journalist if I can do owt to avoid it.'

Thackeray raised his eyebrows. The request, while not precisely illegal, was certainly irregular.

'Minding our backs, are we?' he asked.

'Looking after our own, more like,' Longley snapped. 'Nowt wrong with that, in my book.'

'Wouldn't it be better if you talked to him yourself, sir?' Thackeray asked, suddenly formal, deeply reluctant to be pushed into an unofficial investigation in which he could foresee no winners.

'I'm too close to him. I've known him too long,' Longley said. 'Look at it with a fresh eye, Michael, and tell me what you think. That's all I'm asking.' Longley was not a man to say please to a subordinate, but both men knew that this was a request, could not be an order, and there was a long pause before Thackeray finally nodded his acquiescence.

'I'd better take a couple of days' leave,' he suggested.

'Aye, you do that,' Longley said. 'Go and watch some cricket with old Harry. I know you're a rugby man, but stretch a point, eh? And mind he doesn't bite your head off when he finds out what you're really about. I don't think he'll be right chuffed.'

The long sultry afternoon, with thunder clouds piled up like fantastic leaden grey towers on the horizon but not apparently moving any closer, ended with Laura Ackroyd driving reluctantly back up to the Heights. She had gone back to the office and written her report on the mothers' action group for the next day's paper, only to find that there were a couple of points she needed to check. Neither Linda nor Jackie were on the phone so she ground out of the town again to visit them, her clothes clinging stickily to her body in the hot car, through the stifling fumes of the late afternoon traffic.

Laura was finding the summer in Bradfield oppressive for reasons that went beyond the insupportable weather: reasons she shied away from examining too closely. She had spent a month earlier in the year in the sparkling sunshine of Portugal, overtly resting a broken ankle beside her parents' swimming pool but also nursing less visible wounds.

She had renounced men for the duration, she told her friend Vicky Mendelson on her return to Bradfield, with a toss of that astonishing head of copper hair. Vicky smiled knowingly from the depths of her own pregnant complacency and forbore to tell Laura, as she might have done, that she had heard all that before.

18

Laura would confess to no one that since her return she had sat alone in her flat evening after evening with a bottle of vodka waiting for a phone call which had not come and which she now no longer expected. Only Vicky could have guessed the truth, and she had decided, for the moment at least, to avoid emotional minefields and leave strictly alone the question of who it was who had put the faintly puzzled look of hurt into Laura's grey-green eyes.

Laura edged the car forward jerkily in first gear and smiled faintly at a sudden vivid recollection of her father, spread out pinkly on his sun-bed beside the pool, cigar waving for emphasis, as he had vainly lectured his daughter on the shortcomings of her present life-style: unconcernedly unattached, professionally under-developed and under-paid, and therefore, he assumed, terminally discontented. Most of the time, she thought, it simply was not true.

There were times though, she had to admit, when she desperately wanted to get away from Bradfield, and this sticky, simmering summer was undoubtedly one of them. She had returned from her deeply resented time at a girls' boarding school to study at the local university as a defiant response to her father's insistence that she should go away in the first place. But she had not expected her quixotic gesture of loyalty to Bradfield to last so long.

She had trained as a reporter on the Gazette, expecting to move on, as so many of her ambitious young colleagues had done, to greater things. Her father's heart attack had changed all that. In the space of eighteen months he had sold up his business and retired to his bougainvillea-draped villa near Estoril, leaving Laura as Joyce Ackroyd's only living relative in England, and her dearest anywhere.

While Joyce was alive, Laura told herself grimly as she waited at traffic lights to turn right, feeling faintly nauseous from breathing the diesel fumes from the bus in front of her, she would stay in Bradfield, however frustrating that might prove to be. But she sometimes wondered, in moments of depression, whether she would have any career prospects left worth speaking of when she was finally free to look elsewhere for a job.

The call from the London TV company had come as a welcome relief – a break, however temporary, in what threatened to become the terminal monotony of a Bradfield summer. True, they were making no extravagant promises, she thought: just a small commission for a film which might never be made if the story did not stand up to investigation. The interviews would not take long, the promised cheque would not be large, the project would not interfere with her normal job. Even so it was a welcome sighting of a succulent big fish in the wider sea in which she sometimes ached to cast her net.

The flowers left in a mound in front of Bronte House were already beginning to wilt in their Cellophane wrappings. Laura tried to raise Jackie Sullivan on the entry-phone but got no reply. As she pushed her damp hair out of her eyes for the hundredth time that day and thought longingly of a cold shower – and even more longingly of that sparkling blue pool in Estoril – a bulky middle-aged woman pushed past her to open the door with a key.

'Who did you want, love?' she asked. And when Laura told her she pointed off to the right where the main road dropped away slightly and a huddle of prefabricated buildings backed on to a patch of waste ground, bright with yellow ragwort and pink willow-herb.

'She'll have taken t'kids down to t'playground. They've got a paddling pool down there for t'little 'uns.'

Laura left her car parked outside Bronte and walked slowly down the dusty pavement to the adventure playground which was run every summer holiday in the hope of keeping at least some of the estate's children off the streets and out of trouble. The playground itself was fenced off from the road and the waste ground behind the doctor's surgery and clinic by a rusting chain-link fence.

As she reached up to open the gate, which was secured by a high bolt inaccessible to small children, it swung open and a tall man in dark jeans and a white shirt came out. They narrowly avoided a collision and Laura was

20

conscious of an intense look before the man turned sharply and made his way briskly towards the flats.

Laura smiled faintly before going in, securing the gate behind her. Since her early teenage years, she had taken male interest for granted, knowing that more often than not it was merely her hair that caught the casual eye. Skinny, her father used unflatteringly to complain every term when she came home from boarding school. And pretty skinny, she thought wryly, she remained.

Children were milling around just inside the playground gate but she found herself face-to-face with a tall black woman in shorts and skimpy sun-top and, to her surprise, a dark-haired man in worn jeans and tee-shirt whom she recognised and who seemed desperately anxious to speak to her before she could speak to him.

'Hi, Laura,' he said urgently, almost pushing his way past the woman to greet her, though not forbearing to give her waist an apparently obligatory squeeze as he passed. 'Kevin, Kevin O'Donnell? We met during the by-election campaign in the spring. You remember?'

Laura remembered Detective Sergeant Kevin Mower very well, though at the time his hair had been shorter, his clothes a whole lot smarter and he had lacked the outbreak of dark designer stubble which did not conceal his embarrassment at her arrival.

'I'm helping out here for the summer,' Mower said, quickly overcoming his confusion. 'This is Sue, by the way, Sue Raban, the play-leader. Sue – Laura Ackroyd from the Gazette.'

Sue cast an unenthusiastic eye over Laura. She looked hot and harassed and at the end of her tether.

'If you're looking for comments about last night, you've come to the wrong place,' she said uncompromisingly, in an accent which Laura could not instantly place. She looked, Laura thought, an uncompromising sort of person – dark skin untouched by make-up, hair cut close to her head, slim figure, though not without enviable curves, entirely unadorned except for a pair of dangling silver hoop earrings which swung gently as she moved.

21

'I'm looking for Jackie Sullivan,' Laura said unemphatically. 'I was told I might find her here. I'm writing about her campaign.' Sue's expression softened slightly at that and she waved a hand across the playground, where groups of youngsters, oblivious to the heat, were climbing and swinging and running in what looked like a cross between a jungle gym and an extremely dusty football pitch. At the far side of the enclosure a crescendo of screaming and splashing was coming from a bright blue plastic structure which evidently contained water.

'I'll take you over,' Kevin Mower said, putting a proprietorial hand on Laura's arm. 'I think she's in the pool with her kids.' Sue gave Mower a speculative look before giving Laura a considered nod of approval and turning her attention to two small boys who were tugging at her shorts and shouting at her in a simultaneous and incomprehensible frenzy of excitement.

Once out of ear-shot Laura disentangled herself from Mower's grip.

'So what's all this about?' she asked, in a tone that demanded an answer.

He smiled placatingly, reminding her just how good-looking he was beneath the incipient beard which gave him an unexpectedly disreputable air.

'I'm doing my "Miami Vice" bit,' he said. 'Surveillance. I just happened to be the one no one round here knows by sight – being a foreigner in these parts, as it were – a bloody southerner and all that. This is a good base. They expect the odd harmless do-gooder up here during the summer so they don't notice me.'

'The joy-riders?' she asked softly, but he shook his head quickly.

'Not primarily,' he said. 'A number of little girls have been complaining about being approached in dark corners around the flats by a man. Nothing very definite at first but getting worse and definitely not nice.'

'Not nice,' she agreed soberly, recalling Jackie Sullivan's impassioned plea for somewhere safe for her children to grow up. 'So who knows who you really are?'

'No one knows,' he said quickly. 'Not even Sue – especially not Sue. She's from South Africa but went to university in the States, some mainly black college in New York, or wherever. She's got no time for cops. She makes that very clear. As far as she's concerned I'm a mature student on vacation, doing social work – which is what my boss thinks I'm doing half the time anyway.' He gave Laura a disarming grin.

She flashed him a sharp look but he had turned away, diplomatically she was sure, to help a child untangle a rope on a climbing frame. When he turned back his dark eyes were full of innocence and he made no further reference to his chief inspector, Michael Thackeray, whose recent silence irked her almost as much as she was irked with herself for expecting anything more.

'There's Jackie,' said Mower, waving at a familiar figure wrapping a towel around a small child on the far side of the pool. 'I'll be through here soon. Do you fancy a drink? I'm gasping for a pint. All I get here is cola till it runs out of my ears. And there's no fridge so it's lukewarm cola most of the time.'

'Sue won't mind?' she asked, recalling his casual familiarity with the South African.

'She's got a date,' he said dismissively. 'He just dropped in to see her.' Laura recalled the tall man with the speculative eyes.

'Why not then?' Laura said. 'I'm parked up by Bronte. I'll wait for you there.'

They were early enough at the Malt Shovel in Broadley to secure one of the wooden tables in what had once been the inn's cobbled stable yard. A pergola now dripped swathes of climbing roses, fading in the heat, where once shire horses had rested prior to the climb over the moorland road to Wharfedale. This had once been a farming village, its cottages housing the families of shepherds and carters instead of retired bank managers and aspiring artists, its fields home to over-wintering flocks instead of four- and five-bedroomed executive residences for professional families working in Milford and Bradfield and beyond.

Laura had deliberately chosen an out-of-town pub. After phoning in the brief additions she wanted to make to her story for the next day's paper she had driven the temporarily car-less Mower, keen to maintain his impoverished student image, out of Bradfield with a sense of relief. Above the valley a whisper of a southerly breeze made the humid evening slightly more bearable as they respectively started into a vodka and tonic and a pint of Tetley's bitter. Laura watched Mower sink half his glass in one deep draught and smiled faintly.

'You're not a teetotaller, then, like your boss?' she said.

'Not bloody likely,' he said, knowing she was fishing but willing to indulge her, so far at least. He was content for the moment simply to be in the company of a woman whose startling red hair tumbling around an oval face and pale Renaissance skin, apparently untouched by the sun except for the freckles she hated, turned heads at the other tables. The yard was quickly filling up with youngish regulars looking for the relief of cool drinks in the marginally less sweltering shade beneath the pub's old stone walls. 'But then I don't have his reasons.'

She raised an eyebrow at that but would not be drawn into another overt question. Coming to the Malt Shovel, which she had not visited since an emotional trip in the company of that same boss, had been a way of challenging her own feelings and she was not at all sure what conclusion to draw from her equivocal reaction to the noisy, convivial scene.

'It's turned into a long hot summer,' she said neutrally. 'Especially up at the Heights.'

Mower smiled a faintly knowing smile, running a hand down the unfamiliar stubble along a jaw-line that he knew was not unattractive.

'Long, hot and quite likely very violent before it's over.' His assessment was unemotional and all the more chilling for that.

'Do you think so?' Laura asked, her mind switching sharply back into a professional mode.

'I don't think it's over up there,' he said. 'The word on the street is that there'll be a reaction to the smash last night. I reckon the plods were lucky not to have a riot on their hands. You'll get plenty more headlines out of it, I'd guess. Another?' He nodded at her empty glass.

'I'll get them,' she said firmly. Mower nodded with a smile and a shrug of acquiescence which said he could live with her independence – and an intensity in his dark eyes which spelt out a desire for rather more than a drink.

'Only if you come out to dinner with me,' he said casually.

Laura hesitated for a moment and then gave a near imperceptible shrug herself.

'Why not?' she said again, with a smile that held only the merest hint of mockery.

THREE

CHIEF INSPECTOR THACKERAY HAD PUT off his meeting with Harry Huddleston for as long as he dared. He had spent the next morning at home reading through the file on the death of Tracy Miller until he knew the outline of the case almost as well, he suspected, as Huddleston himself would be able to recall it after a ten-year interlude. He sat in an armchair close to the open window of his sparsely furnished flat, a Billie Holiday blues playing softly on the stereo and reflecting his sombre mood.

It had been, he could see through the unemotional prose of the official record, a traumatic case for all those involved: not, it was true, one of those agonising affairs conducted under the glare of the television lights when a murdered child is missing for days or even weeks, but brutal and distressing all the same.

Tracy had been discovered, half naked, sexually assaulted, and bundled into a black plastic dustbin bag only hours after she had been reported missing by her father when she failed to return home from school. The anguished suspense of waiting had been short but the discovery of the body no less shocking for that. The ten-year-old had been strangled and her body hidden close to the huge dustbins at the foot of the rubbish chutes at the rear of Bronte House, where her family – her natural father and younger sister, her stepmother and older stepbrother, Stephen – lived on the top floor.

She had, Thackeray had thought grimly, as he had sat gazing sightlessly at Amos Atherton's ten-year-old forensic report, been dumped like so much garbage by the rubbish

26

spilling from the overflowing and no doubt stinking bins behind which her body had been concealed. A more suitable place than most to hide a horrific crime, he thought, and one which had offered the media no opportunity to wax sentimental about some little lost babe in the woods. In Thackeray's experience death was no less shocking for a covering of leaves and flowers.

It had taken Huddleston a week, the record showed, to arrest Stephen Webster, who had not adopted his unofficial stepfather's name. Tracy's father Paul and Stephen's mother June had apparently not bothered with the formalities of wedlock during the two years or more that they had lived together.

The file, with its bald summaries of interviews and statements, gave no flavour of what that other hot summer week must have been like, but Thackeray could imagine. There was nothing like the death of a child to send hundreds of determined police officers onto the streets, many of them volunteers working in their off-duty time and thinking inevitably of the vulnerability of their own sons and daughters.

And nothing was more likely to inflame communities far more stable than that living on the Heights even ten years ago. The combination of anger and fear which would have seized the estate's other parents, the brew no doubt stirred by the media, would have been palpable in the heavy summer heat. It would have born down on Huddleston and every officer on his team like a goad, just one more pressure to add to their own understandable determination to clear the case up and clear it up quickly.

There would have been an overwhelming need to make an arrest, Thackeray thought, and within seven days Huddleston had done just that. But was it just any old arrest? Thackeray could see no evidence for that unwelcome conclusion as he went meticulously over the files. Stephen had been vague about the time he had got home the evening Tracy died. The caretaker at Bronte House said he had seen him going out when he claimed he was already at home watching television. The boy had changed his story and floundered even more about his timings. And when Huddleston finally took him to the police station on the Sunday following the murder, he had eventually broken down and admitted to killing Tracy.

Photocopies of his statements were there in the file, signed carefully in a looping childish hand, each giving a slightly different and cumulatively more damning version of events that afternoon. Thackeray had no doubt that, given the evidence on offer, he too would have charged Tracy Miller's stepbrother with murder and slept soundly in his bed for the full ten years which had followed the boy's conviction, in spite of his withdrawal of the confession at the trial.

But Thackeray knew there were still questions to be asked. Those ten years had not just made television reporters and the public more sceptical as convictions had been regularly overturned and the veracity of police officers increasingly put in doubt. The whole criminal justice system had also become more rigorous.

There was no Police and Criminal Evidence Act then, no tape-recording of interviews, few doubts about the confessions of the weak and suggestible, no genetic fingerprinting to confirm the identity of killers and no tests which could indicate whether a confession had been tampered with. It had been a rougher, tougher world into which Thackeray had himself been inducted as a young detective and to which he occasionally still looked back with something close to shame.

He had closed the file with a heavy sigh, not relishing the task Longley had thrust upon him. Yet he was quite sure that if Stephen's mother had enlisted the support of a television programme he would be only the first to question Huddleston, and undoubtedly the most sympathetically disposed.

He had reluctantly drained the glass of lemonade which he had put on the window-sill beside him and glanced out at the view of Bradfield his third-floor flat offered him, dispirited by the endless repetitiveness of crime. The modern block where he had set up a sort of home was perched high on one of the seven hills down which the suburbs tumbled to the huddled industrial town centre in the valley.

Local wits of a classical turn of mind had not missed the comparison with Rome although for most of the couple of centuries that Bradfield had spread outwards and upwards from its low-lying heart around the squat parish church, the citizens of ashy Pompeii might have felt more at home within its sooty walls than the Romans. A hundred years of smoke haze and grime had only recently been banished, the Yorkshire sandstone gradually restored to its soft natural gold, the meanest of the slums and most satanic of the mills demolished to make way for smart new housing and industrial estates.

And yet, Thackeray thought, as he gazed down at what had so recently become his patch, the old evils were still there and if one sort of disease and squalor appeared to be vanquished another quickly rose up to take its place. He was not, he thought, much of an optimist where human nature was concerned. As Billie Holiday bade good-morning to heartache, he switched the stereo off with a feeling that the song might suit the raking of old ashes well enough.

He had arranged to meet Harry Huddleston at a pub some distance out of the town, on the main Manchester road beyond the suburb where the ex-DCI was beginning his retirement. The Yorkshire county cricket team, Thackeray had carefully ascertained, smiling faintly in recollection of Longley's suggestion of a pitch-side encounter at Headingley, was playing in Essex. There, the car radio told him as he drove up towards the moors to the west, a humiliating defeat seemed in prospect unless it could be averted by the thundery rain which was apparently forecast for Chelmsford.

The Fox and Hounds seemed an odd venue for Huddleston to have chosen, a huge red-brick roadhouse surrounded by an extensive car park where coaches were ominously welcome. Thackeray guessed that the former chief inspector was wary of meeting his successor in any of his old haunts in the town centre. In the Woolpack, favourite watering hole of Bradfield CID, tongues would wag all the sooner if he and Huddleston were observed in confidential conversation.

The two men knew each other by sight, although their careers in the county CID had never brought them into more than occasional casual contact. Their eyes met appraisingly across the almost empty bar without much warmth on either side, both knowing too much, perhaps, of the other's weaknesses.

'Now then, Michael,' Huddleston said, assuming seniority by age which he could not claim by rank. He was dressed casually in slacks and a blue polo-shirt, open at the neck and straining ineffectually over his belly. Thackeray felt absurdly formal in his shirt and tie, glad he had at least left his jacket in the car.

'It's been a long time, Harry,' Thackeray said. 'How does retirement suit you?'

'It doesn't, lad,' Huddleston said flatly. 'I'm bored out of my bloody mind already, looking for a job in security or summat like that. I can't be doing with all this gardening and house-painting my missus has got lined up, and it'll be even worse when the cricket season finishes. She wants to wallpaper the bloody lounge.'

Thackeray gave a thin smile. His unease made the heat seem even more oppressive than it really was and he hoped that Huddleston did not think that the beads of sweat he could feel on his forehead were caused by nervousness. He brushed his unruly hair away from his brow with careful casualness.

'What can I get you?' he asked. Huddleston did not contest the offer, settling himself complacently again in his seat and handing Thackeray his already empty pint glass for a refill of Tetley's bitter. He did so with every appearance of unconcern, although when Thackeray turned away he watched his progress to the bar through narrowed eyes, full of suspicion.

When Thackeray returned to the corner table Huddleston had selected, carrying a pint of bitter, a lemonade for himself and a plate of ham sandwiches, Huddleston had pulled a small transistor radio from his pocket and was holding it to his ear with a satisfied smile splitting his broad face like a trench.

'No play before lunch,' he said. 'They'll inspect the wicket again at two. Wi' a bit of luck it'll be raining again by then.' He laughed, but Thackeray thought there was no humour in the sound, and a coldness about Huddleston's heavy features that did not alter, even at the good news from Chelmsford and his apparent satisfaction that God was still on the side of His own county.

When Huddleston had taken a draught of his beer, given Thackeray's drink a disgusted glance and demolished half a sandwich in a single gargantuan bite, he switched the radio off again and stowed it away, his expression hardening. He was a big man, as tall as Thackeray and distinctly heavier around the waist and belly, his hair a streaked iron grey and his pale blue eyes watchful above the broad fleshy nose and thin lips.

'So why's Jack Longley sent a lad to do a man's job?' Huddleston asked offensively. 'Summat's come back to haunt him, has it? Some alleged miscarriage of justice?'

Thackeray did not reply for a moment, keeping his resentment at this assault well concealed while he absorbed the evidence that firstly Huddleston was no fool and had quickly worked out why he had requested the meeting, and secondly that if Huddleston's professional judgement was about to be questioned he would fight for his reputation every inch of the way.

Huddleston's glance relaxed the tiniest fraction as he took another gulp of his bitter, the sharp eyes never leaving Thackeray's somewhat nonplussed expression for an instant.

'He was always a bit of a mardy bastard, was Jack,' he said. 'Too bloody scared to come and see me himself, I suppose.'

Thackeray smiled faintly at this assessment of the superintendent and guessed that where the belligerent Huddleston was concerned there just might be a grain of truth in it.

31

'There's a TV programme called "Case Re-opened",' he said.

'Aye, I know it,' Huddleston said. 'So what are they pushing their dirty little snouts into? Summat to do wi' me?'

'The death of Tracy Miller,' Thackeray said quietly, watching Huddleston's face intently as he took in this information. But there was little enough to be gleaned from his impassive expression.

'Bollocks,' he said flatly. 'That little toe-rag was as guilty as hell. He confessed, for Christ's sake. Has no one read the case file?'

'Read, marked and inwardly digested,' Thackeray said. 'I can't pick any holes in your case unless . . .'

'Unless what?' Huddleston asked, his colour rising and the real anger beginning to thicken his voice now. 'Unless what? What are they saying?'

'Unless you pressured him.'

'Thumped him, you mean?' Huddleston snapped back. 'He didn't complain. No one laid a finger on him that I know of.'

'You know it doesn't have to be as crude as that,' Thackeray persisted. 'I think what Jack Longley wants to know is that we're fireproof: that the confession won't turn out to have been written at different times if it's tested, that if there's any possibility of genetic fingerprinting after all this time we won't find that this lad couldn't possibly have done it, like that poor sod in Lancashire who did sixteen years for nothing.'

'She wasn't raped,' Huddleston said angrily. 'Interfered with, but not raped. There'll be nowt to test as far as I can remember. You must have read the forensic report.'

'Nothing under the fingernails? No sign she'd scratched him?'

'Nowt. You know how she was found. She'd not have had much of a chance to scratch anyone.' Huddleston's restraint was beginning to wear thin now and one or two of the other drinkers in the bar glanced curiously his way as he stuffed the last of the sandwiches into his mouth as if to prevent the glowing fires of anger within from bursting into an unstoppable conflagration.

'But they'll test the confession statement, if it comes to a formal investigation,' Thackeray said. 'Will it stand up? All his own words? No one suggesting anything to him? All written up contemporaneously? You know all the bloody silly things people have been caught out at recently. You know why Longley's worried. It was ten years ago. Things were done differently then – sometimes.'

'There was corroboration, lad,' Huddleston snarled. 'We didn't rely on the bloody confession, did we? We had witnesses. Go back and read the file again and get your facts straight. Webster was seen. He lied about where he was and when, and his story fell apart because his stepfather contradicted it – at least he did when he got his timings sorted out – and because Jerry Hurst saw him where he wasn't supposed to be. Unless the witnesses were lying through their teeth, that lad was as guilty as Old Nick himself.'

Abruptly the big man got to his feet, rocking the table and sending the glasses sliding dangerously close to the edge as if on a ship in a high sea. Thackeray steadied them and himself as he stayed seated, allowing Huddleston to loom over him threateningly, keeping his breathing even.

'Tell Jack it's watertight,' Huddleston said through clenched teeth. 'And tell him to come and do his dirty work himself next time.' Fascinated, Thackeray watched the sweat roll down the older man's brow to be dashed away with an impatient hand, before he spun on his heel with surprising lightness for one so heavy and marched out of the bar without looking back.

Thackeray sighed and finished his drink. So much for tact and diplomacy, he thought. Though on reflection, he conceded wryly, there may not be any inoffensive way of asking an ex-copper if he had knowingly put an innocent boy away for life.

Restless and dissatisfied, he called back at police HQ instead of heading back to his empty flat. To his surprise

33

he discovered the rangy figure of Kevin Mower half sprawled across his desk with the telephone clamped to his ear. The call was evidently not an official one and the sergeant hung up quickly with a look as close to embarrassment as Thackeray had ever seen him achieve.

'I thought you were off duty, guv,' Mower said, sliding into his chair and affecting nonchalance. 'I came in on the off-chance of catching you, but they said you had a couple of days off.'

'I have,' Thackeray said shortly, not willing to admit that the prospect of hours of free time filled him with more dread than pleasure. 'I just came in to pick up a file.' He rummaged not very convincingly in one of the drawers of his desk. 'You look as if you've slept in those clothes,' he said, casting a chilly eye over Mower's torn jeans and grubby sports shirt. 'Has something come up?'

Mower shrugged.

'It's all rumour, guv. The young lads are full of threats. They're going to get the pigs for what happened to young Mark and Gavin. There's talk of a protest march, petrol bombs, you name it. And the mothers are all in a state of high old tension anyway because of the assaults. There's a couple of traumatised little girls up there being shown off like prize exhibits in a bloody peep show. The victims. It's sick. And its racking the tension up another couple of hundred notches.'

'Have you told uniformed?' Thackeray asked wearily. 'They'll be the ones who'll have to deal.'

Mower nodded.

'I'll talk to the duty officer,' he said. 'The Gazette doesn't help much either. Have you seen this?' He tossed a crumpled copy of the local paper onto Thackeray's desk and pointed at Ted Grant's vitriolic editorial. Thackeray cast an eye over it without much interest. The scatter-shot of blame and recrimination which Grant aimed at the police amongst others was familiar enough and offered no solutions.

'Talking of the Gazette, guv,' Mower said slowly as Thackeray passed the paper back. He was aware he was pushing his luck, as Thackeray's expression perceptibly froze. 'Did you know Laura Ackroyd was snooping around asking questions about an old murder case? Tracy Miller, was it?'

'How do you know that?' Thackeray asked, giving no indication whether what Mower was telling him was news to him or not.

'I bumped into her yesterday,' Mower said innocently. 'She'd been talking to the kid's father for "Case Re-opened" – you know, Channel 4? Got that woman who killed her husband off last year?'

'I remember,' Thackeray said. 'So how long has Miss Ackroyd been working for television?' He spoke quietly, aware of his heart quickening slightly. Damn Mower, he thought. He had an uncanny knack of probing that extra millimetre too far into areas which Thackeray would rather keep deeply buried. Mower continued with apparent insouciance, but Thackeray was aware that he was watching him intently. He glanced down at his hands to make sure they were not shaking as much as he imagined.

'She's not working for them,' Mower went on. 'Just doing some preliminary research, she said. Though I should think she'd like it to turn into something more permanent. They all want to go on telly, don't they, journalists? Wasn't it one of old Harry Huddleston's cases?'

'I think so,' Thackeray lied non-committally. 'I was on the other side of the county then.' And not conscious enough most of the time to know what was going on in my own home, let alone in Bradfield, he thought bitterly.

A tap on the door put an end to a conversation which Mower was as eager to pursue as Thackeray was reluctant. But as Thackeray took his leave to resume his interrupted day off he could not restrain the smallest of smiles at the thought of Laura Ackroyd confronting the formidable Huddleston. Beauty and the beast, and no bets on who would triumph, he thought, wondering why he felt unaccountably more cheerful as he ran down the steps and out again into the humid afternoon.

Laura Ackroyd floated on her back in the shallow end at the local swimming pool, keeping a lazy eye on two dark-haired little boys who were playing ducks and drakes close by. The pool was a modern one, all glass and tubular steel balconies painted bright blue, and in spite of the hot weather was less crowded than she had expected it to be when she had agreed to take her friend Vicky's two small boys swimming on her day off.

There had been a time when the pool would have been a magnet to every holidaying child in Bradfield and for miles beyond on a day like this with the temperature in the eighties, but she had noticed that since the pool had been sold to a private firm and the entrance fees had been raised, the patrons had diminished in number and become distinctly older.

Vicky, luxuriantly pregnant in a loose flowing cotton dress of bronze and gold, which flattered her honey coloured skin and rich brown hair, was sitting close by in the front row of the viewing balcony, watching what had started as a swimming lesson turn into a joyful splash-about. Catching Laura's eye she waved and held up her watch.

'Boys,' Laura called. 'I think your mum wants you out. Tell her I'm going to do a few lengths. I won't be long.' She shepherded six-year-old Daniel and four-year-old Nathan to the steps, noting affectionately their dark curly hair plastered to their heads like sealskin and the water dripping off their sturdy bodies, which were deeply suntanned after a recent holiday in France. She watched as they joined their mother who wrapped voluminous towels around them before they all made their way to the changing rooms.

Laura launched herself strongly back into the water and did a length of the pool in a powerful crawl, exultant at the feel of the water parting to let her through. As she kicked vigorously, she could feel a faint twinge from the ankle she had recently broken. But she felt fit and healthy again, she

36

thought with a sense of relief. She should get back into the habit of swimming here, as she used to do before the leg injury put her in hospital for a week and out of the country for a month. All that, she thought, was behind her now and best forgotten – a time of torn loyalties as well as physical pain, and of disillusionments that were still too tender to explore. She was not one to brood, she told herself, and almost believed it.

She had almost believed it the previous evening, too, as she had let Kevin Mower wine her and dine her, not lavishly, it was true, but generously nevertheless at Bradfield's classiest Chinese restaurant. He had been good company, with a fund of sharp, ironic stories about his time with the Metropolitan Police, a ready wit with the less grim aspects of his work and the sensitivity, which she found surprised her somewhat, to edit out the harsher detail. He was sparing, though, with details of his own private life, and more cautious still about his current ambitions, although it was plain that he did not anticipate remaining a detective sergeant for long.

On the way out of the restaurant, Mower had put an arm lightly around her waist, and she had not objected. But when she had asked him if he wanted to come back with her for coffee he had hesitated for a moment and then refused. She had glanced quizzically into those dark eyes, which had been openly admiring all evening but now revealed a reticence which she was sure was uncharacteristic.

She had not repeated the invitation, half-relieved it had been rejected. He had walked her back to her car and said good-night without touching her again, leaving her to drive home with a faint feeling of dissatisfaction, as of business unresolved, which, she thought wryly later as she got into her solitary bed, was perhaps precisely what he had intended.

Surging through the water head down to begin a third length, she grinned to herself, exhilarated at the thought of the previous evening's entertainment and by a sheer physical energy that had been drained away in the humidity of the day beyond the pool and its echoing coolness. Two lengths more, and slightly breathless now, she pulled herself from the water and made her way to the changing rooms where Vicky was still supervising the boys' dressing.

She showered and wrapped herself in a towel and released the clips with which she had fastened up her hair, letting it fall in damp copper filaments around her face.

'I'm beginning to feel fit again at last,' she said.

'Well if you feel like bringing these wretches here regularly until the baby arrives, feel free,' Vicki said, patting her bulge proprietorially. 'I'm not much for maternity cozzies – they tend to float around you in the water like a barrage balloon.' She sent the two boys to put coins into hairdryers, which would keep them occupied for five minutes, and when they were out of earshot looked at her friend with some concern in her eyes.

'Is this telly thing likely to lead to a new job?' she asked.

Laura shrugged as she slipped a tee-shirt over her head, aware that however ambitious Vicky might pretend to be on her behalf, she would be devastated if and when she did decide to leave Bradfield. They had been close since their student days when Laura had stood side by side with Vicky against her family's icy reservations about her proposed marriage to David Mendelson: an ideal match to a lawyer fatally flawed by the fact that he was a Jew. They remained determinedly oblivious to David's family's equally fierce objections to Vicky's status as a Gentile whose children would not be of their father's faith.

'Chance would be a fine thing,' she said. 'All they want me to do is a bit of snooping around for them. It all depends on what I think of the boy's mother. She may just have got herself into a panic because she thinks he's never going to get out of gaol.'

Vicky's eye's shifted to her sons, jumping up and down beneath the drier, their dark curls swirling in the hot air.

'I can imagine,' she said quietly.

Laura took a brush to her own damp hair before tying it back loosely. She looked thoughtful.

'Is it worth it?' she asked. 'Motherhood? All that pain?' She glanced at Vicky's bulge, but it was not just her forthcoming labour she was thinking about. Vicky smiled the pre-Raphaelite smile of contentment which often infuriated Laura but which today she half envied. She called her sons to her to have their hair combed and their hastily donned tee-shirts and shorts straightened out from the damp tangle they had achieved alone.

'Oh, it's worth it, isn't it, boys?' she said over the two bright-eyed, inquisitive faces which held no comprehension of what they were agreeing to so eagerly.

'Do you want to come again, Daniel, Nathan?' Laura asked, and was rewarded with a boisterous hug from the younger boy and a grave 'Yes, please,' from Daniel, who at six was already taking seriously his responsibilities as the first born.

'It's a date,' she said lightly, pushing to the back of her mind the half-formed conviction that she was using Vicky's children as some sort of surrogate for those she had not herself conceived and in her darkest moments feared she never would.

FOUR

'YOU'D BEST COME IN,' PAUL Miller said grudgingly. 'I know I'll get no peace else.' He was a small man, grey-haired, parchment-skinned, a sharp nose and chin giving him the air of a ferret or some other small rodent. Pale eyes quivered behind round glasses with slightly tinted lenses, as if he hid from a world which had served him ill.

Still damp and glowing from her swim, although the freshness was soon dissipated by the cloying heat, Laura had driven up to the Heights and parked outside her grandmother's bungalow. She knew that Joyce would not be there: it was her morning for attending a women's committee meeting at the Town Hall, an appointment she kept with dogged determination as her ability to get about unaided declined.

Laura had decided to begin with what she guessed would be the more difficult of the two interviews she had been commissioned to conduct. Surprisingly, she thought, Tracy Miller's father still lived in the top-floor flat in Bronte House that the whole family had shared at the time of the murder. He had opened the main door promptly when she rang and announced herself on the entry-phone, and was waiting on his threshold when she emerged from the creaking, smelly lift.

He waved her into the living-room, where a well-developed teenaged girl still in short satin pyjamas was sitting on a worn sofa gazing at a morning chat show on a large-screen television. She looked up irritably as her father showed Laura in, switched the set off and flounced out without a word, leaving a faint odour of sweat and heavy perfume behind her.

'That's Kelly,' Paul Miller offered. 'She were just a little lass when we lost our Tracy. I'm not right sure she even remembers her now.' Miller's eyes flickered towards a series of photographs on a wooden sideboard which took up one whole wall of the small room. There were five of them all told, each of the same child growing up, golden-haired and blue-eyed, from the chubby toddler to the thinner-faced, already faintly sophisticated blonde ten-year-old in school uniform, which must have been taken shortly before her death. It was the picture of Tracy that had appeared in blurred black and white in the Gazette and Laura recognised the Technicolor version with a shudder. There was no photograph of Miller's younger daughter Kelly on view.

She turned her attention back to the dead girl's father, taking in the thin disappointed mouth, the lines of strain around the eyes and the prematurely aged hands, which he twisted nervously in his lap as he sat slumped in the corner of the sagging sofa as stained and frayed by the years as he was. He looked at Laura with a faint interrogation in his eyes.

'You said you wanted to talk about our Tracy,' he said, unable to suppress a tremor in his voice. Laura had been deliberately vague on the telephone when she had asked for this appointment and knew that her deception of this still living victim of that old crime had been unconscionable. There was no alternative now, she thought, but to be straightforward. It was the least the man deserved. She told him why she had come and pulled out a notebook, guessing that a tape-recorder would panic him.

'Did you know that your wife – is it ex-wife? – is trying to get Stephen's case re-opened?' she asked bluntly. Miller looked at her without apparent comprehension for a moment, before two spots of angry colour appeared high on his thin cheeks.

'She weren't my wife,' he said. 'She were never my wife. She just . . . she just . . .' he searched for the word he

41

wanted and failed to find it. 'She just lived with me,' he said at last, loading the phrase with contempt for a situation in which he must at the time have been a willing partner. 'What's she saying now?' he asked. 'That he never done it?'

Laura nodded and told him what she knew of the letter the former Mrs Webster, now Mrs Baker – Laura was not sure whether she had reverted to her maiden name or had remarried – had sent to the television programme. Miller sat for a moment gazing out of the window at the heavy sky outside with unseeing eyes. The atmosphere in the room was insufferably stale and airless, the windows tightly closed, and Laura felt the sweat prickling her back and beginning to form damp patches beneath her loose shirt. From the next room came the incessant thudding beat of pop music, switched on and turned up as if deliberately to cut out the conversation taking place in the living-room.

Miller's face hardened.

'He were crazy for sex,' he said harshly. 'Don't you know what they found in his room when they searched it? It all came out at t'trial. Great piles of them magazines, stuff they put on t'top shelf. YOU know. Dirty pictures.'

'It's not uncommon for teenaged boys,' Laura said mildly. 'It doesn't mean they'll turn round and murder their little sisters.'

'She weren't his sister, and June weren't her mum neither. I never said nowt at the time, but I'd not be surprised if June didn't know what were going on. They were my girls, both on 'em. I should never 'ave let that young bugger in. I told June I didn't want him when she first moved in. He were a sly little beggar. He should 'ave stayed with his own father. That's what I wanted. But no, he had to stay with his mum, he needed his mum, and look where that got us.' The depth of the man's bitterness filled the room with a sourness which could almost be tasted.

In the next room the insistent pop beat reached a new crescendo, resonating through the thin walls. Laura flinched and even Miller seemed affected. He dragged himself wearily to his feet and opened the door.

'Turn that effing noise down, Kelly,' he shouted, and the sound decreased by a fraction in response.

'How long were you all together?' Laura asked.

'Two years, more or less,' Miller said. 'Two years too bloody long. We were all right on us own, the girls and me, before June came along organising things, moving in, shifting t'furniture.' He lapsed into silence.

'And the girls' mother?' Laura prompted.

'Did a flit, didn't she, when Kelly were born. Never wanted either of them, if you ask me. "Took precautions", she said. Never wanted kids in t'first place, she said. But Kelly turned up when Tracy were just on five. That finished her off, she said. Any road, she were off before Kelly were out of nappies. I brought that babby up, fed her, put her on her pottie, the lot. And much thanks I get for it now from the little tart. Out all hours. Tracy weren't like that. Tracy were a good little lass. She'd come in from school and help me get the tea ready, set the table, the lot.'

'You weren't working, then?'

Miller looked at Laura with an expression of near contempt.

'How can you work when you're left with a couple of bairns to bring up?' he said. 'I've not worked for fifteen years.'

'And how soon before you met June Webster and she and Stephen moved in?'

'Aye, that were when Tracy were about eight. Kelly'd be three or four.'

'And Stephen?'

'He were older. He were fifteen when it happened. A big lad for his age. Like a baby elephant about t'place. And noisy.' Miller's eyes flickered towards the music still hammering through the adjacent wall. If two people seemed to fill the flat with noise and tension, Laura thought, what must it have been like with five crammed here on top of one another?

'And you never had any idea he might have been a danger to Tracy?' Laura chose her words carefully, but

43

Miller responded with fury anyway, his face contorted and his fists clenching and unclenching impotently as if deprived of the physical revenge they sought.

'I'd have effing killed him if I'd known,' he said.

Laura was suddenly conscious that they were no longer alone, and turned to see Kelly standing in the doorway listening. She had changed into a short, tight skirt and a skimpy sun-top. She did not speak, turning away abruptly when she was spotted and slamming the living-room door behind her.

Laura was suddenly overcome with a deep depression at the unresolved pain of this shattered family. There would be no comfort for Paul Miller from young Kelly as she grew up, she thought. Tracy might have turned out much the same as her sister but Miller would never suffer the disillusion of that adolescent transformation. Tracy had died the innocent child who set the table and adored her dad, and Kelly had paid the price.

'You've no doubts, then, about Stephen's conviction?'

Miller looked at her again with that cold contempt which threatened to dry up her questions completely.

'What do you think?' he asked. 'I'm just sorry they couldn't hang the little bastard.'

Outside on the concrete walkway which linked the flats, Laura took a deep breath of warm air. Over the balustrade she could see figures moving languidly in the oppressive heat, and a couple of cars parked well out of range of the missiles which occasionally hurtled from these balconies in apparently random protest, accepted by the world below as one of the natural hazards of life on the Heights.

On the landing she waited impatiently for the lift to come, but insistent pressing of the button brought no response and she began to walk irritably down the littered, graffiti-ridden concrete staircase where obscenities vied with anti-police slogans and a strange logo – the letter J linked to a shape like a crown.

On the next landing she discovered the reason for the lift's non-appearance. The doors stood wide open on this level, and a body lay slumped across the threshold, effectively preventing them from closing. For a moment Laura stood paralysed by a cold fear that the sprawled body of indeterminate sex in jeans and a tee-shirt was dead. But as she approached the figure groaned faintly and gave a convulsive movement, like a marionette twitched into life by strings.

Behind her the clatter of heels on concrete caused Laura to turn. Kelly Miller was following her down the stairs and was also brought to a halt by the scene on the landing. She pushed past Laura impatiently and rolled the body onto its back with scant respect.

'It's Gaz,' she said. 'He's one of t'squatters. He's always OD'ing on summat. Tell Jerry the caretaker on your way out and he'll get an ambulance.' The girl's face was cold, evidently neither surprised nor moved by the plight of the boy of about eighteen who lay between them, moaning faintly now, his eyes beginning to flicker and focus intermittently on Kelly.

'Jerry?' Laura asked.

'Flat two, next to the front door. He'll fix it,' Kelly said, backing away. 'There's nowt you can do for him.' As if to confirm that diagnosis the boy struggled convulsively into a sitting position, where he stuck, leaning against the wall and grinning inanely at them both.

'Kelly,' Laura said sharply, seizing the girl's arm before she could get away, reassured now that the boy was recovering. 'I wanted to ask you. Do you think Stephen killed Tracy?'

Faced with this unavoidable question the girl hesitated, her eyes blank as she ran a hand through her spiky blonde hair.

'I dunno, do I?' she said dully. 'I can't hardly remember her. But I'll tell you summat for nowt. Kids who can remember her say she weren't such a little angel as my dad thinks she was. He thinks the sun shone out of Tracy's backside.'

Laura digested this slowly.

'What else do kids say about Tracy? And about Stephen?' she asked. The girl shrugged, as if the events of

45

ten years ago were no concern of hers.

'You should talk to Stephen's girlfriend,' she said.

'I didn't know he had one,' Laura said, surprised. Nothing in the briefing she had received from the television company had mentioned a girlfriend.

'I remember her,' Kelly said. 'She used to come round our place when my dad were out sometimes. She were called Lyn or Linda. They used to give me sweets to keep me quiet and then shut themselves up in t'bedroom. I didn't know what they were at, did I? I were only a little kid.'

'Lyn who?'

'Don't ask me. I never saw her after Tracy were killed.' Laura glanced at the boy, who was now holding his head in his hands.

'Hey, Gaz, d'you want the doc?' Kelly asked without much warmth. The boy shook his head from side to side, although whether this was to indicate a negative or simply to clear it was not immediately apparent. He pulled up the bottom of his tee-shirt and used it to wipe his mouth and eyes, revealing a thin pale stomach and chest as undernourished as some Third World refugee's.

'Nah, I'll be all right,' he mumbled. 'I gotta go in a minute. Gotta go.'

'And I gotta go,' said Kelly. 'Talk to Lyn. I would,' she said, and swung away down the walkway leading to the front doors on this level.

Laura looked at the boy dubiously, noting that a little colour was returning to his hollow cheeks.

' 'S all right,' he said. ' 'S all right.'

With a sense of utter impotence she turned away and continued on her way down the stairs. At the bottom she hesitated for a moment before knocking on the door of Flat 2, which had 'Caretaker' scrawled in marker pen where a more official notice had clearly been wrenched from the woodwork. There was no immediate response, and Laura had almost given up hope of an answer when she heard a shuffling sound behind the door. It eventually opened, with much noise of bolts being pulled and chains being unfastened.

The caretaker evidently found it necessary to barricade himself into his home as if against a marauding army of vandals, which was probably not an inaccurate description of the gangs that did roam the walkways in broad daylight as well as by night. Eventually the door opened a crack and a heavy, pasty face appeared in the gap and scowled at her in interrogation.

'Are you Jerry, the caretaker?' she asked. The face pushed itself a little further forward, revealing an equally heavy body dressed only in boxer shorts and a grubby white cotton vest which barely stretched across a flabby expanse of heavily tattooed chest and stomach.

'Who wants to know?' The eyes were bleary and hostile, as if the man had just woken from a long sleep.

'I just thought you ought to know that there's a boy on the landing up there who looks ill,' Laura said irritably.

'It'll be one o't'squatters,' the caretaker said. 'They're all bloody druggies. Nowt to do wi' me.'

'What do you mean?' Laura asked angrily. 'He could die, for all I know. . .'

'Nowt to do wi' me,' the man repeated, slowly and loudly, as if Laura were deaf and had not quite heard him the first time. 'The council know they're theer, it's up to t'council to get 'em out. They're not my responsibility. I'm here for tenants who pay their rent.' And with that he slammed the door in Laura's face.

'Jesus wept,' Laura said furiously to the pockmarked woodwork. She glanced up the stairs and was relieved to see that the boy was apparently fit enough to be making his way slowly down the second flight of stairs, clinging to the iron banister for support but none the less upright and apparently not too seriously the worse for wear. Thankfully she turned and pushed through the main doors and out into the open air, resolved to persuade Ted Grant to let her write a series of features on the degradation of the Heights. If the blocks could not be renovated, as Ted had suggested, then it really was about time someone decided to pull them down.

Police Constable Alan Davies sat uncomfortably in the front seat of Chief Inspector Michael Thackeray's car surveying from the anonymity of plain clothes and an unmarked vehicle the beat which he normally patrolled in uniform. The Heights was his patch, and in normal circumstances he would have felt flattered that a DCI had requested a background briefing from him personally. On this occasion, though, there had been a perceptible frostiness in his own inspector's mien when Thackeray's request had been granted and Davies was an old enough hand to know that he was a pawn in a much bigger game which was being played by his superiors at division.

Davies had been a community police officer at the Heights for three years, ever since a directive from the chief constable had attempted to reinstate something like the traditional bobby on the beat. A dogged man, Davies had done his best to fulfil his brief, which was to keep his ears open and feed regular intelligence back to HQ. More hopefully, and it was very hopefully he felt with an increasing sense of impotence as time passed, he was supposed to win friends and influence people to occasionally help the police stem the rapidly rising tide of crime around the estate.

It was, he had concluded reluctantly over the years, an impossible job. It had now been effectively derailed by the recent collision between lawlessness and brute force in which the two joy-riders had been killed. Davies had bluntly enough made his views on that score known to his own inspector at HQ, but was wary of sharing his reservations with a senior officer from CID.

He eased a finger between the collar of his short-sleeved cotton shirt and his neck, and lifted himself gently off the car seat for a moment, feeling the sweat run down the small of his back in rivulets. Even with all the windows open, the heat in the car was almost intolerable. Thackeray had parked opposite Bronte House, where half an hour before there had been a patch of shade. But the morning advanced, and the sun now shone directly onto the rear windscreen. Davies glanced at the chief inspector in word-less entreaty, but he was watching intently the comings and goings on the estate, apparently oblivious to discomfort.

Thackeray too was casually dressed. This was the second of the two days Longley had allotted him to talk to Huddleston and his sergeant about the Tracy Miller murder, but he had decided to use the morning to talk to Davies as informally as he could manage about the more immediate problems at Wuthering. So far without noticeable success.

Davies was a stocky, sandy-haired man with a broad, untroubled face, whose career had remained obstinately on the bottom rung for much longer than it had taken Thackeray to climb to his present relative eminence. He evidently regarded this intrusion by CID into the affairs of the uniformed branch with deep suspicion.

'I don't know what more I can tell you, sir,' Davies said, his uneasiness showing in his pale blue eyes.

'It's not facts I'm after,' Thackeray said, taking pity on him at last. 'More impressions. We know what we know about what's going on up here, we know the established villains, we can haul them in any time we like. But this is different. This is new. And there has to be more to it than uncoordinated mayhem caused by a few young tearaways. Why was that car nicked in Harrogate, for instance? That's a long trip for youngsters of that age. And why a mobile phone? That was nicked too, but not with that car. It came from an Escort which disappeared in Leeds and hasn't turned up since.

'They weren't carrying that on the off-chance their mums would call them up, were they? Did they organise all that themselves or were they helped? Don't tell me about the villains we know. Tell me about the ones we're only guessing at. Give me the whispers, the rumours, give me a feel for the place, Alan.'

Davies hesitated, wondering how far he could trust the dark, impassive man who had only recently arrived in Bradfield and who remained something of an enigma, apparently, even to his junior officers in CID, still more to the uniformed branch whose efforts to contain the simmering lawlessness on the Heights had so far been so conspicuously unsuccessful.

Davies looked for veiled criticism of his own role in Thackeray's unexpectedly blue eyes but could read nothing there except curiosity – an apparently genuine desire to know and comprehend the towering blocks looming above them, the rubber-streaked streets, and the occasional aimless group of young people who drifted across the estate like so much flotsam on the tide.

'The kids who were killed,' Davies said. 'They were the usual young tearaways, done all the usual things, been cautioned, been on probation. But I did think the Astra was out of their league. A cut above – you know? It's usually lads a bit older.' Thackeray nodded thoughtfully.

'Fourteen and thirteen. That's what I thought,' he said. He watched intently as two teenaged girls in extremely tight, short shorts and loose tee-shirts pulled provocatively off-the-shoulder swaggered towards Bronte House. He glanced up at the flats, their façades smoke-stained and blanked off by boarded windows here and there.

'Those two look as though they're asking for trouble,' he said, nodding at the girls. 'And an Asian girl? That's unusual, isn't it?'

'There's no Asian families up here,' Davies said. 'The council allocated a couple of flats in Priestley to Paki – sorry, Asian – families a couple of years back but the yobs soon drove them out. But you come across a few Asian runaways around town now.'

'Are they local or just visiting, then?' Thackeray said, watching intently as the girls picked their way past the heap of wilting flowers in the doorway and used a key to open the entrance door to the flats.

'Difficult to tell,' Davies said non-committally. 'I don't know everyone by sight and there's at least a dozen flats in there with squatters in and out, mostly youngsters. The lasses are on the game. That, or they're nicking some very classy gear.'

'So it's not just the lads running wild?'

Davies shook his head.

'There's very few of them under twenty-five who've ever had a job. If they get dole – which the younger ones don't – it barely covers their keep. If they want booze, or fags, or drugs – and most of them are into that too – they'll nick summat just to set themselves up. And for kicks, there's the cars.'

Davies's eyes smouldered with an anger which had burned slowly within him ever since he had watched the stolen Astra and two young lives disintegrate in the harsh light of the police helicopter.

'Hard times are no excuse,' Thackeray said. 'There's plenty resist the temptation.' It was a view offered without much conviction by a man who had fought temptation himself and lost far more often than he had won, but he wanted to hear Davies's reaction.

'Aye, well, I dare say that's right,' Davies prevaricated, unwilling to contradict, but a streak of stubbornness resisting the analysis. 'But if I'd been brought up in these rabbit warrens I'd not put money on which side o't'law I'd be on now.'

'You don't think we should have come in mob-handed the other night?'

Davies looked away and shrugged dispiritedly.

'Not my decision, sir,' he said.

'But if it had been?' Thackeray persisted. Davies turned and looked Thackeray full in the face.

'I told you, sir,' he said, his fury barely suppressed now. 'I've flogged my guts out up here for three years trying to win us a few friends. This morning no one would even give me the time of day.'

'But there've been people asking for tougher action,' Thackeray objected.

'Some,' Davies conceded. 'There's more been out on the streets enjoying the fun. Any road, the law-and-order brigade are keeping their heads down this morning. Wuthering's closed ranks.'

Thackeray sank into a watchful silence again. He agreed

with much that Alan Davies had said. So-called community policing threatened to become a waste of time in communities like this, he thought, communities tacitly left to rot as the blocks of flats disintegrated and decency ebbed away. He glanced up at the battered grey hulk that was Bronte House and wished it wiped off the face of the earth.

Outside the sun beat down on the dusty, yellowing grass and a straggle of women with pushchairs and small children in tow made their way from the adventure playground towards the flats. As several of the mothers approached the doors of Bronte House, Thackeray was surprised to see a figure he recognised come out. Laura Ackroyd glanced somewhat wearily around but apparently failed to notice the police presence. She pushed her hair away from her face with a slightly dispirited but familiar gesture before making her way towards her own car across the street.

Thackeray's lips tightened perceptibly and he took a deep breath as he watched Laura stride across the road, her short cotton skirt swinging above slim, lightly tanned legs, her hair like a beacon above her pale face in the bright sunshine. What, he wondered, is she doing up here – which, given the tension on the estate, was a legitimate question. And why, after all this time, does the unexpected sight of her still take my breath away, he thought, which was a question he did not want to answer at all.

Almost in spite of himself he told a curious Davies to wait and got out of the car. Laura saw him immediately and her smile was as welcoming as his was uncertain.

'How are you?' Thackeray asked. 'How's your ankle? I've been meaning to call you ever since you came back from Portugal . . .'

'You knew I was back, then?' Laura asked lightly. 'I was tempted to stay. There was this gorgeous PR man from Lisbon with an unpronounceable name my father invited to dinner. Had a look of Tom Cruise . . .' But as she caught the gravity of Thackeray's blue eyes, the mischief in her own faded. 'I'm fine,' she said quietly, remembering, as she knew he was, the horror of their last meeting when he had found her lying half-conscious and in pain. 'The leg's healed now, and for the rest . . .' She shrugged. 'It fades slowly.'

He nodded at that, knowing how slowly. The silence between them lengthened as if each had too much to say to know where to begin.

'Are you writing about the joy-riders?' Thackeray asked at last, opting for safety as he glanced at the tape-recorder which was clearly visible in Laura's open shoulder-bag. She hesitated, not wanting to lie and yet reluctant to tell him the real reason for her visit to Bronte.

'I had an interview to do,' she said non-committally.

'For your television programme?' Thackeray hazarded.

'How did you find out about that?' Laura asked, suddenly feeling at a disadvantage as she picked up the note of disapproval in his voice. She flushed slightly.

'I suppose it was that bastard Kevin Mower,' she said. 'I should have known he wouldn't respect a confidence.'

'Not if there's an advantage to be gained by not respecting it.' Thackeray's assessment was unexpectedly harsh. 'And I think on balance I can do him more good than you can.'

Laura digested that slowly, wondering just how insulting it was supposed to be. She did not reply and the sparkle that had lit up her face when she first saw Thackeray faded. She gazed tiredly across the littered grass towards the flats, embarrassed by her own presumptuous pleasure at meeting a man who clearly was not much moved to see her again. 'You don't have a high opinion of reporters, do you?' she asked irritably.

'They have a job to do,' he said. 'I don't think it should interfere with mine.'

'Even if you've got it wrong?'

'So you are investigating the Tracy Miller case?' he asked.

'Do you have a problem with that?'

'That programme's had more misses than hits,' he said. 'And Harry Huddleston's something of a local hero. You'll get no encouragement on this one.'

'Perhaps that's just because the police close ranks so

53

effectively when their methods are questioned,' Laura came back quickly. 'I didn't expect that from you.'

'I don't like to see honest coppers hounded for no good reason,' he said. 'No one does.'

'Then it's a pity there are so many dishonest ones about,' Laura said sharply, looking slightly flushed now. 'If that boy's been locked up for ten years for no good reason, it's high time someone got him out. Ten years in gaol is a damn sight worse than any embarrassment "Case Re-opened" can cause the police now.'

'He can appeal,' Thackeray said, knowing he'd blown it, as he had half intended, but only half.

'He did appeal, and much good that did him.' She did not bother to hide her anger now. 'If Harry Huddleston got it right, he has nothing to worry about, has he?'

'Just so long as you get it right too,' Thackeray said.

Laura turned away from him to hide the disappointment in her eyes, and unlocked her car. For a second Thackeray looked as though he might reach out and take her arm, but then he shrugged and turned back to his own car to meet the still curious gaze of PC Davies.

'Bloody reporters,' Thackeray said as he turned the key viciously and revved the engine.

'Always poking about where they're not wanted,' Davies offered sagely. 'Not that she's not got nice legs on her, that one.'

Thackeray groaned silently as Laura's Beetle pulled away from the kerb ahead of them and accelerated down the hill towards the town.

'I've never gone much for red hair, myself, though,' Davies burbled from the passenger seat and was astonished when his superior responded with a single and to his mind totally unjustified expletive.

'Take the car back to HQ, will you,' Thackeray said suddenly. 'I feel like a walk.' Without waiting for a response from the astonished Davies, he got out of the car again and walked briskly away towards the centre of the estate.

He had wanted time to think, but as he made his way

past the old people's bungalows which huddled beneath the shadow of the flats, he was surprised to hear a shrill whistle. Nonplussed, he hesitated, searching for the source of the sound.

'Nah then,' said a voice in a piercing whisper which clearly came from the bungalow he was closest to. 'Nah then. You! Copper!' The door of the bungalow was open slightly and as he opened the gate and went slowly across the tiny patch of garden, it swung wider, revealing an elderly man sitting in the hallway in a wheelchair, a maroon muffler firmly tucked around his neck and into his tweed jacket despite the oppressive heat of the day.

'Come in quick, lad,' the figure said conspiratorially. 'I've got summat I want to tell you. Stan Jackson's the name.'

Thackeray followed him into an untidy and sparsely furnished living-room which smelled faintly of cats and disinfectant. The house had been adapted for a wheelchair but its occupant was evidently not much of a housekeeper. The old man looked at Thackcray warily for a moment, his eyes bright with some unfathomable emotion in a face as grey and lined as that of a mummy.

'I want guarantees,' he said at length. 'I need to get out of here, else they'll be chucking bricks through t'window if they find out I've been talking to thee. Or worse.'

'What is it you want to talk about, Mr Jackson?' Thackeray asked cautiously.

'Them bloody joy-riders,' the old man said. 'Some bloody joy they bring. Young Mark, that were killed. He were my great-grandson.'

'I'm sorry,' Thackeray said, understanding the old man's glittering eyes now, the tears held in check by determined pride.

'I'm eighty, you know,' the old man said fiercely. 'I fought at El Alamein. I didn't reckon I'd have to put up wi'this.'

'Is there anywhere you can go, if you feel unsafe here?' Thackeray asked, knowing that the old man's fears were not idle ones. Intimidation was a major industry on the

Heights, 'grassing' a serious offence and age no defence at all.

'If you can get me some transport I can go to my sister's in Halifax. She's always asking. She's seventy-six and nearly as decrepit as I am.' He laughed mirthlessly. 'Do her good to have someone else to look after, silly old cow,' he said.

Thackeray used the old man's phone to make arrangements with social services, who prevaricated until he lost his temper and told them that this was a matter of life and death. Having got the assurances he wanted, he put the phone down angrily and turned back to find the old man offering a toothless grin of appreciation.

'You tell them useless buggers,' he said. 'They're supposed to come and clean this place up twice a week and I'm lucky if I see 'em once a fortnight. Community bloody care!'

'This had better be good,' Thackeray said, wondering if he was being used.

'Do you want to catch them beggars or not?' the old man snapped.

'Of course,' Thackeray said gently and settled down to listen. What Jackson had to tell was simple enough. Confined as he was to his wheelchair, he had become an inveterate watcher of the world as it passed his front window where he sat for hours, concealed behind the net curtains. He had got to know most of the estate's residents by sight and watched their comings and goings with unquenchably malicious curiosity.

The joy-riding had excited him at first as the cars had screamed past his grandstand seat. But infrequent visits from his relatives had intimated that young Mark might be involved and he became alarmed. It was only then that he began to notice that on the nights when displays materialised an unusual number of vehicles had previously made their way to the hollow square of lock-up garages opposite his bungalow, arriving at dusk and disappearing into the complex, sometimes for days at a time, to roar forth, as if at some appointed signal, on the nights of the displays.

'I thought it were a bit o'harmless fun at first,' Jackson said. Thackeray looked at him in despair, although he knew that many, perhaps the majority, of the people on the estate had gone along with that view for a time, and many still did.

'What sort of cars are we talking about?' he asked. 'And how many?'

'I've not counted,' Jackson said. 'And I'm not right good at makes of cars. Fast, though, and expensive. I must have seen a couple of dozen over t'last month or so. They've not all been in t'displays. Some of them come and go without t'lads driving them at all, as far as I can see.'

'Can you see which garages they're using?' Thackeray asked, but Jackson could not be much more specific. His view of the garages was restricted and he could not easily change his position, but that they were being used to store the stolen vehicles he had no doubt.

'Do you think there are any there now?' Thackeray asked, but Jackson shook his head.

'I've seen nowt,' he said emphatically. 'Nowt since the night Mark and t'other lad were killed. They're keeping a – what d'you call it? – a low profile?' Which was not surprising, Thackeray thought, and he wondered how long they would maintain it.

'We'll not rush in,' he said slowly. 'You could help us, if you're going away, by leaving us a key so that we can keep watching from your window. Would you be willing to do that?'

'Oh, aye,' the old man said, a single tear shining in the corner of his eye. 'I'd like to see them beggars hang. They're effing murderers, aren't they?'

FIVE

THE CHURCH OF THE SACRED Heart in Arnedale was as
dim and cool a refuge from the afternoon sunshine as
Thackeray remembered it. It was a modern building,
winner of architectural prizes for its unadorned concrete
echoes of old Romanesque basilicas. The narrow lance-
olate windows were set at an angle and their abstract
patterns of coloured glass cast lozenges of azure and gold
across the tiled floor and the pale oak pews. They filtered
the light and air even on the hottest of days such as this
and maintained an even temperature which as a boy
Thackeray had thought of as an integral part of a holy
place, as essential to achieving a state of grace as the faint
smell of incense and the piercing sound of the choir.

It had been a place of intense joy to him in his youth. He
had taken his first communion and been married here.
The pain of seeing his son's tiny coffin in front of the
golden sandstone altar had drowned those earlier
memories in bitterness, but even now, years later, he was
drawn reluctantly back to the church whenever he had
cause to drive near Arnedale.

He sat quietly in the tiny Lady Chapel facing a rack of
flickering candles in front of a pale, sad-faced plaster
Virgin and Child. He had put his silver into the box and
held a tall translucent candle to a guttering neighbour not
out of any vestigial belief in the efficacy of prayer, but
simply as a remembrance of the faith which, in spite of
what had come after, had made him what he was.

He sat for a long time, hoping to be soothed by the
silence and mesmerised by the flickering flames, as he had

often been before. But today he found that the solace of the place was not so easily come by and old wounds felt newly raw. Laura Ackroyd's sparkling green eyes and guileless smile of greeting came unbidden into his mind again and again, and he cursed himself for his gratuitously graceless response. Laura offered the possibility of a new beginning, something he had scarcely dared contemplate since his son's death and scarcely dared imagine now.

He was unaware of anyone approaching until a hand on his shoulder made him turn round with a start.

'It's good to see you, Michael,' said the priest who had come quietly up behind him. There was an unexpected warmth in Thackeray's smile as he faced Frank Rafferty.

'You're looking well,' he said, taking in the elderly priest's ruddy complexion under the thick iron-grey hair which seemed hardly to have changed over the last ten years of an at times stormy relationship.

'And you're not looking too bad yourself, my son,' Rafferty said, a hint of amusement in his sharp blue eyes and more than a hint of Irish in his voice. 'I take it you've not come to confession – or has there been a trip to Damascus since I last saw you?'

Thackeray shook his head with a glimmer of a smile.

'No chance,' he said. In spite of past battles, he liked the old man and valued the friendship of someone who had been generous enough not to bear grudges and to offer him help when few others would.

'I come to talk to Ian,' Thackeray said, without affectation, glancing at the simple plaque on the wall of the chapel, a memorial to his baby son. 'He'd have been going to secondary school soon. I'd have been taking him training at the rugby club. I wonder if he'd have taken to rugby. He had a good pair of shoulders on him.'

It was said lightly but Thackeray could not maintain the pretence for long and he turned away suddenly to hide the spasm of pain that seized him. A look of helplessness passed briefly across Rafferty's face, aging him even in the soft afternoon light.

'God has forgiven you, Michael,' he said quietly. 'Can

you still not forgive yourself?'

Thackeray turned back, his face set now as immovably as one of the carved images on the stone face of the altar. 'No,' he said shortly, getting to his feet. 'I don't think I'll ever do that. But don't worry about it, Frank. I've learned to live with it.'

The two men walked slowly towards the door of the church, Rafferty's cassock swinging gently and sending motes of dust wafting into the narrow shafts of coloured sunlight where they hung, dancing, like sparks from a fire. As they crossed the main aisle, the priest genuflected towards the sanctuary where a red lamp glowed, while Thackeray stood unmoving at his side.

'Have you seen your mother recently?' Rafferty asked, as they paused for a moment on the threshold, reluctant to pass from the coolness of the church into the glare of the sunshine beyond.

Thackeray shook his head.

'I'm not welcome there,' he said. 'She hasn't forgiven me either.' Rafferty nodded, knowing the truth of that. If Thackeray was implacable in some things it was not difficult for anyone who knew his family to work out from whom he had inherited that iron will.

'She's not well,' the priest said quietly. 'I took her the Sacrament a couple of weeks back and thought she was worse than I'd seen her. If you can find your way to go up there at all, I think it would be a kindness.'

'I'll call my father,' Thackeray conceded. He pulled open the swing door with an angry gesture and Rafferty thought he intended to leave on that note, but at the last moment he hesitated and turned back, his expression softening slightly.

'There's no help for it,' he said. 'There's not a day when I don't think of Ian. Time doesn't heal, it only blurs the edges a bit. But I get by.'

'I'll pray for you,' Rafferty said, and both men knew that he meant precisely what he said. 'Though I know you won't thank me for it.'

'Feel free.'

Thackeray strode back to his car without a backward glance.

'Shut t'door or tha'll let t'bloody sheep in!' Jim Redding was sitting on the customers' side of his almost empty bar and had clearly decided that his role in life after the police force was to become a character landlord, a handy asset to his character pub. The Waggoners was a low stone building, indistinguishable – apart from its gently swinging sign – from the neighbouring cottages on the main street of Culham, a dales village which at this time of the year attracted its share of tourists.

A few visitors were still ensconced to one side of the main bar finishing off late lunches provided by a plump and cheerful woman Thackeray assumed must be Mrs Redding, who occasionally emerged from her steamy kitchen with another portion of cod or chicken or steak pie and chips. Drinks were being desultorily served by a pale young girl in jeans and tee-shirt behind the bar, leaving the landlord to entertain the punters from his tall stool in the corner of the room, where he could keep a weather eye on staff, customers and invading sheep alike.

In spite of a comfortable corpulence, Redding had a sharp eye which sized up the newcomer fast and efficiently and switched his expression from professional bonhomie to deep suspicion in an instant. He surveyed the world from within a luxuriant growth of gingery hair – a long back and sides which would have earned him short shrift on the beat – plus flourishing sideboards and a moustache of Dickensian proportions. But the blue eyes were icily watchful.

'You must be Thackeray,' he said. 'D'you want owt to drink?' When Thackeray shook his head, Redding slid off his tall stool and gestured that he should follow him into a back room. Here he waved him into a battered armchair crammed into a corner beside an untidy desk from which he evidently conducted the administration of his business.

'So what's up, then?' Redding demanded aggressively. 'It must be summat serious to bring a DCI all this way out

61

of Bradfield. Found a few skeletons rattling around in t'cupboards, have you?'

'I hope not,' Thackeray said, irritated by the ex-sergeant's manner. 'And Jack Longley hopes not, too. Do you know different?' Longley's name gave Redding momentary pause. It was clearly not one he took lightly.

'He ran a tight ship, did the super,' Redding said. 'Just promoted and not for standing any nonsense when I were coming up for retirement.'

'He still runs a tight ship. And so do I,' Thackeray said.

'So what's up, then? There was nowt untoward going on when I were in Bradfield CID, nowt I was aware of, any road.'

'Someone's trying to pick over the Tracy Miller murder,' Thackeray said. 'Looking for a miscarriage of justice, they say. You remember the case?'

Redding's face darkened with anger.

'You don't forget that sort,' he said vehemently. 'Poor little beggar, dumped like a sack of rubbish for t'bin men. I remember it. No one who saw her's likely to forget it.'

'And you got the right lad? No mistakes there? No one bullied that confession out of him? Thumped him till he said what you wanted him to say.' There was an edge of anger to Thackeray's voice now and Redding hesitated for a moment, as if weighing his words, before he replied.

'Bullied, no,' he said at last. 'No one laid a finger on Stephen Webster to my knowledge, and I were with him most o't'time right up to when he went to court. Which isn't to say there weren't plenty around the station who'd have liked to have given him a good hiding. Or that Harry Huddleston were a soft touch. Nor me, for that matter. We pushed him hard, very hard. We knew he'd done it. He'd lied to us: statements were contradictory, we had eye-witnesses to say he wasn't where he said he was when he said he was – but we wanted an admission to charge him. You must have read the reports if you've taken the trouble to come all this way to ask. It were a long hot night. I can remember it as if it were yesterday. We ground him down, I dare say, and in the end he confessed. But bullied – no.'

'A lad of fifteen?' Thackeray said, a dangerous softness in his voice.

'Just sixteen, as I recall,' Redding said defensively. 'Old enough.'

'Old enough to be ground down by you and Harry Huddleston?'

'Not a kid. A big lad, not bright, but well capable of killing that child. Well capable.'

'Who wrote out his statement? It's not in his own hand.' Thackeray changed tack.

'I think I did. I took the notes.'

'And it was a true and accurate record?'

'Aye, it bloody were,' Redding said vehemently. 'Do you think we set him up, or summat? You must be bloody mad.'

'It wouldn't be the first time, or the last,' Thackeray said. 'Jack Longley would be pressing for an arrest. And the Press.'

'Aye, they're always pressing for summat, the Press,' Redding said bitterly. 'They don't have to stand up in court and make the charge stick, do they. But Harry Huddleston wasn't a man to give in to that sort of hassle. Took his time, did Harry, played it by the book. You can dig around till you're blue in the face, Mr Thackeray, but you'll not unstick Stephen Webster's conviction because the jury returned a true verdict. The little toe-rag did it and he got what he deserved. Personally I'd have liked to see him hang.'

June Webster had gone to ground ten miles away from the Heights like a frightened animal taking to its burrow. In an anonymous suburb of Eckersley she had metamorphosed into June Baker, mistress of a conspicuously respectable pebble-dashed semi with a neat patch of garden front and rear and a well-polished red Metro on the drive. She opened the door to Laura almost as soon as the chimes of the doorbell had stopped ringing and glanced anxiously up and down the road at the deserted pavements and net-curtained windows of her neighbours before waving her inside.

She was a small woman, dressed in a cream blouse and

blue skirt which were as neat and characterless as a school uniform, her grey hair carefully waved around a face which had been delicately pretty before anxiety and grief had marked it with a mosaic of fine lines which no conventional make-up, however carefully applied, could disguise. June Baker put a brave face to the world, but Laura could see the fragility of her composure and sensed that here she must tread very carefully indeed.

The house had that dustless, highly polished, sterile look only achieved in a home that is little used. Two coats hung on the pegs near the front door, a morning newspaper was neatly folded on the coffee table, the cushions on the settee remained as freshly plumped as they must have been when Mrs Baker had tidied them that morning, and the pale Wilton carpet was innocent of dog hairs and biscuit crumbs, a blank slate upon which Laura felt it would be rash to make any mark.

'I think this was all a mistake,' June Baker said, waving Laura towards an armchair placed at a precise angle towards the gas log fire, unlit but startlingly dust free on this midsummer afternoon. 'I shouldn't have done it really. I can't think what got into me. There's nothing to be done about Stephen now, is there? It's too late. Too late altogether?' Her search for reassurance took on a hysterical edge as she perched herself opposite Laura, her hands clasped tightly between her knees, revealing an edge of white lace petticoat beneath her navy cotton skirt.

'Too late to find out the truth or too late for it to make any difference to Stephen?' Laura asked gently.

Mrs Baker looked at her visitor for a moment as if the question were too complicated for her to deal with. A single tear crept slowly down her cheek, leaving a rivulet in the heavy powder.

'Both,' she said at last. 'It's ten years.'

'But you wrote to "Case Re-opened",' Laura said. 'Did you have any fresh evidence that made you think that maybe Stephen could appeal after all this time?'

'No, it wasn't that. It was all these other cases, people being let out after fifteen years or more, the police making up evidence and that. I never believed Stephen had done it, never. He was fond of Tracy, but fond like a brother, not the way they made it out to be at the trial. Not all that mucky stuff.'

The sheer helpless horror that Mrs Baker must have felt all those years ago as her son was tried and convicted was etched now in her face as she strove to keep control. But that could be genuine, Laura thought, trying hard to be objective, whether or not Stephen Webster was guilty. Mother-love could be famously blind.

'So you don't know of any new avenue we could explore?' Laura persisted, her disappointment evident in her tone. Mrs Baker shook her head.

'It was the state Stephen's got into that made me write in,' she said dully. 'You know what they do with child murderers in jail, don't you? There's a thing called Rule 43. They lock them up in solitary for their own protection. He was in a youth custody place at first and he was always getting thumped there. Then when they transferred him to an adult jail they put him in a cell on his own. It's no life for a young lad. He's got more and more strange. He's all pale and withdrawn, hardly seems to recognise me when I visit sometimes. And now they're saying he'll have to go to a special hospital. But they've made him like that, haven't they? They've driven him mad. And I'm terrified they'll never let him out. He'll be in there for life.'

Tears streamed down June Baker's face as finally she gave vent to the sheer despair which had driven her against all her instincts out of her quiet suburban sanctuary into the public world of television programmes and prying reporters. Laura put an arm awkwardly around her shoulder.

'Do you have any children?' Mrs Baker asked fiercely through her tears. Laura shook her head.

'If you haven't got children you can't understand,' the other woman said with a sort of rough contempt. Laura guessed that she was right and wondered how she could tell her that if there really was no fresh evidence of Stephen's innocence then it was very unlikely that the programme she represented would be willing or able to do anything at all to help her or her son.

'Let's go back to the beginning,' she said gently, switching on her tape-recorder. 'Tell me what happened to you the day Tracy was killed. Where were you that afternoon? She disappeared at tea-time, didn't she?'

'I was at work, wasn't I? I worked as a supervisor at Tesco in town – it was a good job. Paul hadn't worked since his wife left him with the kids. He went to a few interviews when I moved in, but no one was interested in someone who hadn't worked for years. So he stopped at home and made sure they all got their tea when they came in from school, did the shopping – you know? He went on drawing the dole. We weren't married or anything so we reckoned he was entitled.

'Anyway, that night was one of my late nights at work. I was meant to be working until eight, though in fact I got off about half six when Paul rang up and said Tracy was missing. She should have been home from school at half past three.'

'He didn't go to meet her?' Laura prompted.

'She was ten. She said she didn't need meeting any more,' Mrs Baker said. 'Very independent, was Tracy. Felt her nose pushed out of joint a bit with her dad, I think, when Stephen and I moved in. Kelly was still just at nursery in the mornings, so she was home all afternoon. Paul fetched her home about twelve. She was a nice kid. I think she liked having a new mum.'

'And Stephen?'

'Stephen went to St Mark's. Started there when we moved to Bronte House. He came home on the bus and didn't usually get in till about four. But that evening Paul said he didn't come in at all, at least not before he decided to take Kelly out and look for Tracy. Stephen said later that he did come home, and there was no one there, so he watched television for a bit and then went out again down the rec to play football.'

'But no one saw him there until much later?' Laura asked, recalling the summary of the evidence against

66

Stephen that 'Case Re-opened' had provided.

'No one,' June Baker said dully. 'Not until about six. They said Tracy must have been dead by five o'clock. They found her body about eight that evening. It wasn't even dark. The only witness who said he'd seen Stephen at all before six was the caretaker, Jerry Hurst – "Fat Jerry" the kids used to call him. I never liked him and Stephen hated him. Perhaps that's why he never budged over his story. He'd seen Steve going out of the building before five, he said, though Steve swore blind that wasn't true.'

'And at the police station he confessed,' Laura said softly.

'They questioned him for the best part of a day and a night,' Mrs Baker said, the look of pain distorting her features again. 'That big bloke Huddleston, Chief Inspector Huddleston. Steve would never say what happened in all that time they had him at the station before he was charged, but it changed him. He wasn't my boy after that. He looked stunned. He's never been the same since. I lost him then.'

'You think they bullied the confession out of him?' Laura asked, a faint feeling of excitement returning as she broached the other way of approaching a programme about Stephen Webster. 'Put words into his mouth?' she knew that there were ways of analysing both the written record and the language of a confession to discover whether it was in the actual words of the alleged writer or not. At Stephen Webster's trial much had been made of that damning statement, although the boy had denied its veracity later.

'He wasn't bruised or anything,' his mother said reluctantly. 'They hadn't thumped him, if that's what you mean. But that Huddleston looks like a bully. He could scare me, so I don't like to think what he did to Stephen when he had him locked up all that time.'

'He didn't have a solicitor with him?'

'Not till later, after he'd signed the confession statement. Then they got him a solicitor.'

'Did Stephen complain about the way he was treated?'

67

'No, he never said much. Just that he never laid a finger on Tracy and why wouldn't anyone believe him. I think he lost heart, though, when he was on remand. He sort of gave up.'

'Did Stephen have a girlfriend?' Laura asked, remembering what Kelly Miller had said about a girl.

'Not that I know of,' his mother said confidently. 'Friends at school, but no one special. Of course they made a lot of fuss about some copies of *Playboy* they found in his room when they arrested him, but I don't see that proved anything. I'd have given him a good talking-to if I'd found them, mind, but I don't see that a few dirty pictures prove he was a murderer.'

'Given the high circulation of girlie mags and the very low murder rate I shouldn't think there's a very obvious connection,' Laura said dryly.

She switched the tape-recorder off and leaned back in her chair with a sigh.

'There's not much to go on, Mrs Baker, I have to be honest,' she said. 'I'll talk to one or two other people before I write a report for "Case Re-opened", but I can't promise they'll take up the case.'

June Baker got up and stood looking out of her bay window at the sun-soaked suburban street outside, her face tear-streaked but calm now.

'I suppose I'm clutching at straws,' she said. 'Anyway, I'm not sure I could take all the publicity all over again. And my husband would have a fit if he knew I'd been in touch with you.'

'You haven't told him?' Laura asked, surprised.

'He travels for his job. I'm here on my own a lot,' Mrs Baker said dully. 'He's been very good to me, has Tom, but I wouldn't say we're really close.'

'And you didn't have any more children?' Laura asked, knowing that was a superfluous question in this tidy house, as quiet and unsullied as a grave.

'Oh, no,' Mrs Baker said. 'I've lost one son. I couldn't risk another.'

SIX

'HOW MANY ATTACKS IS THIS?' the woman asked angrily, putting a protective arm around the small girl who was huddled on the sofa beside her. 'Where's it going to finish up?' She glanced at her daughter and bit her lip, unwilling to spell out the fear which now overwhelmed her and most parents on the Heights, but no one in the room was in any doubt as to what she meant. A policewoman sat close to the child and Thackeray was opposite in shirt-sleeves in a low chair, a small tape-recorder on the coffee-table between them.

They were in the 'soft' interview room at the central police station, a place reserved for the most vulnerable victims of crime. The pale, thin child was wrapped in a towelling dressing-gown too large for her and in spite of the still stifling heat, she was shivering slightly and kept glancing at Michael Thackeray with a look of sheer terror in her eyes. Her mother tightened her grip on her daughter and glared at the chief inspector, unable to put her feelings into words.

'We're doing our best,' he said quietly. 'Believe me. We take it just as seriously as you do.'

The woman shrugged, rigid with shock and outraged disbelief.

'What am I to tell her dad when he gets home?' she asked helplessly. 'He'll do 'is nut.' The child shuddered and began to sob quietly.

'Mrs Renton, we need to ask Josie some more questions, but if you think she'd be happier with a female detective, I can arrange that,' Thackeray said, feeling the situation

69

drifting away from him. He had only two female detectives on his team and one was on leave and the other off duty and so far all efforts had failed to find her.

'Would you like to talk to a lady policeman?' Mrs Renton asked the sobbing child, who nodded dumbly.

'Fine,' Thackeray said reluctantly, unwilling to waste the time it would need to comply, but he got to his feet.

'I'll send someone in with some tea. Have a chat with Wendy here while you're waiting,' he said, nodding to the WPC and leaving the interview room with a shaming sense of relief. He pounded up the stairs to his own office two at a time to work off some of the anger and guilt this sort of case always engendered. Superintendent Jack Longley was standing by the window in his room waiting for him, a face as thunderous as the threatening weather outside.

'Another one?' he asked. 'Serious, is it?'

'She wasn't raped. She's had a medical, and her clothes have gone to forensic.' Thackeray said shortly. 'Not that that's much consolation. She's in a state of shock and her mother's going bananas. Father's a long-distance truck driver. We're trying to trace him.'

'Statements?'

'Not yet. I can't get hold of either of my women DCs and the kid's scared to death at the sight of me.' Thackeray said bitterly.

'Get on to Milford and see if they've got anyone on duty we can borrow,' Longley said. 'Is the community bobby – what's his name? – Alan Davies on duty?'

'No, I've asked the duty inspector to call him in, and I've sent for Mower. In the meantime the scene-of-crime lads are examining the alleyway where it happened and Craig has started to organise a house-to-house at the flats. We'll not get right round tonight, but they're starting with Bronte House. I'll start on the usual suspects here. We did it last time and they all seemed to be in the clear, but you never know. They'll scream blue murder about harassment, of course.'

'Pull all the stops out, Michael,' Longley said. 'Don't mess about. Four assaults in six weeks is bad news by any

70

standards, and with all this other bother up there we'll have a Toxteth on our hands if we're not careful. I was at a conference about urban tensions last month, all analysis and how to measure the bloody pressure. An unnecessary load of cobblers if you want my opinion. A good copper knows his patch, and if you ask me Wuthering's about ready to blow.'

As Longley swept out, Detective Sergeant Kevin Mower stood aside to let him pass, getting an old-fashioned look from the superintendent for his trouble.

'I thought he was going to tell me to get a short back and sides, guv,' Mower said ruefully rubbing a hand over his stubble. 'What does he want me to do? Wear a little badge saying "I'm a detective working undercover" on my nice clean shirt and tie or what?'

Mower was dressed in jeans and a not very clean tee-shirt, and with his lengthening dark hair and unshaven, sun-tanned face had taken on a distinctly Mediterranean appearance. He slumped behind his desk, unable to disguise his weariness.

'You look as if you're about to audition for a part in Il Trovatore,' Thackeray said sourly. 'So what's all this play-acting come up with? As far as I can see I've got another traumatised child downstairs and not a single clue as to who's terrorising them. So what's the news from the play-group, or wherever it is you've been sun-bathing?'

Mower gave a token smile at the joke, knowing that it was not intended to be entirely humorous. He could see the tension in Thackeray's face and knew that it pervaded the whole station, where off-duty officers had appeared as if summoned by magic to help with the inquiry. Even Mower, as a relative newcomer to the town, knew that the Heights was now threatening Bradfield like some unexploded bomb. He wiped tiny beads of sweat from his brow. It looked as if he too had run up the stairs, although he would never admit to being driven by that level of enthusiasm or anxiety.

'The trouble is, the more frightened they get the harder it is to pin anything down,' he said. 'Most parents are bringing their kids to the playground and fetching them home again afterwards. If you set up a surveillance of the stairways and back alleys between the flats you could be there for a month before you saw a single child under fifteen out alone,' Mower said soberly. 'The older ones go round in gangs, the little ones are being taken everywhere.'

'Until they fail to do as they're told, like Josie Renton,' Thackeray said. 'She went to a friend's flat to watch a video and didn't wait for her mother to fetch her back.'

The chief inspector sat down wearily at his desk and ran his hands through his springy dark hair.

'Each one is more violent than the one before,' he said. 'He had something over her face, his hands round her neck. She's badly bruised. You know where that's leading, don't you?'

Mower nodded sombrely. They both knew that there was a pattern to this sort of crime and that with every attack the risk to a child's life grew more acute.

'It looks as though we're going to have to do this the hard way,' Thackeray said. 'I've asked the boys doing the house-to-house to ask every man they interview not only where he was today at the relevant time, but at the time of the other attacks as well, and who can vouch for them. If we put it all onto the computer we should be able to get some sort of pattern established. It has to be someone local, someone who's on the spot and can seize the opportunity to grab a child when it presents itself. I think it might be better if you packed in the playground now and came back to base. I need you here.'

Mower shook his head angrily.

'Not yet, guv,' he said. 'We knew it would take time. They're just beginning to trust me. Sue, the girl who runs the play-scheme, is into everything up there. She and I are getting on quite well.' He gave Thackeray a faint smile, wondering whether to expand on that remark and thinking better of it in response to the chief inspector's chilly expression. 'Sooner or later it will begin to pay off. They'll talk to me. I'll hear things.'

'We pay Alan Davies and the other community bobbies to hear things,' Thackeray said. 'And there's the lads from uniformed we've put in to watch the garages. There's a limit to the time they can be spared. I can't afford to keep you up there any longer.'

'They won't talk to Alan now,' Mower said, controlling his anger with difficulty. 'I have picked up that much. Since the kids were killed in the car they'll not give any copper the time of day if they can avoid it.'

'If that's the case they're going to find some little girl strangled next time,' Thackeray said. He looked at the sergeant appraisingly, sensing the ambition that drove him and wondering whether it might not one day drive him too far.

'All right,' he conceded at last. 'I'll give you another week. But I want daily reports on what you pick up. And watch what you're up to with your informants. We want a "sex on the rates" scandal all over the Gazette like we want a hole in the head.' Mower grinned disarmingly at that.

'In the meantime, you can hang on and interview the usual suspects with me. I've asked the uniformed lads to pick up everyone on the list again.'

'Right guv,' Mower said, as Detective Constable Val Ridley put her head round the door looking distraught.

'Another?' she asked.

'She's downstairs with her mother and a WPC, who might have got something coherent out of her by now,' Thackeray said. 'What we desperately need, Val, is some identification evidence. On what we've got so far you'd be pushed to produce a photofit more life-like than Frankenstein. We desperately need a result on this one before the inevitable happens.'

'They don't see him, sir,' DC Ridley said angrily. 'He comes up behind them, pulls their clothes or something else over their head – they never get a proper sight of him.'

She was a competent-looking woman. Her fair hair cut short, her white shirt and green cotton skirt well pressed. She was apparently unfazed by the heat, but her grey eyes were bright with emotion. She had been working on the assaults since the beginning and was obviously taking the mounting pressure hard.

'I thought our undercover Don Johnson here was coming up with something special,' she said, giving Mower a distinctly unfriendly nod. 'From what I hear he's more interested in getting into someone special.'

She slammed the door behind her, leaving Mower looking embarrassed under Thackeray's icy gaze.

'One week,' Thackeray said dismissively.

'Sir,' Mower said, knowing better than to argue further, but cursing Val Ridley roundly under his breath.

It was almost eleven before Thackeray and Mower left police headquarters. The sergeant declined a lift, intending to call into a club which he knew would still serve him a drink in spite of the lateness of the hour and disinclined to solicit Thackeray's increasingly ill-tempered company in that particular enterprise. The chief inspector flung his jacket dispiritedly onto the passenger seat of his car, loosened his tie and slid into the driving seat, opening all the windows to let out the stale humid air although even then the car was only slightly more suffocating than the atmosphere in the station car park outside.

He had spent the last three hours with Mower closeted in interview rooms taking statements from the three known child molesters the uniformed patrols had been able to round up. Another on the files proved to be in Spain on holiday and a fifth turned out to already be a guest of the State, on remand in Manchester charged with interfering with a young boy on a train.

As each man with a record of crime against children waxed eloquently indignant across the interview-room table, Thackeray's distaste and depression had grown in tandem.

'Anyone would think you've never laid a finger on a child when you've got a string of convictions as long as my bloody arm,' he had shouted at his last suspect in exasperation as the elderly man had denied for the tenth time that the thought of little girls ever entered his head.

'Not for years, Inspector. Not for years,' the long-ago dismissed school-teacher had said vehemently. 'I promise you, that's all over and done with years ago.'

'You only came out of Strangeways eighteen months ago,' Sergeant Mower came back sharply, checking the computer print-out in his file. 'Been a good boy since then, have you?'

They did not believe his protestations of repentence and reformation but when it came to the nitty-gritty detail of where he had been the previous night, he, like the others, had an alibi which would probably stand up, and, like the others, they had reluctantly had to let him go, close up the files and call it a day.

Thackeray's depression was almost total, and he knew that it was as much due to his own dilemmas as to the inevitably disturbing effect on the whole station of the latest development on the Heights. He knew his mood was dangerous, that it was at times like this that the old craving could return like a form of madness and push him over a precipice which had almost killed him once. He started the car and drove, knowing that the concentration that required would distract him.

His detectives had not stopped knocking on doors at Bronte House until ten o'clock, but at those doors where they got an answer there had been no help in pinning down the movements of Josie Renton or of a possible attacker. No one had apparently seen the child on what should have been a couple of minutes' walk from the flat of her friend on the second floor of Bentley House to her own home on the third floor of Bronte. Her route had taken her between the flats, where most of the ground-floor windows of Bronte were boarded up, close to the rubbish chutes and huge dustbins where Tracy Miller's body had been found ten years before.

It had been seven in the evening, the thunder clouds bringing a premature dusk to an area which was gloomy on even the brightest days. There, in a patch of stinking dereliction, Josie had been grabbed from behind, her head bundled in her cardigan, then fondled, half strangled and dumped just inside the entrance to the flats where she had been found five minutes later, screaming hysterically, by her own mother who was setting out to fetch her.

Thackeray had long ago given up any serious attempt to make sense of the problems of good and evil. Religion had failed him when he needed it most. It had provided no answers when his instinct for self-destruction had destroyed in the end not himself but those he loved best. He had survived almost in spite of himself, and buried himself in his job but in no crusading spirit. He looked to do no more than try to protect those who required protection and pursue with apparent implacability those who sought to do them harm, without too much apportioning of blame. He left that to those who still saw the world in black and white. For his part it looked mostly to be painted in shades of grey, only on the worst days, like this, a murkier grey than on others.

He had found a way of living with the mess he had made of his life and had begun to believe he was invulnerable at work and in what passed for the social life of a man who worked long hours and had few friends. There had been women on occasion, but no serious involvement on his part ever. That side of his life, he had told himself, was over and done with and he had meant it. Until, that is, he had met Laura Ackroyd, who had suddenly caused him a physical ache of desire he thought he was no longer capable of. Laura had erupted into his carefully disciplined life and thrown him into a confusion he was unsure how to deal with.

He drove slowly out of town with the car windows wide open, creating a welcome draught which ruffled his hair and helped him keep his tired eyes focused on the road. The storm that had been threatening all day had still not broken, although he could hear an occasional rumble of thunder far away over the western hills. He was not driving in any particular direction, certainly not home, where an empty and unwelcoming flat would have provided no sanctuary in his present mood. Here and there he passed the pools of golden light which spilled from the doors and windows of pubs on too many street corners. It was turning-out time and groups of happy revellers pitched through swing doors onto littered pavements, buoyed up temporarily at least by the spirits which swilled about inside them. It was, he knew, too late to get served, even in the Woolpack, where CID officers were more liberally welcomed than the law strictly allowed, and he was glad of that. He was not totally sure that his usual resolve was proof tonight against temptation.

It was not until a slight movement at the side of one of the long, steep residential streets which led up to the Heights caught his eye that he realised he had been inexorably drawn to the source of much of his present distress.

He slowed the car and looked again. Several young girls stood on the street corners and there could be little doubt in anybody's mind what they were selling. He pulled into the kerb far enough away for them to be unlikely to approach him and watched. Within minutes another car had pulled up on the corner ahead and one of the girls, in short tight skirt and skimpy top, had evidently agreed a price and jumped enthusiastically into the passenger seat to be driven away.

He sat for a long time, mesmerised by the brisk trade going on at the other end of the street. Even from this distance it was obvious that some of the girls who went off with men either in cars or on foot, up the hill towards the Heights, were very young indeed. The trade disgusted him and fascinated him at the same time and he wondered quite dispassionately how much frustration it would take to drive him a little further along the kerb to open the door for one of the slim young whores and seek oblivion of a different sort, however brief.

A sharp tap on his windscreen made him jump and he looked up to see a uniformed constable leaning down towards him with a distinctly unfriendly look on his boyish face.

'Good-evening, sir. I wonder if you'd mind telling me what you're doing parked here.'

Thackeray laughed without humour, old guilts flooding his mind.

'Thinking, Constable,' he said. 'Although I wouldn't expect you to believe that,' he added, half under his breath.

'I wonder if you'd mind getting out of the car, sir. I'd like to see your driving licence.' Thackeray picked up his jacket and did as he was asked.

'I can do better than that,' he said wearily. 'I can show you my warrant card.' The flush of confusion on the young constable's face was visible even in the bluish glare of the street lights.

'I'm sorry, sir, I didn't recognise you,' he said stiffly.

'There's no reason why you should,' Thackeray said, taking back his warrant and putting it carefully away. 'And you were quite right to question me. Kerb crawling's a menace round here.'

'Sir,' the constable said, uncertain now.

'Where do they take their clients, these kids?' Thackeray asked.

'Some of them go up to the flats,' the constable said. 'There's a lot of dark corners up there. And squatters' places.'

'So I believe,' Thackeray said dryly. 'I'll be on my way then, Watson – it is Watson, isn't it? And no hard feelings?'

'If you say so, sir,' Watson said, but as he watched Thackeray's car accelerate away up the hill there was still a look of profound suspicion in his eyes.

As Thackeray undressed, tossed the heavy cover off his bed and slid naked under a single crumpled sheet he was no nearer deciding what to do about Laura. He fell into a fitful sleep, interrupted by lurid dreams of scantily clad young girls sobbing inconsolably in each other's arms. He awoke soaked in sweat, still exhausted but dragged reluctantly back to wakefulness by his alarm to find the morning almost as dark as night and the flicker of reflected lightning dancing fitfully on the ceiling. He lay still for a moment, one hand behind his head, gazing unseeingly at the ceiling before deciding, with foreboding

78

rather than relief, that he must contact Laura again and to hell with the consequences.

SEVEN

THE RAIN CAME THAT MORNING, a Saturday, in torrents, bouncing off the dusty parched earth to make swirling rivers of muddy brown water along every gutter like some overdue monsoon. At Wuthering it gathered in pools on the flat roofs and cascaded through gaping joints in the prefabricated construction, running down already damp walls and dripping through ceilings where what was left of the plaster sagged under its weight.

Weary mothers bundled children out of bed early and confined them to the rooms that were still weather-proof, rushing with buckets and bowls to catch the drips where the downpour outside became a constant drizzle of dirty water within. In Bronte House, which under this onslaught became as leaky as a sieve, even the squatters, heavy-lidded with drug- or drink-induced sleep, opened bleary eyes long enough to shuffle their mattresses and sleeping bags out of the worst of the wet.

Above the blocks, which crowned the Heights like gap teeth, lightning split the clouds apart and thunder reverberated in the canyons between them. In the seconds it took for Laura to run from her car to her grandmother's front door she was drenched. She stood in Joyce's narrow hall laughing as she pummelled her hair and face with the kitchen towel the old woman had handed her as she bundled her into the house.

'Why can't you wear a coat, you daft ha'porth,' Joyce grumbled contentedly. 'You've not got the sense you were born with.' Laura grinned and kissed her parchment cheek gently.

'And you should know by now that anyone under sixty goes round with the express intention of catching pneumonia just to annoy you,' she said affectionately. 'How are you?'

'Middling,' Joyce conceded, leading the way into her living-room, leaning heavily on her stick.

'The knees are no better?'

'The rain'll likely make them worse,' Joyce said, glancing out of the window at the downpour which almost obscured the lowering flats where half a dozen police cars were still parked. Laura followed Joyce's eyes and her expression became serious.

'They've done the story of the attack for today's paper,' she said. 'It's the front-page lead. Even squeezed United down to two columns. There'll not be anything to add unless they arrest someone.'

'And that's not likely, if the other cases are owt to go by, is it,' Joyce said bleakly. 'They've got nowhere with those. Men! I thought your generation were supposed to have tamed the beggers. If you ask me they're getting worse. Kiddies used to be able to walk the streets without getting molested.'

'Have the police been round here?' Laura asked, not wanting to get into that endless debate between the generations.

'Aye, they came early. Had I seen anything unusual, heard the child screaming, anything.' Joyce's eyes were full of hurt and Laura guessed that it was not only for the assaulted child, but for all the children condemned to the decaying wreckage of the flats that had been her dream.

'You know they're going to pull them down?' Joyce said fiercely. 'They wanted to refurbish them, but that's fallen through. No one's got the brass for ambitious schemes like that now, so they've decided to take them down.'

'How do you know that?' Laura asked, surprised. There had been no hint of that decision in the office when she had left the previous evening.

'I've still got friends at the town hall,' Joyce said with a small smile of satisfaction. 'There was a meeting last night,

81

apparently. I had a phone call late on. The meeting was private but someone thought I should know.'

'Great,' Laura said. 'The places are a disgrace. Can I write about it? Though it's a bit late for today.' Saturday's Gazette was devoted mainly to sport and only the most extraordinary of new stories would persuade the editor to change the front page at this time of day. The likely demolition of the flats would not qualify, Laura was sure. The story would have to wait until Monday.

'Talk to the chair of housing, but don't tell him I told you,' Joyce said, satisfied that even now she could still occasionally prove to be better informed than Laura. A notoriously independent spirit who had driven colleagues and family to distraction in her younger days, she faced old age with a deep and abiding resentment.

'I'm worried about it, even though it is what the mothers were asking for,' Joyce went on. 'The plan is to get the squatters out straight off. There's dozens of them in Bronte. After that, they'll gradually move the legal residents out as houses come vacant.'

'That's sensible, isn't it?' Laura said. 'Bronte has always been the worst block and from what I saw of it the other day it's turned into a complete pigsty.'

'I told them when they were being built they were doing it on the cheap, but no one would listen,' Joyce said sadly. 'What you don't remember are the back-to-back terraces those folk came from. They thought those flats were little palaces when they moved in. We all thought it was the new Jerusalem.'

'It's thirty years, Nan,' Laura said. 'Times change.' She changed the subject, inwardly condemning the cowardice which made her veer away from the disappointments which were souring her grandmother's retirement and which she too resented but felt powerless to address.

'So what's the problem?' Joyce had telephoned her early that morning to ask her to call round but had been mysterious about the reason.

'Jackie Sullivan wants to see you again and she's not got a phone. She's coming over at eleven with that lass who

82

runs the adventure playground. Sue something?'

'Yes, I've met her,' Laura said thoughtfully, recalling the tall equivocal black woman who had allowed her into the playground with a slightly bad grace. Or was it perhaps not her own arrival but Kevin Mower's over-enthusiastic reception of her that had grated on Sue Raban's susceptibilities? Mower, she thought with cynical amusement, was not one to waste his opportunities. 'Jackie will be delighted if they decide to pull the flats down, won't she?'

'Aye, mebbe, but I'd not bank on any of them sorting their problems out that easily,' Joyce said. 'It's not just Bronte that's driving them to distraction.'

Within minutes the doorbell rang and Laura opened it to find a bedraggled cluster of people huddled in the porch for shelter against the rain. She let in Jackie Sullivan and Sue Raban, both with jacket hoods pulled well up against the downpour, and was surprised to see that they were followed by Kevin Mower himself, looking even more piratical than the last time she had seen him with his dark hair plastered to his head and water streaming down his face and thickening beard. He gave Laura a quizzical look but said nothing as he took off his leather bomber jacket, heavy with water, and hung it, dripping, on a hook by the front door.

'You're working overtime, aren't you?' Laura asked.

'As ever,' he said quietly, so as not to be overheard. 'I seem to be part of an action committee, and very curious as to what the action may turn out to be.'

'Well, don't push your luck,' Laura said. 'You may find I'm as bad at keeping confidences as you turned out to be.'

'Ah,' Mower said. 'You've seen Mike Thackeray, then? I'm sorry about that – it just slipped out. I take it the brass are not too keen on having the county constabulary starring in "Case Re-opened"?'

Laura raised her eyebrows at that but said no more, following the two women into Joyce's living-room where they settled down and waited for her expectantly.

'How can I help?' Laura asked. 'Did you get any reaction from the town hall after the piece I wrote last week?'

Jackie Sullivan drew deeply on her cigarette, sucking in her thin cheeks hungrily as she inhaled.

'Not so's you'd notice,' she said flatly. Laura glanced at her grandmother who shook her head almost imperceptibly.

'The talk is that you'll hear something positive soon,' she said carefully.

'It's all promises,' Sue Raban said dismissively. The hint of America in her voice was more pronounced this morning. 'We've decided it's time for some direct action – particularly since the attack on little Josie yesterday. We're calling a meeting at the community centre on Monday night, if you'd like to come.'

'Of course,' Laura said. 'It may not be me but I'll tell my editor and someone will certainly be there. Do you have some particular direct action in mind?'

Kevin Mower looked studiously down at his sodden trainers to hide the inevitable gleam of interest in his eyes.

'We're sick and tired of the police. They're not providing any protection for the kids,' Jackie said explosively. 'We're going to start our own patrols round t'flats at night. We reckon we're going to have to catch this bastard ourselves because no one looks like doing it for us.'

'You're beginning to look more and more like Heathcliff, which I suppose is fair enough at Wuthering,' Laura said to Kevin Mower with an amused gleam in her eyes as she leaned across to open the passenger door of her car to let him in out of the rain.

'Fine, if you feel like playing Cathy,' Mower said. Laura laughed slightly grimly.

'No chance,' she said. 'All that mooning about on the moors in this weather? Not my scene.' She started the car and switched the wipers to maximum speed to try to clear the windscreen of the downpour which showed no signs of easing.

'Anyway, I thought you had other fish to fry? Ms Raban seems to be keeping a very proprietorial eye on you.'

'Huh, only when she feels like it,' Mower said. 'I think

84

she's the one with other interests.'

Laura glanced up at the walkways of the flats, where plain-clothes and uniformed officers, collars turned up against the weather, worked their way doggedly from door to door.

'Shouldn't you be up there helping?' she asked.

'Not yet,' Mower said. 'Michael Thackeray thinks I'm more use on the ground.'

'So I suppose you're going down to the nick to tell him all about Jackie and Sue's little plan?' Laura asked as she edged her way through the traffic towards the centre of town, unable quite to keep a note of contempt out of her voice. 'A bit sneaky, isn't it, all this pretending to be someone you're not?'

'What's sneaky when a kid's been half strangled,' Mower said, an edge of anger in his voice. 'Next time he might try a bit harder and we'll be into a murder investigation.'

'Seriously?' Laura asked, surprised at the raw nerve she seemed to have touched.

'Seriously,' he said. 'So we can't have Sue or anyone else messing with this operation. It's too important for that. Their vigilante games will have to be stopped if they get in the way.'

At police headquarters that afternoon Superintendent Longley and Chief Inspector Thackeray stared glumly at a wall chart of the Heights estate. They had just come back with their opposite numbers from the uniformed branch from a crisis meeting at the town hall.

'It's a compromise, Michael,' Longley said. 'Sometimes you have to compromise. You know that place is like a rabbit warren. This way at least we'll be sure we've had a look at every bloody bunny who's in there.'

'And then what? We just let them vanish into thin air?'

The meeting with the police had been convened by the council's housing officials, who were taken aback by the speed of the previous evening's decision to demolish the Heights and begin the 'decanting' of Bronte House immediately. Someone had realised almost as an afterthought that a decision to evict all the block's squatters, who had already been served with court orders, might hinder the police inquiries at the flats.

A bad-tempered Longley had been summoned from home, where he had been staring at the rain streaming down the windows and keeping him from the golf course where he normally spent his Saturdays. Thackeray, hardly aware that a weekend was in progress, had been prised from the computer screens where CID were collating the accumulating evidence in the Josie Renton case.

They had both asked in vain for a postponement of the evictions. All they had gained was a few days' grace and the promise of immediate access to the tenants' lists from which the bailiffs would decide which flats were legally occupied and which were not.

'You know what politicians are like,' Longley said. 'They're under a lot of pressure from the rest of the town to clean that place up. There's no doubt that those empty flats are being used by kids on drugs and on the game, so there's political mileage in clearing them out. And I guess if you suggested to the mothers on the Heights that the fellow responsible for the assaults would be flushed out with them, they'd not fash themselves overmuch. At least he'd be gone.'

'To start over somewhere else,' Thackeray muttered, not mollified. 'And the devil's own job to track him down if we do come up with some hard evidence.'

'Much sign of that?'

'Damn all,' Thackeray admitted. 'He's careful, this one. We've not had a decent description from any of the kids. It's either been dark or he's bundled something over their heads. And forensic have come up with very little: a few hairs, mostly animal, a few fibres that could have come from anywhere, no bodily fluids. They reckon he must wear gloves and something over his face. We might get a DNA profile but that'll take time and there's no guarantee just with hairs.'

'He'll go too far in the end,' Longley said grimly. 'He's using some self-restraint at the moment but in the end he'll get carried away. And the worst of it is we almost need him to get carried away if we're to catch him.'

They looked at each other for a moment in silence as Longley put into words what Thackeray had been thinking.

'Christ,' he said, appalled at the impasse they had reached. 'There are times when I wonder what I'm doing in this job.'

'You'll get there, Michael,' Longley said, aware that Thackeray's despair was not fuelled simply by the present case, which had inspired a frenetic and in his view not very productive anger in all his men. 'Go steady. Take your time. There's nothing like solid detective work to get you there in the end. If he's made a mistake already, you'll find it.'

'Maybe,' Thackeray said without much confidence. 'There's the other thing too. Huddleston and the television programme. I've seen Harry and Sergeant Redding and there'll be no shifting them. They're convinced they got it right, and Huddleston reckons he's fireproof, by the sound of him, on anything "Case Re-opened" can rake up to the contrary.'

'And do you reckon he's fireproof?' Longley asked, suddenly belligerent again.

Thackeray shrugged, not in a mood to temper his words to suit Longley's prejudices.

'I don't know,' he said flatly. 'Either of them would be capable of a bit of heavy pressurising, not to say a quick thump where it wouldn't show a bruise if they thought they could get away with it. Redding virtually admitted they'd leaned on the lad. Coppers of the old school, both of them, and proud of it. If you want my honest opinion . . .' He hesitated because he was not totally convinced that was what Jack Longley did want in the matter of Harry Huddleston, but he ploughed on regardless.

'If you want my opinion, you don't stand a chance of proving they went further than they should have done, after all this time. You can't get them on disciplinary

87

charges now they're out of the force so we're talking about criminal charges – beyond reasonable doubt.' He shrugged dispiritedly.

'I'll keep trying if you want me to. D'you want me to talk to anyone else who was around the station when Stephen Webster was being questioned? Or the other witnesses at the trial? – the child's father, and the caretaker at the flats – Jerry Hurst. He's still there, as it happens. I was planning to ask him to go through the list of tenants with me on Monday. I thought he might be a useful source of gossip – perhaps more.'

Longley looked thoughtful, half closing his eyes for a moment as if trying to exclude Thackeray from whatever was going on behind that creased brow.

'Don't make a thing of it,' he said at last, jaw clenched tight as if the words were being forced reluctantly from him. 'I don't want it getting out that we're worried about that conviction. But if you make it your business to interview Hurst yourself – and Tracy Miller's father, for that matter – it wouldn't come amiss to remind them of the previous case, would it? Could this be the same man? Could we have got it wrong with Tracy . . .?' He let the question trail away, aware, as Thackeray was, of the implications of that possibility, which were about as unpleasant as they could be. He exploded suddenly.

'If we're going to be crucified by the media,' he said, 'let's make sure we're Jesus and not the other bugger – what's his name? Barrabas? – shall we? We want to be sure we're going to get resurrected, don't we?'

EIGHT

LAURA TOOK A REST AFTER six lengths, floating lazily on her back and gazing up at the complex pyramids of glass and steel which made up the roof of the leisure centre. The sunshine filtering through the angled glass created dazzling patterns of light against the egg-shell blue of the sky beyond. It was a shining Sunday morning after the rain of the day before, promising heat later but with a freshness which had been absent for weeks now.

She had got up early, wakened by the warmth of the sunlight falling on her bed and exhilarated by the prospect of a free day. She had decided when her live-in boyfriend of several years had moved out that this was the day of the week that had to be taken by storm if the single state she half welcomed and half feared was not to become a burden.

Often she fetched Joyce from the Heights to her flat and cooked her a traditional Sunday lunch. They spent the afternoon companionably arguing over the Sunday papers if it was wet or driving out of town to one of Joyce's favourite beauty spots if it was dry. There had been a time when they had been able to tramp over the moors together, but now Joyce had to content herself with sitting close to the car with a rug round her treacherous knees and looking at the spreading panoramas of the dales.

Today Laura was invited to lunch with what she regarded as her other family, the Mendelsons. She had rung Vicky early to ask if she wanted her to take the boys swimming with her, but they had other plans for the morning so she had come alone and set herself a target of twelve lengths. After six she awarded herself a rest, bobbing gently at the deep end, out of the way of the children splashing about in the shallows and the determined swimmers in caps and goggles who ploughed relentlessly up and down the lanes.

The motion of the water was soothing, and she thought idly about men and the lack of them. Joyce, widowed early in the war and left with a son to bring up alone, had survived and triumphed on her own, she thought. Laura herself had as a teenager tagged along behind Joyce on her many passionate crusades, red flag metaphorically flying. If she now needed evidence that it was possible for an Ackroyd to survive alone, then Joyce was the living proof of it.

Not so her mother, she thought, who was no doubt even now fussing around the swimming pool in Estoril making sure that Jack's chair was placed in the morning sun exactly where he liked to slump into it after his first swim of the day, sun umbrella at a precise angle, yesterday's Daily Telegraph and a jug of iced lemonade at hand. She didn't exactly iron Jack's morning newspaper, Laura thought grimly, but she might have done if the thought had occurred to her.

I can live without that, Laura thought angrily, just as easily as I can live without the departed Vince. I can live without a man, whatever Vicky and the columnists in Cosmo advise. I may miss Vince in bed but I sure as hell don't miss him trying to order my life for me. A bloke is an optional extra.

Anyway, she thought ruefully, it doesn't look as though at the moment I have much option. Kevin Mower was a pleasant enough diversion – good-looking, intelligent and no doubt good in bed, if it ever got that far. But not, she thought soberly, a man to be trusted. There was a ruthlessness behind those dark eyes that should have warned her that he would set personal relationships way behind his career. In that at least he was too much like Vince, she thought, and she would not make herself vulnerable in that way again.

Which left her with the enigma of his boss, a man she had been sure had more than a professional interest in her when they had met earlier in the year, but who had resolutely kept his distance since she had returned from her convalescence in Portugal, except for that chance and unsatisfactory meeting on the Heights.

She still recalled with a certain chagrin the time he had found her lying hurt and locked up, her impulsive pursuit of a story having ended in humiliation. She had been in pain and in shock, and she still could not be sure whether there was really no more concern in his eyes than there would have been for any other victim of violence he had stumbled across in the course of his work. And whatever the right-on might advise in the way of assertiveness, there was no way she intended to pursue a quarry who would be at best elusive and at worst positively antagonistic. The first move would have to be his.

At this conclusion, though, she turned in a lazy dog-paddle and glanced down the pool to where young mothers and fathers fussed over children in puffy orange armbands or watched anxiously as their fledglings took off with splashy strokes on their own for the first time. Blast, Laura said aloud, her eyes pricking with tears which she blamed on the chlorine-laden air though she knew she was deceiving herself. Damn and blast, she thought. She might be able to live contentedly without a man, but she was not at all sure that she could live without a child. That was a bleak and barren prospect which filled her with dismay.

She spun suddenly in the water and resumed her energetic lengths of the pool. Returning to the deep end for the final time, she took a huge breath and pushed herself off in a long shallow dive, head down, kicking vigorously, her eyes closed against the pressure of the water. She was only briefly aware that other swimmers had closed in on her before a grip like a vice took hold of her waist and pulled her deeper under the water and held her there.

Her first reaction was one of sheer panic as, heart thudding, she struggled against the two figures whom she

91

could see vaguely through the swirling blue and white vortex around them. But she realised almost as soon as she had begun to try to free herself that this was a futile effort which wasted the small reserves of air she still had in her lungs, the precious air which was now bubbling fast and ominously upwards from her mouth and nose. Instead she tried to reach up to the sparkling surface which she could see above her, but even that was unavailing as her attackers pulled her deeper so that not even a fingertip broke the surface of the pool.

Surely someone must be able to see what is going on, she thought frantically, as a band wrapped itself around her chest, inexorably tightening its grip so that she knew that very soon she would open her mouth and gulp not the life-saving oxygen she craved but the water which would choke her. In a final despairing effort she twisted this way and that, clawing at her attackers, but they avoided her touch, their grip never slackening, one holding her by the waist and the other pressing down on her shoulders so that no attempts to fight upwards towards the air could be even remotely effective.

It's not true you see the whole of your past life flash in front of you, she thought, her mind racing now. What is agonizing is the life I might have had. It's a prank gone wrong, and it's going to kill me, she told herself in despair as the tightness in her chest became unbearable and she felt her eyes bulging with her last impotent effort not to breath in. The effort failed and she felt the water flood into her mouth and nose and throat with a sense of fury at what she would miss in the carefree world which was obliviously going about its business above her.

Then as suddenly and inexplicably as she had been dragged down, she was freed, and she felt herself shoot like a cork to the surface where she floated for a moment, choking and spluttering uncontrollably as she tried to expel the invasive water from her lungs and draw in the life-giving air. Strong hands took hold of her again and pulled her to the side of the pool, and two men in bathing caps and goggles pushed her bodily up onto the tiled edge where she sat coughing and shaking, her head between her knees. A voice in her ear, cold as the grave which had just beckoned, cut through even her wracked breathing and the confusion of her mind.

'Keep away from the Heights,' it said. 'Right away from Wuthering. Mind your own effing business, or you might not come up next time.'

She was aware of other figures gathering round with sympathetic questions, a towel was draped around her shoulders and she heard one of her rescuers – or was it one of her attackers, she could not be sure – surmising that she had had an attack of cramp.

'Are you all right?' asked one of the pool attendants, a plump blonde young woman in shorts and Aertex shirt, who had bustled up from the shallow end looking anxious. 'Do you need a doctor?'

'I'm OK,' Laura said, her voice sounding croaky and hardly her own. 'I'm fine now. I just got a mouthful of water. It's nothing.' She glanced round, but she seemed to be surrounded now by concerned well-wishers. The two men in goggles and swimming caps had vanished.

'You were lucky someone spotted you were in trouble,' the attendant said sharply. And unlucky *you* didn't, Laura thought. She felt disoriented, not sure that what she believed had happened had really occurred. Had no one else noticed anything suspicious going on in that clear blue water? Had she really heard that harsh whisper in her ear? Had she got cramp, gone under and panicked, and simply imagined some bizarre attack?

Helped by eager hands she got to her feet and made her way back to the changing rooms. She dressed and dried her hair slowly, watching dispiritedly as mothers dried small wriggling children and helped them into their clothes. The normality of it all made what she thought had happened in the pool seem all the more unreal. Above her head the glass roof sparkled and glittered just as brightly as it had before, but to Laura it seemed as though a dark cloud had blotted out the sun.

93

On the Heights an acrid haze did exactly that. It drifted around Stan Jackson's bungalow, where the fire brigade was damping down a small fire which had blackened the kitchen and sent oily smoke streaming from the windows, every one of which had been shattered into jagged shards of glass. On the other side of the road, Stan's elderly neighbours clustered in anxious groups, watching the firemen go about their business. A little further away, Chief Inspector Michael Thackeray stood apart from the sightseers with PC Alan Davies facing another younger man in shirt-sleeves and slacks who was leaning against the door of a police car as if he needed its support.

'Come on, Watson,' Thackeray said, not unkindly, for it was the young constable he had last met on the road to the Heights, in plain clothes now and with a succession of emotions contorting his boyish features as he glanced across the road at evidence of what he clearly feared would be taken as his failure.

'Come on, lad,' Thackeray said again. 'You came on duty at twelve, you saw a Sierra go into the garage area at one, and reported in. Right?'

'Yes, sir,' Watson said miserably. 'They told me to hang on and let them know if it moved.'

'You couldn't see which garage it went into?'

'No, sir. It went round the corner, out of sight.' He waved vaguely at the garage blocks which surrounded an enclosed courtyard area littered with the half-dismantled bodies of cars which local residents worked on desultorily at most hours of the day and night.

'They told me to make a point of looking round there on my patrol,' Davies intervened. 'But there was no sign when I glanced in. If there's a Sierra in there, it's safely locked away out of sight now. But there is another way out. If you take it slowly you can squeeze a car out the far side where one of the garages was burned out a while back and has been demolished.'

'It didn't come out this way,' Watson said vehemently. 'I

never took my eyes off the entrance until I heard the glass smash in the kitchen behind me.'

'And then?' Thackeray prompted.

'I looked in the back,' the young constable said, a note of disbelief still in his voice as he contemplated what had happened. 'There was a gang of lads out the back. They'd chucked a brick through and when they saw me they threw another. Just missed me, as it happened. There were six or seven of them so I reckoned it was safer to come out the front way, but by the time I got the door open they'd started pelting the windows on that side as well. I sheltered behind the front door while I called control. There wasn't much else I could do on my own, sir,' he appealed to Thackeray for support.

'How many all together?' Thackeray asked Davies, who had been the first to answer Watson's appeal for help.

'A dozen or more,' he said grimly. 'Fourteen-, fifteen-year-olds. They ran like hell when they saw me coming, disappeared into the flats. They were too far away for me to recognise any of them. And they'd set the kitchen alight by then.'

'A petrol bomb?' Thackeray asked.

'No, just some oily rags,' Watson said, still looking shaken. 'But it had caught the curtains. It was more than I could put out on my own.'

'Old Stan Jackson'll be staying with his sister in Halifax for longer than he expected,' Thackeray said grimly. 'Did you follow instructions about going in there without being seen?' he asked Watson.

'Yes, sir,' the constable said quickly. 'Left the car down in Skinner Street, walked up the back ginnel and in the back door, just as instructed. I was very careful.'

'Right, well, someone found out we were using the bungalow. And someone wants us off this estate pretty badly. And that won't go down too well at county. Or with the Gazette.'

'They're like a guerrilla army, these kids,' Davies said gloomily. 'What I'd like to know is who's the bloody general.'

'You think it's organised?' Thackeray asked, interested, but Davies just shrugged.

'I've got no evidence, sir,' he said. Thackeray turned his attention back to the matter in hand, filing the community man's comment away for future consideration.

'I want those garages taken apart. Stay here and check anyone going in or out until I get a couple of cars up with the right equipment. If that Sierra is still in there, we'll have it.'

'Are you all right?' Vicky Mendelson asked Laura anxiously as they stacked the dishes into the dishwasher in Vicky's well-appointed kitchen that afternoon. A traditional Sunday roast had been consumed and David Mendelson had taken his two young sons for a kick-about in the neighbourhood park, ignoring the two women's only half-hearted jibes about sexual stereotypes and leaving them for a companionable and welcome hour on their own.

'You hardly said a word to David at lunch, and you look pale, but not interesting. Like death, in fact,' Vicky persisted. Laura and Vicky's lawyer husband could usually be relied upon to keep up a humorous but deadly serious debate on local issues over these regular meals.

'Just because we don't all produce a Torremolinos tan like you and David do every time the sun peeps out,' Laura parried, but her heart was not in it and she knew her friend would not be deceived. They had been close since their student days when they had shared a flat for two years, and Laura knew that this afternoon no careful application of make-up or combing of her copper hair loosely around her cheeks when she went home to change for lunch was likely to disguise the faint violet circles under her eyes or the prominence of her despised freckles against her unseasonably pale complexion.

'Tell me,' Vicky persisted, as they settled into garden chairs on the paved terrace outside the French windows of the sitting-room. Laura gave her friend a rueful smile, put her coffee-cup down carefully on the teak garden table, trying to control the trembling of her hands, and told Vicky what had happened at the pool that morning.

'Go to the police,' Vicky said flatly when Laura had finished and was leaning back in her chair looking drained. Laura shook her head emphatically at that.

'To tell them what?' she asked. 'I'm not even sure now what happened. No one seemed to have seen anything odd. I'm beginning to think I imagined it all.'

'You're not the type,' Vicky said scornfully. 'In any case, you might have got into trouble in the water – anyone could get cramp and panic. But you couldn't have imagined the threats.'

'Oh, I don't know,' Laura said. 'Those flats gave me the creeps, you know, when I went to interview Paul Miller. I've been thinking about Bronte House, having nightmares about it even.'

'You're rationalising,' Vicky said. 'It couldn't be because there's another reason you don't want to go to the police, could it?'

Laura shrugged dispiritedly, wondering how she could have been plunged into such a deep depression on such an idyllic day, which had started so full of promise. The sun and a light breeze created a rippling, dappled composition of gold and green broken by an occasional splash of crimson and cream in the Mendelsons' rose-decked mid-summer garden.

'I don't know what I'd tell them,' she muttered petulantly.

'And you're worried Michael Thackeray might think it's an excuse to see him again?'

'I shouldn't think a detective chief inspector would bother himself with a silly complaint like this,' Laura snapped. She saw Vicky flinch at her vehemence, and remembered that she too was fragile, in the late stages of a pregnancy which had become oppressive in the recent heat, and was instantly contrite.

'I'm sorry,' she said. 'You're right, you're always right, you can read me like a book.'

'So you'll go to the police? Seek out some anonymous sergeant, if you like, but go?'

'Maybe,' Laura conceded, thinking of a not-so-anonymous sergeant who might take her seriously.

'And tell Ted Grant that you've been warned off the Heights? You shouldn't go poking around up there on your own after this.'

'Poking around is part of the job. If I can't ask questions where they need asking, I might as well give up,' Laura said irritably. 'Anyway, the interviews I was doing weren't for the Gazette. They were for "Case Re-opened", and I didn't particularly want Ted to know about that little bit of moonlighting.'

'So you think that's what it's about?' Vicky asked. 'I thought you were writing in the Gazette the other night about this campaign to get the place pulled down. Couldn't that be annoying some people?'

'That's a bit like shooting the messenger,' Laura said. 'If they want to intimidate somebody over that campaign I can't see why it should be me.'

Vicky shuddered, pulling a jacket from the back of her chair and slinging it around the shoulders of her thin, voluminous maternity dress.

'Do you ever feel we're living our comfortable middle-class lives on the edge of a volcano?' she asked.

'All the time,' Laura said grimly. 'I peek over the edge occasionally in my job – David must do it more often in his.' Vicky nodded in agreement at that. 'And someone like Michael Thackeray lives permanently on the brink, directing a hosepipe at the flames and hoping to God that the water doesn't run out.'

'You think a lot about him, don't you?'

Laura looked thoughtful.

'I think about him sometimes,' she said. 'If your question was purely temporal. If you meant it the other way, the answer is, I simply don't know what I think about him except that I'd like to get to know him better, given the chance. But he doesn't seem very likely to give me the chance. In fact, to judge by our last meeting, I suspect he disapproves of me, and disapproves of my job. He's not susceptible to your match-making, Vicky, so I should forget it.' It had been at a dinner party at the Mendelsons that Laura Ackroyd and Michael Thackeray had first met, part of Vicky's long-standing plan to find Laura a suitable husband – a campaign she denied as vehemently as Laura resisted it.

Vicky looked at Laura with an expression half of sorrow and half of anger, one hand suddenly on her swollen belly.

'Christ,' she said softly, 'this baby can't half kick. I've got it down for David's football team already.'

'Should you be invoking Him in your Jewish mamma mode,' Laura asked waspishly. But she looked away, afraid of what Vicky might see in her eyes, though she was not to be denied anyway.

'It's not just a game, the match-making,' Vicky said quietly. 'I know you think you're OK on your own, but you're not really, are you? And don't think I haven't seen you with the boys. You can maybe kid yourself you don't want a man, but you can't kid yourself, or me, that you don't want children. It's written all over you.' Vicky flushed with the intensity of saying what she had long thought and not dared to express. She was not wholly surprised to see Laura bite her lip to keep back the tears.

NINE

IT TOOK THE EMERGENCY SERVICES fifteen minutes to arrive at Bronte House, which for Darren Sullivan was at least five minutes too long. By the time the firemen brought his limp body out of his smoke-logged bedroom he had stopped breathing, and not all the efforts of the paramedics in the ambulance or the casualty staff at Bradfield Infirmary could pummel or persuade his small lungs and heart into action again.

PC Alan Davies watched impassively through the small glass window in the door of the emergency room. Jackie Sullivan stood shivering beside the high table on which the medical team had struggled vainly to revive her son. She was swearing monotonously but with immense passion under her breath. Turning away from the small body at last, the young casualty doctor put an awkward hand on her shoulder.

'I'm sorry,' he said, but Jackie did not appear to hear him and he turned away, seized by the bitter depression which follows failure. A nurse covered the child's body with a sheet up to his chin. They had wiped the black smoke-stains from his blotchy, sun-burned face. With his eyes closed, he could have been sleeping peacefully at the end of another exhausting summer day.

'He's not touched,' Jackie said incredulously. 'He's not burned at all.'

'It was the smoke,' the nurse said helplessly. 'All the plastic in modern houses . . . the smoke's lethal. We did everything we could. If you'd like to stay with him for a little while, that'll be fine. No one will bother you.' Jackie

100

brushed a straggle of sun-bleached hair from the child's brow and shook her head.

'There's nowt I can do for him now,' she said, turning away again.

'I thought the noise had wakened him,' she went on in a monotone which the nurse could hardly hear. 'I ran to get Chrissie out of her cot and I thought Darren were following. By the time I got out the flames were right across the hallway. I couldn't get back in to fetch him . . .' She broke off, wracked for the first time by a sob which seemed to come from so far within her that it had to struggle to escape. The nurse put an arm around her and led her from the room into the corridor.

'I'll get you a cup of tea,' she said, showing her into a small waiting-room furnished with a few battered armchairs and a coffee-table piled with bedraggled-looking magazines. 'And then we'll see about some transport for you. And there's a policeman waiting to talk to you, if you're up to it.' Jackie refused to be helped into a chair, lit a cigarette with a shaking hand and stood staring out of the window at the hospital forecourt where ambulances came and went, filling the night with flickering blue light and urgency.

'Yes,' she said vehemently. 'I want a bloody policeman. I want the bastards who did that to Darren.'

PC Alan Davies came into the room quietly, his broad face filled with concern, his tie loose at the neck of his uniform shirt as if it had been put on too quickly.

'I don't know what to say, Jackie lass,' he said. 'I came straight back on duty when I heard.'

Jackie Sullivan turned towards him, her face grey, traces of lipstick creating a bloody gash where her mouth should be. She had still not shed a single tear since she had thrust two-year-old Chrissie into her friend Linda Smith's arms and scrambled into the ambulance to come to the hospital with her son. The tension in her was palpable, from her staring eyes to the trembling nicotine-stained fingers with which she stubbed out her cigarette-end and lit another. Davies knew that it would take very little now to push her over the edge into hysteria. He recognised the signs.

'Sit down, love, while they bring us that tea,' he said, his faith in the old remedies untarnished. She did as she was told, sagging at the knees slightly until she felt the chair behind her legs, and then sitting hunched over her cigarette, the blue smoke drifting defiantly past the no smoking notice on the wall behind her head. She was dressed in a skimpy sun-dress under a sagging cardigan, her legs bare above a pair of high-heeled sandals, hands, legs and dress smudged here and there with dark stains. The nurse brought in two cups of tea and placed them on top of the magazines on the coffee-table in the middle of the room.

'Are you sure you're up to this?' she asked Jackie. 'I'm sure the officer would wait until tomorrow if you preferred.' Jackie glanced at the nurse – girlish in her neat, short blue uniform, her face absurdly young under her white cap – with something close to contempt.

'I'll be right,' she said. 'I want to talk about it now. Tomorrow might be too late. I want those bastards caught.'

Alan Davies pulled out his notebook unobtrusively. It had been an unexplained fire on the top-floor walkway of Bronte, he had been told by the duty inspector at HQ, a fire which had spread too quickly to allow Mrs Sullivan to get both children out. It had been brought under control soon enough, the brigade running their hoses from a turntable ladder especially designed to cope with a high-rise outbreak. Officers in breathing apparatus had gone in through the choking black smoke and had found Darren quickly but not quite quickly enough. It was unlikely he had even woken before the fumes had claimed him. Alan Davies had hurried back on duty as soon as a colleague called him because he knew that for Jackie Sullivan, who had been trying so fiercely for so long to get her children out of Bronte, what had happened would be too much to bear.

'Do you know how it started?' Davies asked tentatively.

'Oh aye,' Jackie said, without hesitation. 'I know exactly how it bloody well started. Some little bugger put a petrol

102

bomb through t'window, didn't he? I were sitting there watching t'telly. You tell your bosses it weren't an accident that killed our Darren, it were murder. And it's about time your lot did summat about that estate before the whole bloody lot goes up.'

Within an hour Davies was back at the Heights with Chief Inspector Thackeray, watching the aftermath of the fire from just outside the garden gate which stood tentative guard on Stan Jackson's forlorn-looking bungalow, its windows now boarded up. The plain-clothes constable who had been on duty in an unmarked car stood slightly behind them, a look of anxiety on his face.

'I was distracted by the fire, sir,' he said miserably, not for the first time, seeing his chance of a transfer to CID slipping away. 'I saw the flames and called in straight away, so I only caught a glimpse of the car.'

Thackeray turned away from his grim-faced surveillance of Bronte House with a sigh.

'No one's blaming you,' he said. The blame for Darren Sullivan's death would brush many people, he thought, not least himself for not having forseen that Jackie might have been at risk, but he saw no need for the young constable who had volunteered for a night's overtime on the Heights to share it. 'Just take me through it one more time.'

'A dark car, black, I think, looked like an Escort. I just caught it out of the corner of my eye as I was talking to control. By the time I turned it was well down the road, heading towards town, moving fast.'

'So no registration number, no view of the driver, right?'

'Right, sir.'

'And you saw nothing up on the walkway until the flames attracted your attention.'

'No, sir. I was looking the other way, at the garages, then.'

'But you're not sure the car came out from the garages?'

'No, sir. It just seemed to appear—'

'From nowhere,' Thackeray said, trying to keep the frustration out of his voice. 'We've taken those garages apart once today, and found absolutely nothing. . .'

'Except the ladders, sir,' Davies reminded him.

'Except the ladders,' Thackeray agreed, 'which provide a neat back way from a first-floor window of an empty flat in Bronte onto the roofs of the garages and then down. Which means people – kids no doubt – can get in and out without being seen. But cars? We still know damn all about cars, and two have been spotted up here today that sound as if they could have been stolen. Someone up here's making monkeys out of us.'

'Do you want me to stay on watch, sir?' the plain-clothes constable asked tentatively, still unsure whether he was being blamed for some sin of omission.

'Yes,' Thackeray said, glancing around to where firemen were still clearing up the debris. He noticed a white VW Beetle parked some way down the street outside one of the old people's bungalows. Just for a moment he hesitated, before shaking his head and opening the door of his own car. 'Reports on my desk by nine in the morning,' he said to the two officers he left standing on the pavement. 'This little lot will have the Gazette calling for public hangings.'

Laura had driven up to the Heights in what she reckoned must be record time after her grandmother called. She found the front door wide open and the tiny bungalow crowded with people. Little Chrissie Sullivan was asleep on the sofa, covered with a blanket, her face flushed and cherubic against the slightly sooty woollen lamb she clutched tightly in both hands. A boy of about ten was crouching close to the television watching a film with the sound turned very low. His back was turned to the rest of the room and he appeared to be concentrating with rigid determination on the flickering images of violence on the screen.

Linda Smith and another woman Laura did not know were standing at the living-room window with their arms around each other watching the firemen. Reduced to dark shadows beneath their yellow helmets, they were still working on the top-floor walkway of Bronte House, dragging smouldering furnishings from the Sullivans' flat

104

in the chilly glare of arc lights rigged up to give them adequate illumination for the work.

At ground level a fire tender was parked close to the main doors, blue light blinking monotonously, with a police car not far behind. The scene was a desolate one, littered with abandoned hoses as groups of disconsolate fire-fighters cleared up their gear, watched over by knots of pale-faced, silently accusing witnesses at windows and on the lower walkways. Laura found Joyce in her tiny kitchen, hobbling from work-top to table in her dressing-gown, brewing a pot of tea with Sue Raban in attendance pouring milk into mugs.

'That was quick, love,' Joyce said, relief in her voice.

'I rang Ted and he said if I was coming up here anyway I was to cover the story,' Laura said. Her editor was never one to duplicate effort if it could be avoided. 'There'll be a photographer on his way, I expect. Do we know what happened exactly?'

Sue glanced at her, her dark eyes full of suppressed fury.

'It's just a question of how this place gets you, isn't it?' she said. 'If it's not a fire when you're five it'll be heroin when you're twelve or a bit of heavy-handed policing when you're fourteen. The kid's probably better off out of it.'

'Do we know he's dead?' Laura asked, ignoring Sue's outburst.

'I'd guess he was dead before they put him in the ambulance,' Sue said. 'I'd been at a meeting at the community centre. I saw them take him away.'

'I'll call the hospital,' Laura said, going back into the living-room to make the inquiry on behalf of the Gazette. The news she was given confirmed their worst fears and Linda Smith turned away from the window in tears.

'The effing lift wasn't working,' she said. 'I'm just four doors along from Jackie and she came hammering on t'door. I ran down t'stairs and couldn't even raise Jerry Hurst to use his phone.'

'That's the caretaker?' Laura asked, remembering her own encounter with the overweight and unhelpful Mr Hurst.

'That's what he calls himself,' Linda said contemptuously. 'Not that he does much caretaking. Dead drunk, more than likely. Any road, I had to run over here to phone – got your gran out of bed – but the flames were out of the effing window by then. I could see folk up on the walkway trying to stop Jackie going back in. Poor little beggar – he never stood a chance, it were so quick.'

Feeling deeply depressed, Laura left her grandmother and Sue ministering to Jackie Sullivan's shocked neighbours and walked across the main road and the grassy surround of the flats to the front entrance to Bronte. The glass doors were propped open with a heavy fire extinguisher and wisps of sickly smoke, fishy with burned plastic, drifted down the stairwell to meet her.

The caretaker was standing in his doorway dressed in what appeared to be exactly the same boxer shorts and dirty vest as he had worn the last time she had seen him. He took time from scratching his armpit to nod to Laura as she passed, his eyes blank and bleary, though whether from sleep or alcohol it was impossible to tell. Slowly she plodded up the stairs to the top floor. A policeman barred her way, but nodded her through when she showed him her press card.

She recognised the senior fire officer deep in conversation with one of his own men and a uniformed policeman just beyond the area where what was left of the contents of Jackie Sullivan's home was being unceremoniously dumped in a black and smoking heap outside the front door and sprayed down with a hose. Laura picked her way through the streams of dirty water and unrecognisable charred debris and joined the group.

'Do you know what caused the fire?' she asked the chief officer bluntly. He hesitated for a moment, pushing his white helmet back from his brow with a smoke-blackened hand.

'You're writing something for tomorrow's paper?' he asked. When she nodded, he shrugged wearily.

'Officially, we think there may be suspicious circumstances,' he said. 'We'll be doing forensic tests. You know the drill.'

'And unofficially?' Laura said, her stomach tightening in fear of what she was certain was to come.

'Unofficially, off the record for the moment, some little toe-rag chucked a milk bottle full of blazing petrol through the window,' the officer said. 'A bit more efficient than this morning's effort at the bungalow. I don't know what Mrs Sullivan's done to annoy folk up here, but someone doesn't like her. It was a bloody miracle any of them got out alive.'

Glancing down from the top walkway on her way back to her grandmother's house Laura had glimpsed the tall, broad-shouldered figure of Michael Thackeray below. Tonight, she thought, he was the last person she wanted to see. Even the faintest unspoken hint that her role there amongst the shocked and bereaved carried with it the taint of the ghoul would tip her into rage or despair, and quite possibly both. She waited in the shadows of the lift-shaft until she saw Thackeray get into a car and drive away before walking slowly back to Joyce's house and slumping disconsolately into a chair with a mug of tea.

Of the crowd of visitors who had been there earlier only Linda Smith, the sleeping Chrissie Sullivan and Linda's son, who was still gazing intensely at the television, remained. Joyce was dozing in her favourite chair, looking tired and fragile. It was after midnight and the latest news from the hospital was that Jackie Sullivan had collapsed and would be kept in overnight. Linda had agreed to look after the little girl, but she too was staring dully into her mug of tea, obviously reluctant to return to her own flat just doors from the devastation.

A photographer from the Gazette had been and gone and Laura had accumulated all the information she needed to be able to write her story when she arrived at the office early next morning. There was nothing now to prevent her from going home to bed except the shared sense of desolation which drifted around them like a fog.

'How do you come to terms with this?' Laura asked

softly, as much to herself as anyone else, glancing at Chrissie, pink and cherubic in sleep and oblivious to the loss of her brother. The boy who still crouched by the television turned briefly to look at her, blue eyes sunk into violet pits of tiredness.

'What's your name?' she asked, more for something to say than with any real curiosity.

'Stephen,' he said, turning indifferently back to his film. He was a stocky, fair-haired child, who did not favour his mother's much darker colouring. Laura glanced at Linda, the glimmer of an idea taking hold in her mind.

'You've waited a long time to have another, Linda,' she said, glancing at Linda's pregnant bulge under her tee-shirt.

'Another bloody accident, you mean,' Linda said bitterly. 'You'd think I'd have learned more sense after the first time.'

'Not Stephen's father, then?' Laura suggested. Linda stared down into her tea for a long moment without replying.

'You must have been quite young when you had him,' Laura persisted.

'Fifteen,' Linda said at last. 'Under age. They were going mad at me to tell them who the father was but I never did. I thought it would get him into even more bother.'

'Does Stephen's father know he exists?' Laura asked.

'No, no one knows who he is. I left the space blank on t'birth certificate. DSS don't like it but there's damn all they can do about it now.'

'The space where you should have written Stephen Webster?' Laura said softly.

'You're too bloody clever, aren't you,' Linda said, but without much heat. She stared into the distance, as if trying to recall what had happened those ten summers ago.

'We used to go back to our place after school,' she said. 'Nobody knew about us. Stephen didn't have many friends because he'd not been at St Mark's long. And my dad would have given me a right hiding if he'd found out. So

108

we said nowt. We both lived in Bronte, me on t'second floor, him on t'top. We just met up at the bottom o't'stairs after school and if there were no one in at home we'd watch telly, have a cup of tea, and then – you know – it all got more serious. It were a case of let 'im do it or lose 'im, so I let 'im. The old old story.'

The prosaic little tale of teenage romance tumbled out, and there was every appearance of relief in Linda's face, as if she had been longing each and every day of those ten years for the chance to tell someone what had happened.

'And on the day Tracy died?' Laura asked, feeling the familiar spark of excitement at where her questions were leading. Perhaps her investigation for 'Case Re-opened' had not run into the sand after all. 'Were you with him on the day Tracy was killed?'

'Aye, but earlier. He went back to his place in a huff because I wouldn't have sex. My mum said she were coming home early that day and I was too scared to do owt in case she came in and caught us at it.'

'So you couldn't give him an alibi?'

'I don't know if I could or not. I were never right clear what time he was supposed to have done what he'd done.'

'You never said anything to anyone?'

'I did, though! After he were arrested I talked to one of t'coppers on the estate and he said he'd tell his inspector, and get back to me, but he never did. . .'

'Do you know his name, the policeman you spoke to?'

'No chance. There were so many of them about. He had a beard, but I never saw him again.'

'And you never pursued it, never spoke to anyone else?' Laura tried to keep her voice neutral as she absorbed the full import of what Linda was saying.

Linda hesitated and looked about her wildly for a moment.

'What could I do?' she exploded angrily. 'I were only fifteen and I thought he'd effing done it, didn't I? I thought he'd killed her. And after what had happened at our house, I thought it were my fault he'd killed her. Don't you see? I were out of my mind they'd blame me as well as him. The whole place were going barmy about him, wanting him hanged and that. And then I found out I were pregnant an' all, and it were his kid. I kept bloody quiet then. What else could I do?'

TEN

'YOU'D BETTER COME IN,' JERRY Hurst muttered grudgingly to the two police officers he found on his doorstep at Bronte House on Monday morning. He unfastened the chain which had restrained the door from opening more than a narrow crack when they had banged on it. Ungraciously he waved Chief Inspector Thackeray and DC Val Ridley into a narrow hallway which reeked of cigarette smoke and stale food and the all-pervading smell of damp decay which had returned to Bronte after the rain. The caretaker locked the door again carefully, revealing an inside surface reinforced with metal bars.

'You look as though you could withstand a siege,' Thackeray said mildly, taking in Hurst's bulk, spilling this morning from a black sleeveless tee-shirt which he wore loose over stained corduroy trousers sagging to buttock height at the back. There were thick folds of flesh around his chin and neck and it did not look as though he had shaved for days. If a bulldozer could have been made flesh, Thackeray thought, Jerry Hurst could have started work demolishing Bronte House single handed.

Waving them into his cluttered living-room, Hurst cleared a pile of old newspapers from one sagging armchair and dumped them on a floor covered with a dark grey spongy material which looked as though it too might be beginning to decay. He chased an obese and bad-tempered ginger cat from another chair to make space for his visitors.

'Town 'all said you'd be coming,' Hurst muttered grudgingly. 'Though there's bugger all I can tell you about

111

t'squatters. They keep out o' my way and I keep out o' theirs. There's no joy in sticking your neck out round here. Look what happened to that silly cow Jackie Sullivan.'

Val Ridley, who had pulled out her notebook and was waiting to follow Thackeray's lead, flinched slightly at that, but the chief inspector remained impassive.

Hurst sat down on a hard chair close to the door, legs splayed, huge hands on his knees, as if ready to spring, although whether into flight or fight it was impossible to tell. He licked his lips as the silence lengthened, eyeing his visitors in turn. His eyes were pale blue, bright in a grey, putty-coloured face which did not look as though it had been exposed for more than a few minutes to the recent brilliant sunshine. His hair a thin receding thatch, thick with grease, which might once have been described as blond but had now taken on the colour of dirty water.

'I'm not a well man, you know,' Hurst said suddenly into a silence which evidently unnerved him. 'It's bad enough here with the lift always out of action. I can't be running up and down those effing stairs after kids who shouldn't be here.'

'I'm sure it's a difficult job, Mr Hurst,' Thackeray said soothingly. 'I don't think anyone's blaming you for what's been going on here recently. But there are a couple of things we think you might be able to help us with, especially since our inquiries now include the murder of Darren Sullivan last night.'

'Murder?' Hurst asked, licking his lips again.

'It'll be treated as murder, Mr Hurst. Whoever threw that petrol bomb should have had a reasonable expectation that it might kill someone,' DC Ridley said. 'Even if the charge was reduced to manslaughter there'd likely be a life sentence at the end of it. Where were you, by the way, when the fire broke out?'

'Asleep,' Hurst said flatly. 'I heard nowt till the fire brigade near knocked the door down to fetch me out.'

'But Linda Smith says she tried to rouse you earlier than that to use the phone,' DC Ridley persisted. 'Did you not hear her?'

'I'm a heavy sleeper,' Hurst came back.

'So heavy the place could burn down around your ears and you'd never know,' Thackeray snapped suddenly. The fat man's eyes flickered momentarily.

'I'd had a skinful, if you must know,' he said. 'It's not as if I'm on duty or owt at night. I'm not a bloody security guard. Any road the Sullivans are five floors up. You could let off a bomb up there and I'd hear nowt.'

'You'd been to the pub, then?' Val Ridley persisted.

'No, not to t'pub,' Hurst said. 'I were drinking here. I fell asleep in front o't'telly, if you must know. I generally get a bottle o'summat on a Sunday, it helps pass the time. I hate bloody Sundays.'

Thackeray glanced towards the television set in the corner where a couple of empty spirit bottles lay alongside a congealed plate which might have been used for a meal at some indeterminate time in the past. It was a sight that roused old memories and old fears which he pushed impatiently from his mind. The past was a ravaged country from which few returned unscathed, he thought. It was best not visited.

Turning back to Hurst with relief if not pleasure, he thought that if the man was lying, he had prepared his ground carefully and without obvious artifice. Indeed the notion of Hurst slumped asleep in this very chair had the ring of truth about it.

'So you saw no one come or go around the time of the fire?' he asked.

'I told you, I were asleep. I weren't on duty on a Sunday night.'

It was pathetic, Thackeray thought, but he reserved the anger which drove him this morning not for this defensive jobsworth, but for whoever had so carelessly snuffed out the life of another child the previous night. He had no reason to suspect they might be the same person. The belated rousing of Jerry Hurst was too well attested for there to be much chance he had been up on the top floor throwing petrol bombs seconds before the alarm was raised.

The police had been expecting a murder at the Heights, he thought, but not this one. Darren had not died because he had been out on the streets slaking a thirst for vicarious thrills by watching the stolen cars. He had not died because he posed a threat to anyone or even presented a fleeting target to the lust of some warped mind. He had suffocated in his own bed, in the care and safe-keeping of a mother who fought like a tiger for his welfare and must have thought him as safe from harm as she could keep him.

Jackie's enemies had not cared whether she lived or died, and had found almost by chance the weapon which Thackeray knew was the cruellest of all. She had been warned, she had told PC Alan Davies, when he had questioned her at the hospital the previous night. She had been told to stop making waves. She had ignored the warnings and had got, she had said in dull resignation, what she should have expected. It was the law of the jungle and had filled Thackeray with near despair as he had read the reports on his desk that morning.

He had instructed Val Ridley to lead the interview with Hurst, preferring to watch and wait for the smallest hint that might unlock the stranglehold of violence and intimidation on the estate which had now claimed three young lives.

He approved of Val Ridley, although he would never have dreamed of telling her so. She was a good detective, cautious and thorough and intelligent; one whose progress in CID he was watching with interest not least because she was a woman, and therefore, like himself, something of an outsider in the clubbable, boozy and often aggressively male world of the traditional copper. Still she waited for his nod to go ahead, not quite sure of him.

'You know that the council intends to evict the squatters don't you?' Val Ridley said at length, switching Hurst's attention to what was in fact their main concern.

'Aye, they delivered t'court orders weeks ago, but they've done nowt about it.'

'Well, I think they may be getting close to doing

something now,' the detective constable said, carefully avoiding any indication of just how close that time might be. That was the deal the police had agreed with the housing department earlier that morning. Not even the caretaker at Bronte was to be told how soon the bailiffs and the police would arrive in force to clear the squats.

'What we want to know,' DC Ridley went on, 'is just who you think is living where, so we've some idea who we should be talking to when the time comes.'

For half an hour Hurst grudgingly went through the lists with DC Ridley, filling in the details absent from the bare record of tenancies: how many adults and children lived in each flat, who came and went at what times of the day and night.

'I don't know what makes you think I've got nowt to do all day but sit 'ere watching folk come in and out,' Hurst complained grudgingly. 'There's always summat. The bloody lifts are out of order more than they're bloody working: I spend half my life on t'phone to the engineers.' Val Ridley raised an eyebrow at that but made no other comment. She opened a photocopied plan of the flats, floor by floor, and spread it out on the low table.

'What I want now is for you to mark the flats that are legally occupied and tell me which of the empty ones have squatters in them,' she said.

Hurst shrugged and moved closer to her, a procedure she did not find particularly pleasant as it was obvious he seldom took a bath.

'All them at that end are empty,' he said, pointing with a stained finger at the northern-most extremity of the block. 'They're all damp, wringing wet, some o'them. Everyone were moved out of them two years ago or more. Even the squatters won't go in theer. And most of the ground-floor flats are empty, except mine. They're all boarded up, but the kids get into them any road. You can't keep 'em out.'

Reluctantly Hurst was persuaded to identify ten flats where the squatters lived, at least intermittently. He refused point-blank, though, to make even a rough guess as to how many of them there were.

115

'They come and go,' he said obstinately. 'I can't be expected to keep track of them. It's not my job, is it? It's yours.'

Thackeray watched and listened in silence for a while before leaving the flat to take a walk up the stairs to the top floor, where a haze of blue smoke still hung on the air and an acrid smell stung the eyes and nose. He strolled along the deserted walkway overlooking the main road. The estate was quiet in mid-morning, although he could hear the shouts and laughter of children from the adventure playground just out of sight around the corner of the building.

He stood watching the scene below until he suddenly felt himself watched. He turned to find a man standing at the door of one of the flats behind him, a tall figure in jeans and trainers and a black sports-shirt. His brown hair was cut short above a thin face and his grey eyes exhibited neither fear nor curiosity at Thackeray's presence on the walkway, more a sort of chilly disinterest.

'Good-morning,' Thackeray said. 'Were you here when all this was going on last night?' He nodded towards Jackie Sullivan's flat, its windows now boarded up, the concrete above the frames stained black by smoke and flames. The man shook his head.

'I got back from walking the dog just as the fire brigade arrived,' he said. 'Are you police? I already talked to one of your lads.'

'Fine,' Thackeray said equably. 'I was just getting the lie of the land, Mr . . .?'

'Stansfield, John Stansfield.' The reply was off-hand as the man turned to attend to a young Alsatian which had thrust an inquisitive muzzle out of the door behind its master.

'Do you have a garage down there, Mr Stansfield?' Thackeray asked.

The man shrugged.

'There's one for each of the flats in Bronte and Holtby at that end, Priestley and Bentley in the other block. But not many of them are used. Not many folk up here have cars, do they?'

'And you?'

'An old banger. I only use it at weekends.'

A female voice from inside the flat attracted his attention then and he turned to go in again with an easy smile.

'If there's anything I can do to help . . .' he said as he closed the front door. Thackeray nodded almost absently himself and made his way back to the stairs and Jerry Hurst's flat five reeking flights below. Val Ridley had packed up her tenants' lists and notes and appeared to be ready to go. But Thackeray was not quite finished, and reinvigorated by the fresh air, he threw Hurst off balance as he had intended to.

'There is the other business to talk about too,' he said.

'What other business?' Hurst asked, all his earlier unease returning.

'It's a pity you don't pay closer attention to what goes on around here when there's someone attacking little girls,' Thackeray said grimly.

'They've bin round asking questions about that,' Hurst said sulkily. 'I talked to your blokes the day after it happened. It weren't in t'flats, any road. It happened round the back. I can't be expected to know what's happening out there, can I?'

'Were you here when Tracy Miller was murdered?' Thackeray asked, knowing the answer.

'Aye, I was,' Hurst said. 'You should know that. I gave evidence at the trial of the little beggar that killed her.'

'Ah, right,' Thackeray said innocently. 'I wasn't in Bradfield at the time. I'm not well up on the details of that case. Someone at the station thought that Josie Renton was attacked in the same way as Tracy Miller. The injuries were similar.'

'Aye, well, if you've not let that little toe-rag out of gaol it can't be t'same person, can it?' Hurst said.

'Not unless they got the wrong person in the first place,' Thackeray said softly, watching Hurst's reaction closely. But the large pasty face remained impassive.

'He were t'right one,' he said. 'No doubt o' that. I saw

117

him going down them stairs out there when he said he were at home watching t' telly. Lying little git. He were t'right one all right, no fear.'

Later that day, Sergeant Kevin Mower pulled his sweaty tee-shirt off over his head as he came into the prefabricated hut which served as office, changing room and tea-bar at the adventure playground and rubbed himself down vigorously with a towel which he took from a hook on the back of the door.

'That's the lot,' he said to Sue Raban, his voice muffled as he wiped the sweat from his face and the back of his neck. 'They've all gone now and I've locked the gate. You know, that lad Terry's not bad. He was running rings round me.'

Mower completed his rub-down and sprayed himself liberally with deodorant. He stood in his football shorts, gazing with some complacency at his tanned, well-muscled chest, where a fuzz of dark hair still gleamed damply after his exertions in the hot sun.

'Are you doing anything tonight?' he asked. 'Do you fancy a Chinese?'

Sue did not respond or even look up from her perusal of the playground's account books. She sat with her dark head bent so low that eventually Mower realised that hers was not the silence of concentration but of something more. He put his towel down and crossed the room to stand beside the desk. Angrily Sue brushed at a splash on the cash-book in front of her and Mower realised that it had been caused by a tear.

'Hey, what's this?' he asked gently, and she turned suddenly in her chair and put her arms around his waist and her damp face against his naked belly. He drew a sharp breath at the instant response of his body to her touch but he knew that this was the worst time and place to follow that instinct to its natural conclusion. Instead he took hold of her arms and loosened their grip, crouching down beside her chair to put himself on the same level with his hands resting lightly on her shoulders.

118

'What's this?' he asked again. Sue sighed, wiping the tears from her face with the back of her hand as if irritated at being discovered in such a state.

'It's this whole awful mess,' she said. 'Jackie told me she'd been threatened after the first article about her campaign appeared in the Gazette. Linda was frightened too. But I told them to be strong and keep going. Lots of stuff about solidarity and being tough – you know? It's important for people to take control of their lives . . .' She broke off, her dark eyes filling with tears again. 'I guess I just didn't think it would come to this. I had this idea, you know, that England is a civilised place? I underestimated those bastards, didn't I?'

'Do you know which bastards we're talking about?' Mower asked, the policeman reasserting himself.

'How do I know?' Sue said wearily. 'Whoever gains from the existence of that dump, I guess. The ones who don't want it pulled down at any price. The squatters, drug-pushers, you name it.'

'Jackie had no idea who?'

'No idea. Hey, what is this?' Sue put her arms round Mower's neck and kissed him on the lips, running dark fingers across brown shoulders in a way guaranteed to set his pulse racing again as her tongue slid for a moment between his lips and met his. It was a promise and he intended to ask her to fulfil it very soon.

'You're good to know, Kevin,' she said. 'And no I'm not doing anything later. But first I must go home and change.'

'I'll walk you down the hill,' he said, jumping to his feet and putting a dry tee-shirt on as Sue locked her books in a drawer and took the keys to the building from their hook.

They secured the playground gates behind them and walked slowly together along the main road which would take them past Bronte House and down the hill towards the town centre. Sue Raban had a flat for the summer in one of the Victorian terraced houses on the lower slopes of the Heights, neat steps of stone dwellings which had once climbed in rank upon rank up the hills that surrounded the town before the redevelopments of the sixties and seventies had claimed most of them.

The Heights were wound up to a quivering pitch that was almost palpable, Mower thought, watching with a wary eye the groups of teenagers on the grass wasteland which surrounded the flats. The gangs of youths and boys swaggered and strutted around the public parts of the estate, the alleyways and walkways, their eyes as sharp and watchful as scavenging animals waiting to move in on a kill. So far as he knew his cover remained intact, but he had no illusions that he would be in some danger if it emerged at this stage that he was a police officer.

By the main door of Bronte a group of women were deep in conversation and as the couple approached, one of them waved at Sue.

'Hold on a minute,' she said to Mower. 'I'll just see what Debbie wants.' Mower watched admiringly as she walked across the grass. A tall, lithe figure in Bermuda shorts and a bright yellow tee-shirt, head held high, she had lost none of the grace of Africa while she had been sharpening her mind in cooler climates. She would not stay in Bradfield beyond the end of the summer, he knew: the playground job was intended to give her some practical experience while she studied at some obscure new university in outer London. If their relationship was to live up to its promise, he thought, they did not have much time.

He perched himself on the arm of a wooden bench with half its seat missing that stood on the edge of the grass and watched idly as the discussion at the door of Bronte became even more excited. He saw Sue glance in his direction once or twice and he pointed to his watch meaningfully, wanting her to hurry, but she turned away again.

He was joined on the bench by a group of boys of about fifteen who occasionally hung around the playground watching the knock-about football games going on inside the wire fence, too old to take part themselves. They were lanky youths, almost fully grown but with muscles not yet filled out to adult strength and bulk, saplings still beside

Mower's fully grown tree, but formidable enough in threes and fours to give even a seasoned copper pause for thought. They were dressed in the latest fashionable jogging gear and pristine training shoes, their eyes bright and confident and cold.

'You going to United on Saturday?' one of the boys asked, making the question into a challenge. Mower shook his head.

'I'll be working at the playground Saturday,' he said casually.

'Young Terry won't be there,' one of the youths said. 'They'll all be going to t'match with their mates. First o't'season. They rate this new striker they've got. Played for Crystal Palace. Have you seen him?' Mower had found no way of disguising his southern accent and freely admitted to being a Londoner when challenged.

'Nope, I'm a Wimbledon man myself,' he said truthfully, knowing that this would provoke the derisive laughter which followed and, he hoped, defuse the situation. Out of the corner of his eye he could see Sue coming back towards him over the grass, closely followed by the half dozen women she had been talking to, and there was a determination in her walk and, glimpsed fleetingly, an expression on her face which caused him some concern. He slid to his feet and went to meet her.

'Ready?' he asked as she approached.

'Not quite,' she said. 'This is Debbie Renton, little Josie's aunt. She's got something she wants to ask you.' Mower's concern deepened slightly. He was uncomfortably aware that the boys he had been talking to were still just behind him, engaged in some horseplay round the bench, while the women, evidently angry, ranged themselves in front of him, accusation in their eyes.

He glanced at Sue but realised with some disillusion from her frozen expression that he would find no support there. Nor, he knew, would there ever be again if he were forced to answer what he guessed they would want to know: whether he was in fact a policeman.

He turned back to Mrs Renton, who stood with solid,

121

freckled arms folded across an ample bosom which strained her cotton dress to its limit, implacable suspicion in her eyes.

'What is it?' he asked with a tentative smile, switching on all the charm he dared although he guessed it would not avail him much.

'We want to know what you were doing round the back o't' flats Friday tea-time,' Debbie Renton said aggressively, her eyes like small glass marbles of icy blue in her flushed and sweaty face.

It was not the question he had expected and it caught him by surprise. It took him seconds to realise what lay behind it and when he did he was horrified. He caught Sue's eye in desperate appeal but got no response.

'You were seen hanging around,' she said. 'Is it true?'

Mower thought fast.

'Who saw me?' he asked, playing for time.

'Never mind that,' Mrs Renton said angrily. 'Someone up on t'top floor were watching, that's all. So what were you playing at?'

'I did see a couple of kids home at about five. They said they'd be OK on their own but I wasn't sure. I thought it was better to keep an eye on them.' He half turned to Sue, appealing for her help. 'Come on, Sue, you know me better than that,' he said. 'What they're suggesting is crazy. I wouldn't lay a finger on a child.' He knew the denial would sound hollow. He had heard it often enough himself from men who had undoubtedly laid far more than their fingers on children.

'I don't know you that well,' Sue said, her dark eyes full of suspicion. 'I never know men, if it comes to that. When you got this job did the committee run a police check on you?'

'Yes, of course,' Mower said, bitter at the irony of the question.

'You should bugger off this estate,' one of the watching women said belligerently. 'We can do wi'out strangers here.'

Sue looked at him, a hint of doubt now in her eyes, but Mrs Renton was not to be mollified.

'We don't know owt about him,' she said, her voice rising

with anger. 'He were there watching little girls and an hour later our Josie were attacked. I want him down at t'bloody nick, else I'll not be responsible for what I'll do to him.' She made a furious chopping motion with her hand that froze Mower's blood.

Afterwards he had no doubt that he could have calmed the women down, if necessary by agreeing to go to police HQ with one of them, and ended the embarrassment that way. But Debbie Renton's outrage had evidently ignited anger which neither she nor he could control. The next thing he knew he had been sent spinning awkwardly to the ground at the feet of his accusers by a blow from behind.

'Bastard,' shrieked the youth he had been talking to minutes earlier, following up his initial assault by aiming a tremendous kick at Mower's head. If it had landed where the boy intended Mower would have been unlikely to take any more conscious part in the proceedings, but he rolled to one side, taking the force out of the kick which merely grazed his shoulder.

'Leave it out,' he yelled at the teenager as he scrambled to his feet, but the boy was past listening, and his mates backed him up by forming a threatening circle in front of Mower while the group of women watched in stony silence, like *tricoteuses* at the guillotine, effectively blocking his escape to the rear. The youth ran at him again, head down, and forewarned this time, Mower with his greater height and strength met him in a bear hug which allowed the boy only to hit him awkwardly around the back and kidneys which he proceeded to do with enthusiasm as the two of them swayed wildly between the watchers.

'Sue,' Mower shouted desperately, as he dodged a leg which another youth had thrust out in the hope of tripping him up. 'For Christ's sake sort them out. I'll go and see the Bill.' The appeal was costly because it distracted him for long enough to allow another of the youths to come round behind him and land a vicious punch which brought him to his knees. He could taste blood in his mouth now and felt a moment of panic. If he could not get away, he thought, he would be faced with a simple choice between doing one of those kids some serious damage or having some serious damage done to him. Either way his cover would be irrevocably blown, the weeks he had worked on the estate wasted and Michael Thackeray infuriated.

The boy he was holding tried to head-butt him and again Mower was quick enough to dodge the full force of the blow which caught him on the temple. With a struggle, he got back to his feet, still holding his first assailant tightly as a human shield against the rest, though very aware that the other youngsters were growing bolder and that if they coordinated their attack the fight would escalate from unpleasant to extremely nasty.

Suddenly he saw his opportunity. He had spun round, with the first boy still flailing about in his unforgiving grip, just as all three of his friends appeared directly in front of him at once. With a tremendous heave he pushed his first attacker straight at them, knocking them all off balance for one crucial second. He put his head down and ran.

More by luck than judgement he found himself heading along the grass parallel to the main road which led towards the centre of the town, and even as his attackers regrouped themselves with yells of fury not far behind him he saw his salvation as a small white VW Beetle started up at the kerb outside the old people's bungalows on the other side of the road and headed in his direction. Mower dashed heedlessly across the road, causing Laura Ackroyd to brake sharply. He flung open the passenger door and got in, fighting for air as he slumped into the passenger seat.

'Get me out of here,' he said, though Laura, seeing four or five hefty youths approaching at a menacing run, needed no telling. She accelerated away, leaving Mower's pursuers standing in the middle of the road screaming obscenities after them.

ELEVEN

KEVIN MOWER WASHED THE BLOOD off his temple and squinted at himself in the mirror in the police headquarters' washroom. He went to his locker and took out a long-sleeved polo shirt and a pair of jeans which he put on over his tee-shirt and shorts and inspected the effect. For the moment, he thought, he could explain the graze away and avoid any chance that Thackeray might pull him off the estate for his own protection before his time was up.

'Some irate husband caught up with you at last, Kevin?' Sergeant Phil Groves said, coming into the room and peering with interest at Mower's injury.

'Sod off,' Mower said irritably, although in truth the question uppermost in his mind was exactly who had just caught up with him. Who, he wondered, had claimed to see him from the top floor loitering at the back of the flats and filled Mrs Renton's mind with that terrible suspicion. And was it just coincidence that a gang of violent lads had happened to be close enough to add their weight to the angry advice that he should get off the estate and not come back? Even Sue Raban, he thought, had been curiously reluctant to intervene on his behalf. Had he, he wondered, been warned off and if so who exactly was doing the warning?

Adjusting his shirt collar so that it concealed the most easily detectable marks on his neck, he strolled into the main CID office where a battalion of detectives was collating information on the escalating situation at the Heights. His appearance led to the usual banter about his undercover role, but Michael Thackeray was unsmiling when he noticed his presence and nodded him into his office.

'Anything new?' he asked.

Mower shook his head.

'Not much, guv, but I thought I'd better check in with you after last night's episode. Word up there is that it was a petrol bomb.'

'Word is right,' Thackeray said grimly. 'It's all in the Gazette. With a leader calling for police heads to roll if the anarchy isn't brought under control soon.' He waved at a copy of that afternoon's paper which lay on his desk with Laura Ackroyd's graphic description of the previous night's events lavishly displayed across the front page.

'And no one saw anything unusual?'

'Not a thing, apart from a car leaving soon after the fire started, but that could be completely innocent. Our man on surveillance failed to get a proper look at it anyway because he was distracted by the explosion on the top floor of Bronte. I increasingly get the feeling that someone up there is playing games with us,' Thackeray said.

'You know Jackie Sullivan was warned to drop her campaign?' Mower asked.

Thackeray nodded without enthusiasm. 'Someone is trying very hard to preserve the status quo up there,' he said. 'And if the child hadn't died in the fire they might well have succeeded. The women would probably have decided their campaign wasn't worth the grief it was bringing them.'

'They're winning hearts and minds,' Mower said soberly. 'All I've picked up today is that Jackie Sullivan got no more than she deserved. She should have kept her mouth shut, in other words. Rough justice but Wuthering's inimitable own. And then there's the bloody vigilantes waiting to pounce on anyone they think has designs on their kids. That could be very nasty too.' He had had a bitter taste of just how nasty, he thought.

'Jack Longley reckons the whole place will explode if we don't come up with something soon,' Thackeray said.

126

'What happened to your head?' he added sharply, noticing the raw patch on Mower's temple for the first time.

'Some little Vinny Jones lookalike brought me down in a football game, guv,' Mower lied easily. 'They reckon because I'm twice as big as them anything goes in the way of a tackle.'

'Good job they don't play rugby. You'd be black and blue all over,' the chief inspector said unsympathetically.

Mower suppressed a groan at that, only too aware of the aching bruises across his back and shoulders where he had been pummelled in what had been more like a no-holds-barred wrestling match than anything known to either football code.

'Anyway, now you're here you can do me a report to justify your wages at that holiday camp you're running,' Thackeray went on. 'And I'll fill you in on what's going down on Thursday when the council's planning to clear Bronte House of unauthorised elements. I'll want you back here for that. There's bound to be umpteen drug arrests and I want every single one of them questioned about the joy-riding, and the assaults and the petrol bombing. You can liaise with your friends at the drug squad.'

That was a sore point with Mower, who had been ambitious to transfer there and had been rejected.

'Sir,' he said stonily, unwise enough to let his displeasure show. Thackeray pounced.

'Don't play the prima donna with me, Sergeant,' he said. 'This undercover ploy was your idea and it's come up with damn all. I want you back on the strength here on Thursday morning.'

'Sir,' Mower said quickly. 'I think I'm running out of rope up there anyway.'

There was a knock at the door and Val Ridley poked her head round. Thackeray nodded her in.

'Something a bit odd, sir,' she said, waving a sheaf of computer print-outs in front of her. 'John Stansfield – the chap you met on the top floor yesterday? I checked with the DVLC in Swansea as you asked and there's neither a

127

driving licence nor a car licence issued to anyone of that address in that name. In fact nothing at that address at all. And according to the tenants' list that flat is let to a Bill Stansfield. It may be nothing. . .'

'Check it out,' Thackeray said. 'It may be something. It's the little things that often turn out to be significant. You never know. And cross-check against the search of the garages too. He definitely said he had an old banger.'

Mower typed out his report, trying to make next to nothing into something himself as he catalogued the detail of what he feared were many wasted days, professionally at least. He still had hopes on the personal front, or had thought he did until he had caught sight of Sue's disturbingly impassive face as she had watched him being beaten up. Now he was not so sure.

On his way out of the station, he met the community constable from the Heights, Alan Davies, plodding wearily up the steps in shirt-sleeves.

'Would you do something for me, mate?' he asked, ignoring the older man's disapproving glance at his unshaven face and grazed forehead. 'Some biddy up at Wuthering near enough accused me of watching little girls for nefarious purposes this afternoon. That's not an idea I want spread around while I'm still working up there. Could you put it about that I've been to the nick to make a statement and have been cleared of any suspicion?'

'Bloody play-acting,' Davies grumbled.

'Come on, Alan,' Mower said, suddenly feeling as weary as Davies looked as his bruises reminded him even more insistently of their presence. 'It may be play-acting but it's my neck on the block if it goes wrong.' And his neck, he thought ruefully, had already taken enough of a hammering for one case.

'Come on, Alan. We're all on the same side.'

'I suppose,' Davies said grudgingly. 'Aye well, I'll see what I can do. I'll put the word about. They might have your goolies else, and that'd never do.'

Laura was writing her report for 'Case Re-opened'. She

was sitting at her kitchen table with a portable computer in front of her, the window wide open and the sound of bird-song and laughing children wafting in from the long gardens outside. She had flung off her office suit when she arrived home and was wearing nothing over her bra and pants except a voluminous white cotton top, half-way between a tee-shirt and a dress. She had loosened her hair from the clips which had barely restrained it by the end of a hectic day in the office, and it fell in a tangle of copper curls around her face. She looked like a rather serious flower-child as she frowned slightly at what she had written.

It was a perfect summer evening but her mood was sombre. It had been a long and stormy day at the Gazette, with Ted Grant in one of his most objectionably censorious moods. The editorial which had excoriated the police in a Force Ten tabloid gale of invective for not bringing peace and tranquillity back to the troubled Heights had been mild compared to the venom Grant had poured privately onto the whole pantheon of villains he believed responsible for social collapse on the present scale.

Architects, planners, rock musicians, parents and teachers, social workers and politicians, and a whole top ten of 1960s demons from Dr Benjamin Spock to Mick Jagger all came in for scorn and derision as he paced up and down the newsroom in a pantomime fury which Laura guessed he had modelled on some high-profile London editor of his vague acquaintance. In the end, as he heaped blame for some misdemeanour on Jane Archer, a diffident young trainee who often bore the brunt of his rages, Laura's own less than certain temper had snapped.

'Come on, Ted, she's here to learn,' she had said, standing behind Jane with a protective hand on her shoulder and trying to see which particular sentence on her computer screen had sparked Ted's wrath.

'She's been here almost a year and seems to have learned nowt,' Grant snapped back. 'I'm sick and tired of arty-farty young graduates off some student paper who think they know it all.'

'It's an easy enough mistake,' Laura had said. The remark may have been reasonable but it was certainly not circumspect. If it served its purpose in deflecting Grant's attention from the bowed head of the unfortunate Jane, who was singularly ill-equipped to deal with his aggression, it did little for Laura's own future prospects. Turning an even deeper shade of purple, Grant had waved her into his office and proceeded to attack her qualifications, her competence, and her ancestry, Grant being an old antagonist of her grandmother's in her political hey-day.

'It's a bloody shame you didn't stay in Portugal with your father when you broke your bloody ankle for all the use you are here,' he concluded, eyes bulging and scalp glowing through its thin covering of grey hair.

'And it's a pity you didn't stay on the kind of London rag which thrives on your sort of bullying,' Laura came back with a vehemence to match her boss's before spinning on her heel and leaving, slamming the door behind her with a finality that shook the glazing in its frame. The newsroom outside was uncannily silent and she knew that the assembled staff had been listening avidly to the confrontation.

'One day you'll go too far,' the chief sub Frank Powers had hissed as she had swept past his desk, head high, cheeks flaming.

'One day he'll go too far,' Laura said. Jane's chair was empty, her computer screen winking away inconsequentially to itself. Laura hurried to the cloakroom where as expected she found Jane weeping quietly into a paper towel.

'I'm not cut out for this,' she said.

'No one's cut out for Ted,' Laura said angrily. 'So don't be so daft. You'll outlast him, you'll see. One day he'll get into one of these rages and just explode all over the newsroom floor in a puddle of beer and chip butties.' Grant's diet, mostly ingested at the Lamb and Flag, was legend on the Gazette and Jane gave a hysterical giggle in spite of herself.

130

'You may not be God's gift to reporting but you can write, Jane,' Laura said. 'Don't let that miserable old sod tell you otherwise. You'll be able to take over the features from me when I pack it in. Don't forget, I've been here ten years. It's just a question for me of getting out under my own steam or waiting to be pushed.'

Jane had shaken her head vigorously at that analysis, but it was not one which Laura had invented simply to cheer the younger woman up. It was a thought which had distracted her all the way home, as it often did. If one day Ted did push her into handing in her resignation, as well he might, or pushed himself into sacking her in a fit of temper – less likely as they both knew that she was too good at her job to be cast aside lightly – it might not be altogether a bad thing, she thought. It would force a move that she would have made years ago if it had not been for Joyce.

Tonight, though, the row in the office merely provoked her into tackling her report for the television company with a grim determination to make it sufficiently enticing to tempt the film crew up the motorway to start a thorough re-investigation of the Tracy Miller case.

Dispassionately she reviewed what she had learned from Linda Smith about Stephen Webster's movements that day. He had come home from school at four as usual, met Linda and gone home with her, leaving her flat on the second floor at about four-thirty, Linda thought. As far as she could remember Stephen had gone up the stairs in the direction of his own home at that point, which was consistent with his claim that he had watched television for some time before going down to the recreation field to look for friends to play football with.

He had said that the flat was empty when he got home, though his stepfather later said that he had not gone out with the younger child to look for Tracy until almost five. Even more damning was Jerry Hurst's claim that he had seen Stephen leaving the flats some time before five, in plenty of time to commit murder at the time the forensic evidence suggested it had been committed.

Linda was right, Laura thought, in thinking that her evidence would not give Stephen any sort of an alibi. But the fact that the police had never followed up her offer of evidence might be important. Even if they thought that Linda was not worth interviewing, they should certainly have told the defence of her existence. It was undisclosed evidence and might be enough to persuade the TV company to let her go a step or two further with her investigation. Harry Huddleston remained a challenge she would dearly like to take up if 'Case Re-opened' thought it worthwhile.

As far as she was concerned, anything the repellent Jerry Hurst said might also be suspect, although she admitted there was no more to that conviction than sheer prejudice. Perhaps, she thought, she ought to make one last effort to pin Jerry down before completing her report.

She closed up her computer with a sigh, poured herself a large vodka and tonic and put an old Queen album onto the stereo. It took her back to her schooldays when she had thought Freddie Mercury was a close approximation to God. That idol had been smashed too, she thought, as she curled up with her drink with her mammoth tee-shirt pulled tight over her knees, looking young enough to be perched still on the top bunk in her school dormitory and wishing, just as fervently as she had then, that she did not have to curl up alone.

TWELVE

'LET ME GET THIS QUITE clear,' Chief Inspector Thackeray said to DC Val Ridley, who was perched slightly nervously on a chair in front of his desk, mid-way through the next morning and with a half-pleased smile on her face. The chief inspector was in shirt-sleeves, his tie loosened, the window behind him wide open but not bringing much freshness in from the dusty square outside. The humid weather had returned this morning with a vengeance, the coolness after the weekend rain no more than a refreshing memory as the heat began to build again.

'Let me get this straight,' Thackeray said. 'According to the council the flat is let to Bill Stansfield, who has lived there for twenty years. The rent is paid like clockwork. His name is still on the electoral roll and he registered for the poll tax. But according to a neighbour on the same floor, old Bill Stansfield died five years ago, and the flat was taken over by a younger man who calls himself John?'

'Just John usually, sir,' Val Ridley said. 'Occasionally he's implied he's old Mr Stansfield's son. But according to the neighbour who knew Bill Stansfield best, he never had a son. Just a daughter who lives somewhere in Leeds and turned up for the funeral. He can't remember her married name, though, so she may be hard to trace.'

'And the council was never told the old man had died?'

'Apparently not. According to his neighbour he was an independent character who never had anything to do with social services. He collapsed with a heart attack one day after walking up the stairs because the lift was out of order.' Val Ridley could not disguise the look of disgust

133

which briefly crossed her sharp features. 'It's a wonder more of them don't drop dead in that dump,' she muttered half to herself. Thackeray permitted himself a faint smile of sympathy but was not to be distracted from her report.

'You just talked to one of the neighbours?' he asked.

DC Ridley shook her neat blonde head sharply.

'I talked to everyone on the top floor, sir,' she said. 'There are ten flats. Three have been boarded up for some time, and the squatters don't seem to have got into them.' She consulted her notes carefully. 'Then there's the burned-out flat, Mrs Sullivan's, which has been boarded up as well now. And her friend Linda Smith has been moved out too, for her own safety, the council says, so that's five of them empty.

'The elderly couple who remember Bill Stansfield live between the Sullivan and Smith flats, name of Garside. She's a bit deaf and not much help, but he's a sharp old boy, quite clear about Stansfield's death. They used to play dominoes together at the social club, apparently. Then there's a black family called Macdonald who haven't been there long. They don't remember Bill Stansfield at all and have only passed John on the stairs. Then there's a man called Miller, lives with his daughter, next door to the Stansfield flat.'

'Paul Miller?' Thackeray asked thoughtfully.

'Yes, that's right. Paul and Kelly. But he didn't seem to know much about the old boy or John, in spite of living next door. "Very quiet," he said John was, "kept himself to himself, just like the old man." But as his daughter seems to keep her stereo on full-blast most of the time I shouldn't think they'd hear anything if there was bloody murder going on next door.'

'Does Miller not remember anything about the old boy?'

'Not much, he said. But he definitely thought John was the older Stansfield's son, though he couldn't remember whether John had actually told him that or whether he'd just made that assumption when he moved in.'

Val Ridley closed her notebook and looked expectantly

at Thackeray, but the chief inspector did not respond to her report with either the praise she sought or the blame she feared. He leaned back in his chair for a moment, eyes closed in thought as he tried to recall his own encounter on the top floor of Bronte with the man who had unequivocally called himself Stansfield, a man with a young Alsatian dog.

'Ten flats,' he said at last, swinging his chair back to the floor with a bump and leaning towards DC Ridley across the desk, his blue eyes bright. 'Ten flats, two murders in ten years, another death not reported to people who should have known about it, a flat occupied by someone who may or may not be the previous occupant's son. Coincidence, do you think?'

'Two murders?' Val Ridley said, surprised.

'Paul Miller's daughter Tracy was murdered ten years ago this summer. Two murders. Two children.' Thackeray glanced away for a moment, his face bleak. So he really does care, his detective constable thought to herself with a sense of relief at having succeeded in lifting, however briefly, that previously impenetrable mask.

'They couldn't be connected . . .?' she hesitated, unable to follow his reasoning.

'No, I don't think they're connected,' Thackeray said. 'Not directly anyway. It's just an indication of how long Bronte House has been at the mercy of predators of one sort and another. Time, I think, it was cleaned up for good.'

'Shall I go and talk to this John Stansfield, then, sir?' she asked enthusiastically.

'Did you run the name through our own computers when you checked his car details?' Thackeray asked. She reddened slightly and shook her head.

'So do that, Val. Have a look at the house-to-house interviews that were done after the Josie Renton attack. Check the names off against the tenants' lists. I want to be sure that there's no one else living there under false pretences. And then we'll both go and talk to our mysterious Mr Stansfield,' he said. 'Another thing I want to ask him is where his car was yesterday. The garage belonging to his flat was empty when we searched them – apart from a can of petrol. Which may be quite innocent, of course. It wasn't the only one. Or it may not. Give me half an hour? And well done.'

She gave him a tentative smile of relief at that before leaving him alone. He sat thoughtfully for a moment, easing his sticky shirt from between his shoulder blades, a look of uncharacteristic uncertainty on his face as he turned his attention to a bright red flyer which had been sitting on his desk for more than a week. It was advertising a jazz festival across the dales in Harrogate and he had been intending to book himself tickets ever since it had arrived.

'Dear God, there's no harm in it,' he said to himself at last, although he was not at all clear whether he was trying to convince himself, the Deity or a third party who tended to always loom large in his private thoughts. With a convulsive movement, he picked up the phone and booked the last two tickets for the festival's opening concert the following week.

Laura Ackroyd turned angrily away from Jerry Hurst's well-defended front door, which had just been slammed in her face, and found herself almost falling into the arms of Detective Chief Inspector Michael Thackeray. Taken by surprise, they stood and looked at each other in disbelief for a moment. Thackeray quickly regained his composure then turned to Val Ridley who had followed close behind him out of the lift after an equally unavailing attempt to locate the so-called John Stansfield on the top floor.

'Wait for me in the car for a minute,' he said to the startled DC, who was too surprised to demur. Thackeray held the heavy front door open for Laura in a slightly ironic gesture of old-fashioned courtesy and she preceded him out into the fresh air, hoping that it would take the heat from her flushed cheeks. She walked quickly down the tarmacked path towards the road where she had parked her Beetle unwittingly behind an unmarked police car where DC Ridley was now sitting studiously looking the other way.

'Wait, Laura,' Thackeray said quietly, catching up with her and putting a hand on her arm. 'Please.'

She turned back towards him, her face impassive, letting her hair fall forward a little to hide the expression in her eyes. She did not, she thought, with unexpected annoyance, remembering their last meeting, want to give this man any encouragement he had not worked very hard for. He owed her that, at least.

'Are you covering the Darren Sullivan death?' he asked, cooler now, responding to her mood.

Laura shrugged.

'Amongst other things,' she said. 'Just a follow-up on the estate. I wanted to talk to Linda Smith but apparently she's been moved out too. I'll have to ask the town hall where she's gone. I don't suppose you know, do you?'

Thackeray shook his head.

'I expect we do, but I couldn't tell you even if I knew the address personally. Which I don't.'

'No, I don't suppose you could,' Laura agreed coldly. She glanced up at the cliff face of the flats above them, no more than half the windows reflecting the sunlight, the rest blind and boarded up, the whole structure disfigured by rain and smoke-damage, a monstrous monument to urban neglect and decay.

'Are you making any progress?' she asked, aware that he was becoming stony-faced in the teeth of her evident indifference. 'Or wouldn't you tell me that either?'

'Of course I would, if there was anything much to tell,' he said, unable to hide his dissatisfaction with the progress of the police inquiries on the estate. 'You think the police close ranks when they're threatened,' he said. 'It's nothing to what this place can do. And you? Have you got Harry Huddleston nicely framed for television yet?'

Laura turned away and walked slowly the rest of the way to her car, giving herself time to think, before turning back to face Thackeray. For the first time since she had met him she felt that perhaps the conflict between their professions might be too much. She knew Thackeray would not want to hear about the flaws she had detected in Huddleston's murder inquiry. Part of him – and she hoped it was only part – would prefer to leave Linda Smith and her son in the decent obscurity they had clung to all this time. She would have to tell him soon, but not, she decided, just yet.

'It'll take a mammoth frame to fit your Harry,' she said lightly, pushing back her wayward hair and revealing a gleam of amusement in her eyes. 'Come on, Chief Inspector, you've done your duty and checked up on me. Was there anything else?'

Looking at Laura leaning slightly backwards against the car door, slim in a cream shirt and demure green skirt, the startling red hair escaping from its clips and the grey-green eyes full of laughter, Thackeray realised he was being teased and felt a sense of immense relief flow through him. He knew very clearly what he wanted to ask Laura Ackroyd, though the time was not ripe and might never be.

'Do you like jazz?' he said instead.

It was the last question she had expected and she laughed in surprise.

'Yes,' she said. 'Within reason.'

'I've got two tickets for the Harrogate festival – Wednesday next week. Would you like to come?'

She agreed quickly, trying to hide her disappointment that next Wednesday was eight days away, but he was too perceptive for her.

'And have supper with me tonight? Though I don't think I'll be free until late. Can I pick you up?'

'Would you like me to cook supper for you?' she asked impulsively. 'I'll do something that will keep, so you can come round whenever you're ready.'

'I'd like that,' Thackeray said. 'Probably about nine?'

He held the door for her as she got into her car and turned away to join Val Ridley, who was waiting patiently at the wheel of the police car. The detective constable looked curiously at him as she drew away from the kerb, but Thackeray's expression had resumed its most formidable impassivity.

Outside Bronte House Laura sat in the driving seat for a moment, trying to disentangle the jumble of emotions which had overtaken her. Suddenly she gave a whoop of triumph which astonished two elderly women passing close to the car. Then she slammed the Beetle into first gear and drove somewhat erratically back towards the town centre and the office from which she had taken an illicit half hour off.

Kevin Mower lay flat on his stomach on the bed dressed only in a pair of Pink Panther boxer shorts. Patches of Technicolor bruising on his shoulder and low on his back bore testimony to his recent unpleasant experience on the Heights. His eyes were closed and he was breathing rhythmically; one arm was trailing over the edge of the bed, the other flung across the half from which Sue Raban had just extricated herself. Slim, elegant and completely naked, she was moving softly around her bedsitter, picking up abandoned items of underwear from the floor and putting them on.

In the tiny kitchen, which was screened off from the main part of the light and lofty Victorian room by a divider luxuriant with trailing plants, she poured herself a glass of orange juice from the fridge and switched on a radio, keeping the volume low so as not to disturb her guest. Glass in hand, she wandered back to her wardrobe and took out a low-cut sun-dress in shocking pink cotton which she slipped over her lacy body. The colour lit up the room like some exotic flower, enhancing her dark skin still damp from the shower. She looked at herself briefly in the mirror, adjusted a gold earring and smiled faintly in satisfaction. She looked good and knew it.

Almost absent-mindedly she picked up the tee-shirt of the man she knew as O'Donnell, which he had discarded close to the bed, smoothed it out and hung it over the arm of a chair. Then she reached for his jeans, which had been flung carelessly across to the other side of the room.

139

Undressing, she recalled with a faint stirring of renewed excitement, had been an impulsive affair as they had fallen into each other's arms almost before they had crossed the threshold of the flat. Little enough had been said when she had invited him in but little enough needed to be put into words. Days of close proximity at the playground had left neither of them in any doubt about that.

A soft thud distracted her attention. She looked down and saw that some sort of wallet had fallen from the pocket of O'Donnell's jeans. She picked it up idly and flicked it open, to find a police warrant card in the name of Kevin Mower in her hand, but the unmistakable image of Kevin O'Donnell staring owlishly up at her, a familiar face, if somewhat more kempt than she was accustomed to.

The expletive she used was not in any language which Mower or anyone else in Bradfield would have recognised. The fury in her face needed no translation.

'You bastard! Are you awake, you bastard?'

She shook the sleeping Mower roughly on the shoulder. He rolled over with a lazy grin of reminiscence on his face, reaching out to take her by the arm and pull her onto the bed. Losing her balance, she sat down abruptly beside him but instead of the embrace he expected, she gave him a sharp backhanded slap which brought him abruptly back to full consciousness.

'What . . .?' he asked, rubbing his stinging cheek and pushing himself upright against the head of the bed and wincing as his bruised back protested. 'What was that for?' She waved the warrant card at him angrily and understanding came quickly.

'You have led me up the garden and back down again, you pig,' Sue said, her dark eyes blazing. 'You are a devious, lying, shitty cop. John said you weren't to be trusted.'

'John?'

'Never mind,' Sue said quickly. 'It's you I'm bothered about, you bastard. How dare you do this to me?'

Mower held out his hands in a gesture of mock surrender.

140

'I was watching out for the kids,' he said. 'I'd have told you but it's better not, you know? It's so easy to let it slip out. It's better not to tell anyone, however much you trust them.'

'Trust,' she said. 'You talk about trust? How dare you con me like that, you bastard. You'd better get out of my flat now, straight away. And if you've any sense, you'll keep off the Heights if you know what's good for you. I wouldn't vouch for your safety after this. You nearly got done over the other day. Next time there may not be anyone around to help you.'

She flung the warrant card at him contemptuously and moved over to the tall window where she stood with her back to him, breathing heavily. Mower shrugged, stood up and slipped quickly into his jeans and tee-shirt. Cautiously he approached Sue and put a tentative hand on her shoulder. She shrugged him off immediately and turned towards him, and he was shocked to see the fierce dislike in her eyes.

'We're on the same side,' he said.

'Oh no,' she said bitterly. 'You can't believe that. You are there to protect the status quo, Sergeant. You're not there for the kids, not for the mothers, not for blacks like me, not for the homeless youngsters squatting in that dump of a block of flats. You weren't there for those two boys in the stolen car. I know about the police, remember? I've seen them in New York. I've seen them in South Africa, for God's sake. And don't tell me it's any different here. You Brits are great hypocrites, very good at pretending the world is what it's not. But I *know*. I've been there.'

'This isn't Africa.' Mower responded angrily, guilt and fear of the damage Sue might do to him on the Heights making him doubly edgy. 'There's some pervert up there molesting little girls, for Christ's sake. Don't you want him caught?'

'Of course I want him caught,' she said, wiping away her tears with an angry gesture. 'But if the people on the Heights have any sense they'll catch him for themselves. You bastards can't come up there one day and wipe out

141

one lot of young kids and then persuade us the next day that you're there to protect the rest. Who do you think you're kidding?'

Mower thought quickly. She would not be moved by any appeal to her better nature, that was clear. There was a lifetime of fear and resentment in Sue's eyes which would be more than proof against any charm offensive he might launch. But if persuasion failed then coercion might just possibly buy him the time he was determined to have.

'I've got a job to do,' he said, 'and I need your help for one more day. Then I'm due back at HQ for a big operation. I need to stay at the playground tomorrow and I need you to keep stum.'

'No way,' she said, turning away angrily again. 'I won't cover for you.'

'We could do it the hard way,' he said, his eyes cold now, and his face as hard as hers.

'Meaning?'

'Meaning – maybe there's some irregularity in your passport, or your work permit . . .' He hesitated deliberately, knowing very well that her main reason for being in the country was to study. 'You do have a work permit, I take it, as you're working? These immigration problems do take a hell of a lot of time to sort out with the Home Office, though they say Holloway's very comfortable now it's been refurbished. . .'

She turned towards him again, striking out wildly, but he took hold of both of her wrists and with difficulty forced her hands to her sides until she relaxed and sank down onto the bed, her shoulders sagging.

'OK, OK,' she said wearily. 'One more day. Then get the hell out of my life.'

'I can understand why you're angry,' Mower said more gently, moved in spite of himself by her defeated look.

'Can you? Can you really? Can you really imagine how sick it makes me to think that I've just been to bed with a cop?' The contempt in Sue's eyes was absolute.

'I'm sorry,' he said, turning away.

'I'm sorry too,' she spat after him. 'I'm sorry we had safe

142

sex, because if we hadn't you'd never be sure I hadn't given you AIDS, would you, you bastard? Which would be no more than you deserve.'

'Jesus,' Mower said to himself as he closed the door of the flat behind him. Deprived of that bizarre revenge Sue might well think up some other just as threatening if she put her mind to it. His presence on the Heights, he knew, had always carried some risk. From now on it would be distinctly dangerous. And just who, he wondered, was John?

THIRTEEN

LAURA STOOD IN THE MIDDLE of her kitchen in a frenzy of indecision. She had come home from work with a bulging carrier bag of groceries which she had earlier hurled almost at random into her supermarket trolley, quite unable to decide what to cook for her supper guest. A jumble of mushrooms, new potatoes, red peppers, onions and aubergines lay on the work-top, next to packets of boneless chicken breasts, tagliatelle verde, egg noodles, pesto and sweet and sour sauce, like some manic internationalist illustration for a cookery book.

'Help,' she moaned, flinging open the door of her freezer and surveying the contents with a frantic eye. Slamming it closed again, she picked up the phone.

'Vicky?' she said. 'I've been trying to get you all afternoon.' She barely listened to her friend's perfectly reasonable description of her afternoon at the ante-natal clinic and her equally rational complaint that this was not a good time to talk because she had to get the boys' supper.

'It's supper I'm ringing you about,' Laura said vehemently. 'I've invited Michael Thackeray to supper and I haven't a clue what to give him.' That piece of unexpected news distracted Vicky instantly from her domestic chores.

'Hey,' she said, surprised. 'So how did you achieve that after all this time?'

'Oh, I ran into him this afternoon – literally,' Laura said airily. 'We're going to a concert next week . . .'

'A concert? What sort of a concert?'

'Jazz, for goodness' sake,' Laura said soberly, suddenly

144

brought up against her own impulsive deceit. 'I don't know the first bloody thing about jazz. Wasn't David in the jazz club? He'll have to fill me in or I'll look a complete fool.'

'I never got the impression it was your knowledge of jazz which interested Mr Thackeray,' Vicky said drily. 'And I doubt if it'll be your cooking, either.'

'Vic,' Laura said. 'This is serious.'

'I know,' Vicky said, meaning it. 'Cook him something simple. Policemen are always late. Almost as bad as Crown prosecutors.'

'Chicken,' she said. 'I bought chicken. In a sauce. And rice. When he gets here.'

'Sounds fine,' Vicky said. 'Listen, I must go. Daniel and Nathan are yelling for their fish fingers. Call me tomorrow and tell me all? Without fail?'

That agreed, they hung up and Laura went into her bedroom, straightening the duvet distractedly and wondering when she had last washed the sheets before looking at herself in the tall mirror on the wall. She had changed into her only cotton dress as soon as she had come in from work, and she examined the jade shirt-waister minutely, piling her hair, which hung loose to her shoulders, on top of her head and assessing the effect critically.

I look like a child with it down, she thought, and a child pretending to be a grown-up with it up. Why couldn't I have been born with conventional looks instead of this outlandish colouring and a baby face? And why, oh why, did I have to be drunk the first time Michael Thackeray came here? He's bound to remember and despise me for it. Those watchful eyes, she knew, missed little and judged much, and she could not yet gauge how ready they were to understand. The evening, she concluded, looked likely to be a complete fiasco.

Back in the kitchen, with her hair demurely pinned up, she poured herself an abstemious tomato juice, shook in a hefty dose of Worcester sauce, and began to slice onions and mushrooms thinly, her eyes filling with tears as the

145

juices reached them. Outside the open kitchen window, evening scents rose from the long luxuriant garden, unkempt now as the collective of flat dwellers neglected what had been provided in abundance for a Victorian family. A blackbird sat on the nearby branch of a Japanese cherry tree and offered an aria which would have moved a treacherous Pinkerton to relent.

Over the hills, though, the evening was turning threatening, dark clouds piling up on the western horizon and the sun reduced to a pale pinkish gleam between the towering cumuli. It would be dark unseasonably early and the night would bring thunder again. It was weather to reflect her tumultuous mood, she thought, still uncertain that her invitation had been wise.

Neutral ground might have been preferable, she told herself irritably. He was not the sort of man who would look for a one-night stand – altogether too remote, too serious, too old, perhaps, for casual sex. And yet – he had accepted easily enough, giving her that slow half-smile which lit up his normally grave features and took years and a certain sadness from around his eyes.

She finished her cooking and glanced at her watch. It was eight o'clock, the stormy evening already drawing in. She went back into her living-room with another tomato juice, tidying up the detritus of days and closing the bedroom door firmly on the neatly smoothed duvet.

She watched television edgily for a while, getting up every now and again to glance out of the living-room window at the street below where large spots of rain were now disturbing the dust and streaking the windscreens of the cars parked on either side of the suburban avenue. There would be nowhere for him to park when he did arrive, she thought anxiously, and then grinned at her reflection in the rain-spattered window. You're behaving like a teenage virgin, she muttered, settling herself down again in front of a sit com which on past form might conceivably raise a couple of laughs in the course of half an hour.

The phone call, when it came, made her jump. He's

crying off, she thought at once. Policemen do it all the time. They lead even more disorganised and irregular lives than reporters do. Her mind was so distracted by her anticipated disappointment that it took her long seconds to realise that the voice on the line was, shockingly, not Thackeray's but another entirely. It was a voice she recognised with a horror that sent her shuddering back across the room to crouch on the sofa with the receiver clutched rigidly to her ear. It was the voice she had last heard at the swimming pool as, half drowned, she had gasped for life-saving breath after being pulled from the water. And if the menace it had held then had been terrifying, this was infinitely worse.

'Can you hear me, Miss Ackroyd?' the voice repeated, insistent, demanding response. Whatever sound it was that Laura dragged from the depths of herself it seemed to satisfy him, at the same time confirming what she thought she had heard him say at first and had refused to accept.

'I am at your grandmother's house,' the caller said again, and this time in the background Laura thought she heard a faint cry – though whether of pain or fear she could not tell and dared not guess. 'We told you to stay away from the Heights. Remember?'

Again she offered an incoherent response, which the caller appeared to take for agreement.

'You didn't take any notice. That's a shame.' This time there was no mistaking the sound of someone in pain.

'Stop it!' Laura screamed at the receiver. 'Leave her alone!' The line went dead then, leaving her clutching the receiver in a shaking hand, shivering with a dread she did not dare define.

Laura could never remember driving back to the Heights that night. Outside her grandmother's house she found an ambulance and a police car, blue lights flashing on both. Running through the open door she pushed past a tall uniformed officer in the narrow hallway and went into the living-room where she discovered Joyce, evidently unbowed if not unbloodied, sitting in a chair and issuing instructions to an ambulancewoman who was examining her solicitously.

147

Joyce turned to Laura as she rushed in, and gasped as much in irritation at her own weakness as in pain. One side of her face was bruised and raw, her thin white hair was dishevelled but her eyes were as bright and as combative as ever. Laura was overwhelmed with a fierce emotion which combined relief and anger and admiration in equal parts.

'You're all right?' she asked, finding it difficult to speak.

'I'll live,' Joyce said. 'If only to spite the buggers.'

'We'll take her down to casualty for an X-ray,' the ambulancewoman said, getting to her feet. 'I don't think anything's broken, but we'd best make sure.'

'I'll come with her,' Laura said faintly, wondering if in fact she was not as much in need of medical help as her apparently indestructible grandmother, who declined a stretcher, consented to a wheelchair and preceded the official procession from her house to the waiting ambulance like a queen with her retinue behind her and a distinctly aggressive gleam in her eye.

By the time Laura returned to her own flat with Joyce in the car the defiant façade had begun to crack. Joyce had been examined for signs of concussion – none – and fractures – none – and had described in detail to PC Alan Davies, whom she treated as an old friend, how her bungalow had been invaded by two men she did not recognise.

They had smashed open her flimsy front door under cover of the early darkness and rain, and the distracting presence of a couple of youths circling the flats in spectacular fashion in an evidently stolen Sierra Cosworth. If anyone in the row of old people's bungalows had noticed the noise of splintering wood and glass above the squeal of tyres and shouts of encouragement which were echoing round the estate, they had not dared to investigate its cause.

The intruders, it was soon apparent, had not come to steal. They had burst into Joyce's living-room before she could struggle to her feet from her chair by the fire. She had been roughly forced back into her seat and hit about the face, hard and deliberately, when she protested. She had been quiet then, accepting of what she could not change, unwilling to provoke the incipient violence which filled the tiny living-room with menace, conscious of her own frailty, flesh thin over bones which might snap like twigs in a gale if she provoked further assault.

They had telephoned Laura then, the taller of them using the phone, the smaller, fatter figure, as anonymous as his companion in dark clothes and a black balaclava, hitting her again twice simply to emphasise what was being said and making her cry out in mixed fury and pain. Laura had herself cried out inwardly as she listened to her grandmother's outraged description of what had happened, as unable as Joyce was to comprehend the callous brutality which had been, Laura had no doubt, aimed primarily at her.

'What's it all about?' Davies had asked Laura in bewilderment as they waited for Joyce to come back from X-ray. 'She says they took nowt. I've done my best with that estate but if they've taken to beating up old ladies just for kicks I think I've had it. The women are at their wits' end, the kids are out of control, the old folk aren't safe. I can't see where it's all going to end.'

'Did they say why?' Laura had herself whispered on the way home, after Davies had wearily closed his notebook and Joyce had refused to stay in the hospital overnight. But the older woman had shaken her head, exhausted now as the bruises around her eyes swelled up and the light of battle faded and shock took hold. The description of her assailants that she had been able to give PC Davies was sketchy in the extreme – dark jeans, dark jackets, dark gloves and those balaclava masks so comfortably familiar in television films but hideously menacing in reality. White men, not black, she said, judging by the glimpse of flesh and light eyes which was all she had been able to see of their faces; local men, from their accents; ruthless men from their actions.

'If I'd been twenty years younger I'd not have been able to fend them off,' Joyce had said sadly as Laura and an ambulanceman half carried her up the three flights of

149

stairs to Laura's flat. 'There's always been crime up at Wuthering,' she said. 'You'd expect it. Folk up there are at the end of their tether in the good times, never mind now. But this? I don't understand this. What is it they're after, love? What do they want?'

'I don't know,' Laura said helplessly. 'That's the trouble. I simply don't know what it's all about.'

She had put Joyce to bed in her tiny spare bedroom, tucking her up gently under the unfamiliar duvet and watching her fall into an uneasy, drug-induced sleep, her bruised face cruelly dark against the white pillows. It was only then that she glanced at her watch and saw with a sense of shock that it was almost eleven and realised that the whole flat was filled with the smell of burning food. Her supper guest, she thought dully, must either have been and gone while she was out, or had not turned up at all. In the urgency of her departure she had forgotten to turn her answerphone on.

She glanced at the telephone uncertainly, realising that she did not know where Michael Thackeray lived and felt disinclined to try to find out. She went into the kitchen and switched off the oven, too disheartened even to open the door to examine the cremated chicken within. Instead she poured herself a large vodka and tonic, took it back into her living-room and slumped in a chair, depressed to the point of despair by the evening's events.

The raw alcohol kicked at her empty stomach and she felt her cheeks flush and anger begin to push her brain back into gear. Step by step she began to go over what she had done on the Heights over the last two weeks which could have provoked this level of intimidation. Someone, she concluded grimly, must be very frightened indeed of what she knew, or perhaps just what they thought she knew, to go to these lengths.

But the more she went through a mental roll-call of all the interviews and conversations she had had around the flats the more she became convinced that the nest of vipers she had evidently disturbed had been hidden there long before the current outbreak of unrest. The venom with

150

which she was now being pursued must surely go back to the death of Tracy Miller ten years before. In which case her report to 'Case Re-opened', now sitting on her commissioning editor's desk in London, was a time bomb which might explode any day.

The doorbell interrupted her reverie, but she had so far forgotten how the evening had begun that the voice on the entryphone took her by surprise.

'Am I too late?' Michael Thackeray asked, the voice cool, neutral, through the crackle of static. 'I'm sorry. I got held up.'

'Come up,' she said, opening the front door for him and unlatching her own door onto the landing. He doesn't know what's happened, she thought angrily. He's a bloody policeman, how could he not know what had happened to Joyce?

They stood for a moment on the threshold, staring at each other, nonplussed. He looked weary and slightly dishevelled, his hair untidy and his tie loose.

'I'm sorry,' he said again. 'It's been a bad night. There's all hell let loose up on the Heights again. The joy-riders are out in force. I got delayed at headquarters. I tried to call you but I couldn't get through.'

'It doesn't matter,' she said shortly, turning away from him. 'I must have forgotten to switch the answerphone on. I wasn't here myself for most of the evening. I went out in a hurry. But I suppose an old lady getting mugged is too minor a case for you.'

He moved quickly for such a big man, and was behind her in an instant, taking hold of her arm and spinning her round towards him with a force which could have become violent if it had not been so carefully controlled.

'An old lady?' he said sharply, the blue eyes alert again. 'Your grandmother? What's wrong? I haven't seen any report . . .?'

Laura shook her head wildly as if to blot out the reality of what had happened, her knees giving way on her and her eyes filling with tears, and he took her in his arms as she swayed on her feet. She relaxed against him and for a

151

moment he buried his face in her hair, breathing in the sweet smell of her, as her arms slid around him and they clung to each other. He broke away first, disturbed by the fierceness of his reaction. He led Laura to a chair and guided her into it.

'You look like death,' he said gently, examining her pale face and the dark circles beneath her eyes with concern. 'Tell me what happened.'

Haltingly, she told him, her usual felicity with words deserting her as she shivered with delayed shock.

'It's my fault,' Laura said, wrapping her arms around herself desolately when she had finished. 'I should have guessed they might try to get at me through Joyce. I'll never forgive myself.'

Thackeray got up from the arm of the chair where he had been sitting with one hand protectively on her shoulder and turned away. He looked grey as fatigue took him over again and he tried to conceal the pain which her words involuntarily provoked. He knew only too well, he thought, what it was to count oneself amongst the unforgiven.

'Don't say that,' he said, keeping the emotion carefully out of his voice. 'You're not to blame. You couldn't have foreseen this. I just wish you'd come to me when you were threatened at the swimming pool.'

'So do I – now,' she said soberly. 'Though at the time it seemed too unreal to take seriously. No one else seemed to have seen anything untoward. I began to doubt my own senses after a while, began to think I had imagined it all.'

'But tonight? It was the same man on the phone? You're sure?'

'Quite sure. I'd recognise the voice anywhere,' she said, shuddering.

'Who knew you were making inquiries into the death of Tracy Miller? Apart from Kevin Mower?' She was conscious of Thackeray watching her now and uncomfortably aware that she did not know whether the question in his eyes was professional or personal. She took the personal first.

'He bought me a Chinese meal, that's all. It was a sort of reward for not blowing his cover, I think.' Laura knew that this sounded like an excuse for choosing to do what she had a perfect right to do. She was annoyed with herself for feeling the need to offer it and with Thackeray for silently appearing to expect it. Sod you, Michael Thackeray, she thought as he continued to watch her gravely as if expecting her to go on. You can whistle for more information about my night out with the dishy Kevin. Thackeray nodded, almost as if reading her mind, and waited impassively for her to continue.

'Apart from that I've talked to Paul Miller and Stephen Webster's mother.' And Linda Smith, of course, she thought, but some professional instinct prevented her from telling Thackeray that. Linda had kept her secret for ten years and was not likely to be broadcasting it around the estate at this late stage, she thought.

'And did they tell you anything which someone else would rather you didn't find out about the Tracy Miller case?' He was very evidently back in his neutral, policeman's mode now.

'Nothing that incriminates anyone else, if that's what you mean,' she said. 'Though I was hoping it might be enough to persuade the programme to ask me to do some more interviews, at the very least. I was hoping to ask Jerry Hurst, the caretaker, a few questions when I bumped into you at Bronte House,' she said. 'But he didn't want to know. So I posted off my report to "Case Re-opened" anyway.'

'You haven't talked to Harry Huddleston yet?' Thackeray asked, a shade too casually, Laura thought. She looked at him sharply.

'Not yet,' she said. 'I'm waiting to hear from the commissioning editor in London to see what he wants me to do next.'

Thackeray recalled Huddleston's fury at the implied accusation of impropriety he had made himself and gave a thin smile.

'I'd like to be a fly on the wall if you get near Harry,' he said. 'He won't be pleased to see you and I'll put money on the fact that he'll deny any irregularities point-blank. He gave me short shrift.'

'Stephen's mother's sure he'd been bullied into making that confession,' she said. 'Is covering their backs all the police can find to worry about?'

'It's all some of the police can find to worry about,' Thackeray admitted soberly. 'My boss has nightmares about the Birmingham Six and the Guildford Four.'

'And you?' she asked. Thackeray gave her another ghost of a smile.

'I think if we got the wrong man it's about time we began looking for the right one. I like to think the wheels of justice are a bit like the mills of God – slow, but exceedingly certain in the end. And I happened to notice that there are a few similarities between the recent attacks on little girls up at the Heights and Tracy's death. Not carbon copies, exactly, but similarities.'

'Such as?'

'The fact that they never see their attacker because he covers their head and face up, half smothers them, in fact. Tracy was wrapped in a bin-bag when she was found. What was never reported in any detail at the time, although it was touched on at the trial, was that she had been bundled into it before she died.'

'How do you know that?' Laura asked, her eyes full of horror, not really wanting to hear the answer.

'Because she bit through it. Forensic found the holes, and there were bits of black plastic between her teeth.'

'Dear God,' Laura said faintly. 'How do you cope with that?'

'By keeping my eye firmly on the bastard who did it,' Thackeray said. 'How else?'

'And you're sure Stephen Webster did it?'

'I've honestly no idea. It wasn't my case and it was a long time ago. Given the evidence, I'm sure the jury was right to convict. And Harry Huddleston is still convinced he got the right man. He has no doubts. I've asked him. But if new evidence turns up then it should be looked at. Naturally.'

154

'And if Huddleston bullied the boy?'

'Then that ought to be looked at too,' he said levelly, but as she continued to look at him with her eyes full of doubt he sighed and shook his head in exasperation.

'Think, Laura, use your imagination. Think what it's like to find a child who's been used and killed like that. It's easy to get angry if you think someone might get away with it, easy to press too hard, threaten, bully, hit out even.' He had been trying to come to terms with the prospect of exactly such a case for days now and still found the threatened horror blotted out rational thought.

Laura considered what he had said in silence for a moment.

'Have you ever hit someone in anger?'

The question lay between them like a trap. Thackeray looked away for a moment, taking in Laura's comfortable, secure living-room, the thick curtains tightly drawn against the night. There were hundreds of thousands of citizens like her who would rather not know what was done in their name on the violent margins of society where he earned his bread. Laura, he hoped, would not want to be deceived or to deceive herself.

'Yes, I've hit people when there was no lawful excuse for it,' he said quietly. 'Three, four times, maybe – not in an interview room, not in cold blood, but in the heat of the moment, making an arrest. And been torn off a strip in court for it once, too, which didn't do my prospects much good. You'd be hard pressed to find a copper who hasn't. Most just never admit it.'

Laura sat looking down for a moment, unsure whether he was waiting for sympathy or just an acceptance that life was seldom simple. She gave him a tentative smile.

'I'd be very tempted to do something very unpleasant to the men who hit my grandmother.'

Thackeray shook his head angrily.

'I'll find them,' he said.

'You're very defensive. You don't need to be.'

'We should have protected her.'

'So should I,' Laura came back quickly. She pushed her

155

hair away from her face wearily in a tired echo of the gesture which Thackeray found irresistible.

'I was looking forward to this evening,' she said too exhausted now to care how far she gave herself away.

'So was I,' he said. 'One way and another it's been a sod of a day.' She nodded, looking down at her hands which she had knotted together again on her lap and untwining them slowly.

'Have you got anything to help you sleep?' he asked. She shrugged and shook her head, smiling slightly at the thought that his presence in her bed, if only she dared to engineer it, might be better than any drug.

'I'll be OK,' she said, driving the temptation from her mind. 'It's not turned out to be a very romantic first date, has it?' He could see how much she had wanted it to be and he was suddenly seized by a wave of panic. He took a deep breath.

'Laura,' he said quietly, 'I don't think this is going to work. I'm not good at relationships. And there's the job. How many hours late was I tonight?'

'Stop it,' she said sharply. 'We haven't even begun yet.'

'It might be better if we didn't . . .'

'Balls,' she said vehemently, making him smile again in spite of himself. 'Sit there and I'll get us a drink.' She stood up abruptly and then hesitated, remembering. 'You don't, of course. Can't or won't?'

His face tightened again and he glanced away, unwilling to answer.

'Can't,' she said quietly, almost to herself, divining what he did not want to admit but she had already half guessed.

He nodded and wondered why he was telling Laura things he had not discussed with a living soul since he left Arnedale. But looking at Laura's concerned face he knew why and he felt that tiny shiver of apprehension again.

'I must go,' he said. 'Don't bother with a drink. We both need some sleep.'

If I didn't think it would shock him rigid I'd ask him to stay, Laura thought again. She glanced at the two bedroom doors, behind one of which her grandmother slept soundly. Joyce, she thought, would approve of Michael Thackeray. Following her eyes, Thackeray guessed what she was thinking. He put an arm around her and kissed her on the cheek.

'I'll call you about the concert next week,' he said. 'Let's take it a step at a time, Laura. As for the other business – come in tomorrow and make a statement and we'll see if we can nail these toe-rags before they kill someone. Wuthering is a top priority this week, anyway. The council's taking the squatters out on Thursday. All right?'

She nodded and watched him go, curbing every impulse to call him back until the front door had slammed shut and the sound of his car had faded away into the faint pervasive hum of the urban night. Only then did she pull back the curtains and press her hot forehead against the chilly glass with a sound half-way between a sigh and a sob. She knew now with absolute certainty what she had only half allowed herself to believe before, that she wanted Thackeray with a desire that she had not felt for anyone for a long time. What frightened her was the knowledge that all her considerable charm and guile might smash themselves to pieces against the rock of his reluctance to commit himself. 'I'm not good at relationships,' he had warned, and she believed him.

FOURTEEN

AT THE HEIGHTS, PC ALAN DAVIES started his day's work in the small office the council had allocated him on the ground floor of Priestley House in a more than usually gloomy frame of mind. His mood would have been even more pessimistic had he been able to eavesdrop on the meeting of senior officers taking place at police HQ that very moment.

The place had been buzzing with suppressed tension as Davies had left to come on duty. The assistant chief constable (crime) had already swept in to chair the final planning meeting for the next day's evictions at Bronte House.

'There would have been questions in Parliament by now about Wuthering bloody Heights if MPs had been sitting,' the ACC had said flatly after outlining to the station's senior officers just why the chief constable himself expected the forthcoming operation to be thorough, efficient and effective. 'When they're trying to nail us to the floor with performance indicators, this anarchy is the last thing we want.'

But while the ACC's expectations might be high, Constable Davies's were not. He knew the place too well by now to have any confidence that the massive operation planned for the next day would bring results. And if it failed, he saw little future for community policing in general and himself in particular at Wuthering.

The house-to-house inquiries which had been going on around the flats ever since the attack on Josie Renton had been temporarily suspended. He knew there would be regular car patrols around the flats today, in response to the defiant antics of the joy-riders the night before, but essentially he was back on his own, the sole representative of law and order for half a mile in any direction. Knowing what was coming the next day, he felt increasingly like a very small Dutch boy plugging a very large hole in a very leaky dyke.

Even before he had got out of his car he had been assailed by an angry middle-aged woman, her face creased with tiredness. Just when, she had wanted to know, would 'his lot' get the car hooligans off the streets and give everyone a bit of peace.

'It's not much to ask, is it?' she said shrilly. 'I've not had a decent night's sleep for a week.'

'It's not much to ask, madam,' Davies agreed pleasantly. 'But we need a bit more help from you folk – someone must know who these lads are but no one's telling us owt.' She scowled at that, brushing strands of greying hair from her broad face, her eyes suddenly blank.

'Aye, well, that's for you to find out, isn't it?' she said, backing away. 'There's nowt we can do. Look what happened to Jackie Sullivan.'

She turned away then and stumped off, stiff-legged and stony-faced, leaving Davies to unlock his office, dispirited. There had been times when he thought being a community bobby might work. This last week had not been one of them. Residents he had known for years walked past him with their eyes on the ground, or crossed the road to avoid meeting him entirely, youngsters taunted him obscenely from the walkways, but when he looked up to try to locate them the grey pock-marked façade leered down at him, apparently devoid of life. He had begun to think that even the dogs which raced in snapping, snarling packs around the grassy spaces between the blocks were avoiding him.

From the vantage point of his office, the window open only as far as the wire mesh which protected the glass from attack allowed, he had to squint slightly to get a good view of the outside world. He could just see the length of

159

Priestley House itself, and most of the semi-derelict façade of Bronte.

Outside Bronte a group of teenaged girls sat on the dusty grass gossiping over cans of cola. He recognised Kelly Miller, perched on a stone balustrade, her short skirt hitched up almost to her knickers, her long legs swinging. The way they dressed, he thought, it was no wonder there were attacks. Not that Kelly needed much persuasion to give the lads what they wanted, he thought sourly. The only thing he was unsure about was how much she charged them.

A mother with a push-chair came out of Bronte and headed off towards the shop, a neatly dressed woman who looked as though she might be a nurse or a social worker parked a red Metro opposite the flats and went in. A tall man in dark slacks and, for Bronte, an unusually formal shirt and tie, whom Davies recognised by sight though he could not put a name to him, came out, spoke briefly to Kelly and her friends and drove away in a Sierra which had been parked out of Davies's sight at the side of the building.

The smart black car stirred his interest and Davies jotted down its registration number on the pad on his desk, intending to check it out later. The fact that he did not know the man's name, although he had seen him about Bronte often enough, niggled him. With a sigh, he picked up his helmet, locked the office door carefully, and strolled across the grass, avoiding the tangible evidence of the semi-wild packs of dogs as he went.

'Morning, girls,' he said to the little group who had watched his approach in sulky silence. 'Morning, Kelly.' She was the only one whose name he knew. 'Not patronising the adventure playground this morning?' This provoked an outbreak of snorts and giggles.

'We're too old, aren't we?' a tall, pale girl in an extremely short pink skirt and black top said contemptuously. 'You've got to be under fourteen, haven't you?'

Davies nodded absent-mindedly at that and turned back to Kelly Miller.

160

'That lad who just came out,' he said casually. 'What do they call him?'

'You mean John,' she said.

'Does he live here?' Davies asked.

'Of course he does. He lives next to me, doesn't he? He's lived there for bloody yonks, hasn't he?'

'He's a right raver, is John,' one of the other girls offered helpfully. 'I don't know where we'd be without our John.' This remark set off a small gale of giggles but when he pressed them to define just exactly what they meant by that the girls became evasive and decided as one that they had to catch the bus which was just grinding its way up the hill towards them.

Davies took off his helmet and mopped his brow in exasperation as the scantily clad group ran off across the grass to the bus-stop, still laughing. If John lived in Bronte House, he thought, then how could he afford the high-powered car in which he had just sped down the hill towards the centre of Bradfield? Even more slowly than he had strolled from his office, he strolled back to check it out.

At the adventure playground the long hot day had passed slowly. Sue Raban had found it hard to even bring herself to speak to Mower. Mower had responded with a flippancy which had infuriated her further and the children, made fractious anyway by the increasingly sticky heat as the day wore on, became cheeky and impossible to please.

By four o'clock Mower found himself by the gate watching as anxious mothers began to straggle from the flats to take children home. He recognised Linda Smith coming in and raised a hand in greeting. He had not seen her since the fire at the Sullivans' flat.

'Steve's in the pool,' he said. 'They got so hot and dusty that Sue made them strip off and cool down as soon as the small children had gone home.'

'I wouldn't mind joining him,' Linda said, running a hand through damp straggly hair. 'This isn't the weather to be pregnant.'

'Are you back in Bronte now?' he asked.

'Aye, Steve wanted to get back to his mates so we moved back up there yesterday. They've found Jackie a flat over at Sutton Park for her and little Chrissie. She won't be coming back.'

She put a hand on the small of her back as if to relieve a pain and gazed up at the blank façade of Bronte with an expression of bewilderment.

'We were both desperate to get out, Jackie and me,' she said. 'But for it to be that way! The world's gone bloody mad.'

'Did you get your patrol going last night?' Mower asked. The meeting earlier in the week had, at the women's insistence, drawn up a rota of somewhat less than enthusiastic men who would take turns to walk around the flats between tea-time and nightfall to watch out for the attacker of Josie Renton.

'Bloody men,' she said. 'They won't get off their backsides. They come in from work, have their tea and fall asleep in front o't'telly until it's time to go t'pub, and they won't be shifted. We'll have to do it ourselves if it's going to be done at all. The women's group is meeting tomorrow to talk about it again, tell Sue.'

'I'll pass it on,' Mower promised.

'Usual time, usual place,' Linda said. With a bedraggled son in attendance, she made her way back towards the flats at a slow and weary waddle, like an overweight mother duck towing a gawky adolescent duckling in her wake. Back in the office, Mower wrote Linda's message down for Sue and stuck it on the notice-board. Relations had sunk into such a wasteland that he preferred not to distract her from her conversation on the other side of the playground. In any case his attention had been caught by something else.

Curiously he watched from the window as a small girl of about eight, dressed in brightly patterned shorts and a white tee-shirt, slipped cautiously out from the side of the hut and scuttled towards the playground entrance. Standing on tiptoe, she unlatched the wire mesh gate and slid out, closing it carefully behind her.

Mower hesitated for no more than a second. Grabbing his jacket from its hook behind the door, he followed with a growing sense of excitement. But he was not unobserved. From the other side of the playground Sue Raban saw him go and moved quickly to the gate herself. From there she watched grim-faced as Mower quietly pursued the unaccompanied child, a careful distance behind, across the dusty grass towards Bronte.

'You're pushing your luck, my lad,' Sue said to herself with some satisfaction. 'And perhaps it's about to run out.'

Nicky Tyson was not reported missing by her mother until eight o'clock that evening. In the circumstances, the police were not disposed to take the telephone call as lightly as they would normally have done if a schoolchild had been reported as coming home late. On the Heights these days they took no chances, and by nine Chief Inspector Michael Thackeray and DC Val Ridley were sitting in Mrs Tyson's cramped living-room on the fourth floor of Bronte House trying to extract information without fuelling her incipient hysteria.

'I've been meeting her every day,' Shirley Tyson said for the fourth or fifth time. Thackeray had lost count but did not complain. He recognised and to some extent shared the deep sense of guilt that was driving Mrs Tyson.

'But today I knew I had to work late so I told her to walk home with her friend Samantha and then run like hell up the stairs and stay inside with the door locked till I got in.'

'But she wasn't here when you got back?' DC Ridley asked. 'And what time was that, exactly?'

'About half seven,' Shirley Tyson said. 'I went straight over to Samantha's. She lives in Bentley, top floor, but they'd not seen her, and Sam's mum said she'd taken Sam off from t'playground at lunch-time because she had to go to the dentist or summat.'

'You hadn't made a definite arrangement, then, for the girls to go home together?'

'No, nothing definite. I didn't need to, did I? It's what they did every day until . . .' She hesitated and her face

163

crumpled into an expression of near panic.

'Until the attack on Josie Renton,' Val Ridley suggested gently, and the woman nodded dumbly, screwing the paper tissue she held in her hands into a tight ball. She was a slim woman in her mid-thirties, carefully though not expensively turned out and, Val guessed, still dressed for work, in a short, straight skirt and a formal blouse, her hair shining, her make-up carefully applied, although the mascara was beginning to run now where tears had already been shed. She was not now, Val thought, nor ever likely to be, a mother who neglected her children or took an unexplained absence casually. If Shirley Tyson said that Nicky's behaviour was out-of-character, then that was likely to be the simple truth.

'I thought it'd be all right, two of 'em together,' Shirley said desperately.

'I'm sure she would have been quite safe if they'd been together,' Val Ridley said quietly. 'Now just let me check what she was wearing, and then if you can find me a photograph?' Shirley Tyson stood up with some difficulty, evidently uncertain that her legs would support her, smoothed her skirt with an almost automatic gesture, and went into her bedroom. She returned quickly with a school photograph of Nicky, a rather plain, solemn little girl, blonde-haired and blue-eyed, in a white uniform blouse and red sweater, staring at the camera.

Thackeray, who had been listening impassively to the two women, took the photograph off her and gazed down at it for a moment with a frozen expression before hauling himself mentally back to the neatly if sparsely furnished living-room. He had come to Bronte personally when he had been called back to headquarters instead of delegating the interview to a more junior officer because of a deep conviction, which knotted his stomach up with dread, that the missing child was the murder victim he and Jack Longley had been expecting.

'Is there a Mr Tyson?' he asked at last.

'There is if you look for him in Portsmouth,' she said disparagingly. 'He walked out six years ago and I've heard nowt from him since.'

'Is Nicky the only one?' Val Ridley asked.

'My lad, Carl, he's out with some of the men searching,' Shirley Tyson said. 'He's fourteen.'

'There's no need for them to bother now, Mrs Tyson,' Thackeray said. 'I've got men searching all round the flats, the stairs and walkways, the recreation field – even the adventure playground. We'll do as much as we can tonight before it gets dark – which won't be long now.' He glanced out of the window where a murky dusk was already closing in and the street-lights were beginning to flicker, each with a misty halo in the damp air.

'In the morning, if she hasn't turned up, we'll do a complete search of the flats, house-to-house inquiries. Very often in these cases children turn up unharmed, you know. Perhaps she lost her key, or got anxious because she hadn't done exactly as you'd told her and is too frightened to come home.'

To Thackeray himself the reassuring words sounded hollow and he hoped that for Shirley Tyson they carried at least a little conviction.

'Do you have anyone who can sit with you?' Val Ridley asked.

'Our Carl'll be back directly,' Mrs Tyson said.

'I'll get a policewoman to come up,' Val Ridley promised as they left.

At the head of the stairs Thackeray hesitated for a moment.

'One thing's for sure,' he said to Ridley. 'The big effort in the morning won't be wasted, will it? If we needed any further excuse to search this rabbit warren we've got it now.' He glanced over the balcony at the road and grassy areas below where uniformed officers were moving away from the immediate area of the flats to search further afield.

'Let's go up to the top and see if the elusive John Stansfield is at home, shall we? According to our community bobby he was spotted driving a very smart car this morning with a registration number that doesn't exist, rather than the old banger he claims he owns. He's not been seen since.'

Sergeant Kevin Mower drove up to the Heights at a speed likely to incur the wrath of any traffic policeman he encountered, a fierce anxiety gnawing at him. He pulled to a tyre-squealing halt outside Bronte, switched off his lights and looked around cautiously. In the distance, on the waste ground by the adventure playground, he could see uniformed officers conducting a search, already needing to use powerful torches to cast flickering pools of light into the dense undergrowth.

Twenty minutes earlier, he had put a ready-prepared meal into the microwave and gone for a quick shower, anticipating a relaxing evening at his local. He had emerged again cursing, with a towel wrapped around his waist, to answer the phone which had been barely audible through the rushing water. Thackeray had been brief and curt. A child was missing and he was to meet him at Bronte House at once.

Mower locked his car carefully and walked directly across the grass to the main door of Bronte. There was no sign of a police presence here, although the door was unlatched and swung open to his touch. The lift was not in evidence so he began to walk up the ill-lit stairs.

They were waiting for him on the second-floor landing. For a fatal second Mower did not perceive the threat and made to pass the group of half a dozen burly men before he realised that this was not what they had in mind at all. In the confined space and with his mind already engaged with Thackeray and the self-justification he might have to indulge in to explain how a child had vanished in spite of his regular surveillance of the area, his street sense had temporarily deserted him. It took a swift kick from a heavy boot to make his mistake very clear and by then it was too late. The blow took his legs from under him while a well-aimed fist in the stomach doubled him up, before he could even cry out for help.

There were too many of them crowded onto the narrow

landing to make resistance feasible even if Mower had been able to do more than gasp for air. Far from gentle hands hauled him upright again and held him with his face against the rough concrete of the wall with one arm pinioned behind his back. It was a position in which he had held a few suspects in his time and he knew that if he struggled it could get very painful indeed. Another blow across the back of the neck jerked his forehead against the concrete and he felt blood begin to trickle down his face and a tiny worm of fear begin to burrow into his guts.

'Now tell us where that little lass is, O'Donnell, you effing pervert,' a voice demanded, distorted with raw emotion.

'You're crazy,' Mower said hoarsely. 'I'm a police officer . . .'

Scornful laughter greeted that, emphasised by another couple of heavy blows to the head and back. Taking the occasional thumping, Mower reckoned, was all part of the job, an inevitable consequence of living almost as close to the edge as many of those whose activities he was paid to deter. But to get thumped twice in a week was careless, he thought, and to get thumped in a situation where he was alone and heavily outnumbered and at least one of his assailants was using force with murderous determination was positively unhealthy. The tiny worm of fear grew larger and developed sharp little teeth.

'You were seen following that little lass,' another voice broke in, cold and confident this time. 'Now tell us where she is, pretty boy, or they'll be pushed to stick you together again when they pick up the pieces.'

'You come up here and work with our kids all summer, just to get your dirty hands on them in back alleys. You should be bloody castrated,' another voice added for good measure.

'Where's our Nicky, you bastard,' a much lighter, younger voice with an edge of hysteria to it added.

'You tell 'im, Carl,' someone shouted approvingly.

'I'm a bloody copper, you idiots,' Mower yelled in desperation, trying to look round in spite of the vicious twist to his arm the attempt provoked. But the blood from his head-wound was running into his eyes now and he could see very little in front or behind, though he could feel the heat and smell the sweat of the bodies crushing him against the rough concrete of the stairwell. Where the hell was a policeman when you needed one, he thought, beginning to panic slightly as the increasing vulnerability of his position grew on him.

'Where's Nicky?' the youngest of the voices repeated more shrilly and Mower guessed that the sharp kick on his ankle came from the same source.

'I don't know where Nicky is,' Mower said desperately. 'That's what I'm here to find out.' He never knew whether he would ever have convinced them because the noise of the lift clanking into action above them silenced the general hubbub at that point.

'Teck 'im up onto t'walkway,' one of the voices said urgently and to Mower's horror several hands began to push and shove him in the direction of the door leading out into the open air. Once out there, he thought, it would take no more than a moment to hurl him over the edge onto the concrete almost forty feet below, even if only one or two of the men seriously wanted to fulfil their threat to kill him.

With the upward pressure on his arm released he wasted no time and by a combination of long practice and good fortune dodged momentarily beyond the reach of his captors just as the lift door opened and threw a pool of brighter light onto the landing. Sue Raban stood in the lift doorway surveying the crowd with a look of some satisfaction on her face as a couple of the men, evidently determined that Mower should not escape, pressed close to where he stood, while he backed defensively against the concrete wall, not sure whether to be relieved or even more alarmed at the sight of Sue.

'Having fun, Sergeant?' she asked, her dark eyes full of dislike.

Mower took a handkerchief from his pocket and held it to his forehead, where the jagged gash was oozing blood.

'For Christ's sake, tell them who I am,' he said, his voice hoarse. If she wanted him to beg, then in this situation he would beg, he thought. She let him sweat for a minute and then shrugged slightly.

'If you look in the back pocket of his jeans you'll probably find his warrant card,' she said contemptuously at last and watched as one of the men took hold of an unresisting Mower and unceremoniously emptied his pockets. He held up the warrant card disbelievingly.

'So what the 'ell have you bin doing at the effing playground?' the vigilante's apparent leader came back, his voice still full of suspicion. 'You've been there weeks.'

'Watching after your kids,' Mower said bitterly, addressing the burly man who had spoken but also acutely conscious of a slimmer, taller figure, wearing a dark shirt with some sort of logo on the breast pocket, on the edge of the group with his face half hidden by a scarf. He was sure that he was the author of the most vicious blows, the ones which had been intended to hurt.

'Well you've not been much cop at it,' the burly man said, spitting derisively in Mower's direction. 'We'd have done better oursen if we'd got ourselves bloody sorted.' I'll recognise you again, you bastard, Mower thought angrily. And I'll have you.

'You'd all have done better, if you'd listened to your wives,' Sue said sweetly.

'So what if he is a copper,' another voice broke in. 'Who says coppers can't be perverts an' all? They get up to every other bloody thing.'

'He were seen following Nicky,' said Carl Tyson, a tall, skinny youth in jeans and white tee-shirt, his fists still clenched and his face blotchy and twitching with suppressed hysteria. 'So what's the difference if he's an effing police sergeant?' There was a murmur of approval at that, but it was less convinced now.

'His boss is upstairs, I've just seen him on the top floor,' Sue said placatingly. 'You come with us, Carl, and we'll take Sergeant Mower to him.' She flashed a look of sheer malice at Mower, who also took on board that the tall

169

member of the group was slipping away down the stairs.

'Seriously,' Sue said, addressing herself to the now uncertain vigilantes. 'Sergeant Mower may be a lying bastard but I don't think he's been laying fingers on little girls. Have you, Kevin?'

Mower shook his head wearily, leaned back against the wall and closed his eyes for a moment. That the last extremely unpleasant five minutes were down to Sue Raban he had no doubt. And her revenge would be all the sweeter for knowing that he would never accuse her of it, because to do so would be to admit that she had good cause. And that was one aspect of his brief stay on the Heights that he did not want Michael Thackeray to uncover.

Silently the rest of the men drifted away, muttering their discontent, leaving Sue propping open the lift doors and Carl Tyson, his face still flushed with a mixture of excitement and fear, alone with Mower. Carl hopped impatiently from one foot to the other, waiting for one or other of the adults to make a move.

Mower wiped most of the blood off his face and gave Sue a thin-lipped smile of defeat before turning to Carl. The boy's state of high emotion he could forgive, but he knew there had been a sadist in the group of angry men whom he was very anxious to meet again on more equal terms.

'Let's see if we can find out who's really got your Nicky, shall we?' he said to the boy. 'It's true I followed her back to the flats. Unfortunately, the door slammed shut behind her and I lost sight of her before I could get it open again. I'd no reason to think she wasn't safe enough then, once she was inside.'

'You should have known better,' Laura Ackroyd said, making all three of them jump. She had come up the stairs quietly behind them, dispatched back to the flats by an almost apoplectic Ted Grant who had been tipped off about a child's disappearance at Wuthering by a source he regarded as highly reliable on police matters.

'Eavesdropping, Ms Ackroyd?' Mower said sharply,

170

disconcerted that she should have heard his last remarks.

'It's a public place, Sergeant Mower,' Laura retorted. 'And you seem to be hogging the lift.'

'The vultures are gathering already, are they?' Sue Raban said, not moving from her position which secured the lift doors open and unavailable to anyone else. Laura glanced at her without much warmth.

'I should think if a child is missing the sooner the fact is broadcast to anyone who might have seen her the better,' she said. 'Or have you found her?' She addressed the last question to Mower, noticing his dishevelled appearance and the still oozing cut on his head for the first time as he shook his head.

'You don't seem to be very popular on Wuthering,' Laura said. 'Who's been having a go at you this time?' Mower glanced at Sue and the boy Carl and grinned faintly, some of his self-confidence seeping back.

'I was resisting arrest,' he said with more truth than Laura could guess.

'And I wasn't here to whisk you away to safety this time,' Laura said in mock sorrow. 'I am sorry.' Sue Raban listened to this exchange with growing irritation.

'Are we interested in finding Nicky Tyson or are we just passing the time of day here?' she asked and Carl nodded his agreement.

'We're wasting time,' he said, his voice cracking, not entirely broken yet.

'And you are . . .?' Laura asked. Carl told her.

'Do you think your mum would talk to the Gazette?' Laura asked him, because that was the reason Ted had dispatched her so urgently to the Heights. In his book the only real justification for having female staff at all was for the occasions when a feminine shoulder might prove more enticing for the victim of a tragedy to weep on than a masculine one.

This time, though, Laura did not feel she was intruding when Carl took her home with him, leaving Mower and Sue Raban to go one floor higher in the lift to track down Michael Thackeray. Laura did not particularly want to see

171

Thackeray at that moment. However justified she might feel in her own mind about the call she was about to make, she wondered if Thackeray's level blue gaze might not hold a hint of disapproval. She knew he did not wholly warm to her job, and he would warm even less to the news that 'Case Re-opened' had called her that afternoon and asked her to interview ex-Chief Inspector Harry Huddleston about the Tracy Miller murder as a matter of urgency.

She did not want to analyse her reluctance to see Thackeray again so soon. She had lain awake half the night furious that her every encounter with him seemed to put her at a disadvantage, and furious with herself for caring. But she did care, of that she had been just as convinced when the grey dawn crept into her bedroom, making her screw up her gritty eyes, as when he had left her the previous night.

Here at Bronte and on the fourth floor walkway safely out of Thackeray's sight, Shirley Tyson welcomed her into the flat enthusiastically enough when Carl explained who she was.

'Can you put her picture on t'front page of the Gazette?' she asked.

'Certainly, if she's not turned up by tomorrow morning,' Laura said.

'I gave one snap to the police, her school photo, but I've got another here somewhere,' Mrs Tyson said, rummaging in a drawer in the sideboard. 'It's of her and her friend Samantha, but it'll do, won't it? This one's our Nicky. It were only taken last Whitsun. We all went to Bridlington for the day.'

Laura looked at the two little girls in shorts and anoraks, grinning cheerfully against a background of windswept beach and choppy grey sea. It seemed inconceivable that one of them might not still be alive. She shuddered, as if a cold draught had cut through the stuffy room.

'I'll show you her room, if you like,' Mrs Tyson said helpfully. 'It might give you some ideas for your article.' She led Laura out of the living-room and across the

172

hallway to a door with a small name-plate inscribed 'Nicola's Room' and decorated with pink and blue flowers. Laura gritted her teeth as Mrs Tyson opened the door and ushered her into a small bedroom decorated entirely in pink and pale blue, the curtains held back by bows, the duvet and pillows in a matching print, toys and books and drawing and painting equipment neatly stored on open shelves. Carl crowded in behind them and Laura heard him give a muffled sound, half groan, half sob, before he turned away down the hallway, where a door slammed behind him and loud and insistent pop music was turned on.

'He thinks the world of our Nicky,' Mrs Tyson said, a tremor catching at her voice now. 'I don't know what we'll do if owt's happened to her.'

Laura stood by the child's bed, fingering the shiny nylon of the quilt cover, feeling helpless to offer any comfort.

'She enjoys painting,' she muttered, glancing at the shelves.

'Yes, she's right good at art, her teacher says,' Mrs Tyson said. She followed Laura's eyes and looked puzzled. She crossed the room and picked up a drawing book and a pencil box.

'I thought she took these to the playground this morning,' she said.

Laura understood the significance of the remark at once.

'Are you sure?' she said.

Mrs Tyson glanced through the book.

'Look,' she said, pointing to the last page that had been used — a pencil drawing of children splashing in a pool, carefully coloured in vivid primary colours. 'She said they were going to do some drawing with Sue today. That wasn't there last night.'

'You mean she's been home?'

'She must have. She must have been in and put this away. She's right tidy, is Nicky, not like Carl. You can't get into his room for the mess. I tell him and tell him about it but he takes not a blind bit of notice.'

'You'd better tell the police straight away,' Laura said. 'It might be important.' The flat did not have a phone so Laura offered to go and look for whichever of the police officers already on the estate was nearest. In the event it was Sergeant Mower she found outside the main door, just about to get into his car. She told him what Mrs Tyson had found and Mower looked at her strangely.

'Thank Christ for that,' he said, to her surprise.

'Does it make a difference?' Laura asked.

'Only to me,' Mower said. 'It means that she did get home safely after I lost sight of her going up the stairs.'

Laura hesitated for a moment, not liking the implication of Mower's comment.

'Did you set that child up?' Laura asked, understanding now what had been worrying him. 'Did you use her as a decoy?'

Mower glanced away, refusing to meet her eyes.

'Not exactly,' he said. 'She set off from the playground on her own.'

'But you could have stopped her? You could have taken her home and made sure she got there safely?' Laura guessed.

'I suppose,' he said.

'You really are a bastard, Kevin, aren't you?' Laura said.

'Comes with the job,' he said. 'You won't tell the sainted Michael Thackeray, will you . . .?' His voice faded away uncertainly, his bruised face haggard in the harsh street-lights. Laura ran a hand tiredly through her hair.

'I won't tell the chief inspector anything,' she said. Chance would be a fine thing, she thought. 'Whatever you did, you evidently got away with, though God help you if you hadn't. It seems to be my role in life at the moment to find you up to your neck in trouble. But tell whoever needs to know what Shirley Tyson's found, will you? I'm going home to bed.'

FIFTEEN

THE CONVOY OF POLICE VEHICLES followed two bailiff's vans up the steep hill to Wuthering just after dawn. It was another muggy, heavy morning with dark clouds piled high on the western horizon and a hint of rain in the air. Chief Inspector Thackeray sat silently at the wheel of an unmarked police car parked unobtrusively where he could obtain a good view of Bronte House.

Kevin Mower was slumped silently in the passenger seat, a plaster covering the cut on his forehead, and a polo-necked sweater concealing most of his other bruises. He looked haggard, in spite of the fact that for the first time in days he had shaved. He had collected Thackeray from his flat well before six as instructed the previous evening by an unsympathetic superior. Thackeray had sent him to the hospital casualty department for a check-up with the comment that at his age he ought to know better than to get himself mugged on a dark stairway.

The silence in the car was strained. It was Thackeray's idea to observe the uniformed operation planned for the Heights before going in to headquarters to await developments and Mower, aching and short of sleep, dared not demur. In as far as his brain was working at all, he was trying to deduce just what effect the previous night's debacle would have on his career. Today, he thought sourly, he needed Brownie points as he had never needed them before.

Unusually it had been a peaceful night on the Heights. The joy-riders had not emerged, no doubt deterred by the heavy police presence earlier in the evening. They had dashed the expectations of the excited knots of teenagers who had waited on the street corners until well after midnight, ignoring the imprecations of Old Testament ferocity from angry residents above.

The young people had drifted home gradually, leaving a litter of lager cans to roll tinnily in the gutters as the wind rose, driving the roaming dogs to distraction. After they had gone, a herbal scent wafted in stairwells and lifts and along the walkways, an overlay to the more usual sour smell of dirt and damp decay.

Within the grey concrete walls of Bronte itself there had been the usual thud of heavy bass music, giggling and scuffling, and the occasional muffled squeal which could have been provoked by fear or laughter. Few of the legitimate residents would ever venture beyond their front doors after dark. By dawn, though, the flats lay silent, like some huge exhausted animal, hardly breathing in the humid air.

Thackeray glanced at his watch as he caught a glimpse of the first police vehicle in his mirror.

'They're here,' he said. 'On time.'

Mower pulled himself upright in his seat, wincing as his bruised muscles protested. Thackeray gave him an unfriendly look.

'Are you quite sure you can't identify any of your so-called vigilantes, now you've slept on it?' he asked, returning to his previous night's somewhat bad-tempered interrogation of his sergeant. Mower shrugged and decided the experiment was not worth the candle as pain shot from his neck across his shoulders.

'It was too dark and they had their faces well hidden, guv,' he said. 'I'll talk to Carl Tyson again if you like, but in the circumstances I didn't think it was a good idea to lean on him too hard.'

'It's not going to be a good idea to lean on Carl at all until we find his sister,' Thackeray said. 'The Gazette would take us apart.'

The police convoy had pulled up quietly in a side-street

176

well away from the flats. Only the first two police vans moved closer, following two car-loads of civilian bailiffs. They contained uniformed officers who would support the bailiffs and organise the transport of the squatters down to the central police station for questioning. Half a dozen more police vans, with heavy mesh guards across their windows, waited out of sight. Only if there was violent resistance would the heavy mob move in with shields and batons to impose order.

The devoutness with which the police wished the riot squad to remain firmly behind their reinforced vehicle doors diminished sharply down the ranks. The chief constable might prefer a peaceful outcome to the operation, but the young men in their heavy protective gear looked forward to making their early morning overtime worthwhile by seeing some action. In the meantime, they sat where they were, high and ribald on adrenalin and hot sweet tea, sweating already in their thick blue overalls and itching for the order to move.

At six o'clock precisely a car drew up alongside the vehicles parked directly outside the flats and a man in a grey suit got out and went to speak to the uniformed inspector who was waiting with the bailiffs at the door of Bronte.

'Good morning,' he said cheerfully, shaking hands with the senior bailiff and nodding to the inspector. 'Ken Lawson, Bradfield Housing Services. I've got all the paperwork here, so we can go whenever you're ready.' He took a bunch of keys from his pocket and opened the main door and went in, followed closely by the bailiffs.

'We'll be here if you need us,' the inspector said, and deployed his men close to the door and at the back of the block and close to the garages, in case any residents decided to make an unorthodox exit via the not very securely boarded-up windows at the rear. The inspector called headquarters on his personal radio.

'Stand by,' he said. 'They're just going in.'

'Right,' Thackeray said, starting his car and pulling away from the kerb. 'We'd better make sure the reception committee is ready down at the nick.'

'Why the hell didn't we know about it?' Ted Grant asked his hastily convened news conference for the fourth time at eight o'clock that morning. 'We should have had pictures at the very least.' He scowled at his picture editor, Larry Savage, who sat opposite him wreathed in smoke, lighting one cigarette from the butt of another with hands that were not quite steady, although whether that was a result of the previous night's excesses or the early hour Laura could only guess.

Grant had phoned all his senior staff at seven o'clock that morning when news of the evictions on the Heights had reached him second-hand from the young reporter on the early shift. Laura bent her head over the elaborate doodle on the notebook in front of her. As features editor, a failure on the news front was not strictly her responsibility, but in one of these moods, Grant would not be deterred by that, hitting out in all directions like some small child in a tantrum.

And in this particular matter she was far more culpable than Grant could possibly know. It was not until the editor's early morning reveille had roused her from an uneasy sleep that she recalled she already knew not only that the evictions were planned but that they were planned for this morning. Michael Thackeray had actually told her so, and it had completely slipped her mind.

'I'll get onto the press office at county,' the news editor, Steve Hardcastle, said placatingly, surprised himself that Grant's own network of contacts had not come up with the merest whisper of the dawn raid which the police had concluded by seven a.m. 'I'd guess it was a last minute thing, with this kid missing. They must be planning to take that place apart now they've got the squatters out.'

'Right, so we make that connection in the intro, then run two parallel stories, one about the eviction, one on the hunt for little Nicky. Make the kid the splash. Laura's got us a nice pic. I want that run big on the front page. Right? Who's on today?' Laura smiled faintly, unaccustomed to

178

even this faint praise, and aware that she could find herself back in the firing line as abruptly as anyone else.

Steve ran through his summer-holiday-depleted list of reporters and Laura knew, her heart sinking, that she was going to get dragged away from the office to supplement the news staff again even before Ted Grant's unfriendly blue gaze swivelled her way.

'You get back up to the Heights, Laura,' he said. 'See if you can get in to Mrs Tyson again. If the kid went home before she went missing – check that out with the police, Steve, we've had no confirmation yet – any road, if she went home, someone may have seen her going out again. Your grandmother's got plenty of contacts, hasn't she? See what she's heard on the grapevine. You know what the old biddies in these places are like – all gossip over cups of tea. Plug into it, will you.'

'My grandmother's staying with me at the moment,' Laura said carefully, knowing just how vitriolic Joyce's response to being called an old biddy would be. Laura had said nothing in the office the previous day about the assault and somehow the news seemed to have slipped through the net which the Gazette normally cast around the emergency services each morning. She wondered if she had Thackeray to thank for that. And not for the first time she wondered about her own commitment to the job, which seemed to evaporate whenever a story came too close to home. The thought of anyone writing about Joyce's ordeal filled her with revulsion.

'That'll clip your wings a bit, won't it, having granny living in?' asked the chief sub, Frank Powers, with a smile that bordered on a leer. Laura had repulsed Frank's advances years ago and had never been forgiven. She refused to rise this morning and contented herself with a small, private smile. She knew how little Joyce's presence would have inhibited her two nights ago if the moment she had regretted ever since could be re-lived.

The day's assignments allocated and Ted to some extent mollified now that firm plans to catch up on the morning's events had been made, Laura walked slowly back across the office to her desk. It looked like being a hectic day. She picked up her phone and called Vicky Mendelson.

'I don't think I'm going to be able to find time to take the boys swimming this afternoon,' she said. 'Tell them I'm sorry and I'll make it up to them next time I see them, will you. All hell's broken loose here. There's a child missing on the Heights, and the police have evicted all the squatters ... you name it. Perhaps tomorrow? It's supposed to be my day off.'

Vicky acquiesced in that. Laura could almost feel her flinch at the news of a missing child and could imagine her instinctively anxious glance at her own boys whom she could hear chattering, probably around the breakfast table, in the background. But Vicky did not cut the call short.

'I thought you'd ring me yesterday. I was dying to know what happened to your dinner date,' she said.

'Ah,' Laura said softly. 'That's a long and bruising story, and this is not the moment.'

'Not a culinary triumph, then?' Vicky persisted. 'Or any other sort?'

'No sort of triumph,' Laura said, as Vicky's cheerful curiosity roused emotions she had spent more than twenty-four hours carefully burying. 'I can't talk now, Vic,' she said. 'I'll ring you this evening, I promise.'

'I thought you had real prospects there,' Vicky said. 'I'm sorry.'

'Blast,' Laura said loudly as she hung up, attracting a surprised look from Steve Hardcastle who was passing her desk, stripped down to shirt-sleeves and braces ready for the day's action.

'Cheer up, it may never happen,' he said. 'Will you call me as soon as you get anything up at Wuthering?'

'No, I'll send the news by carrier pigeon,' she said unhelpfully. 'Will that suit?'

'Nope, they've all OD-ed on dope up there,' Steve said. 'Even the bloody sparrows are as high as kites.'

Feeling ratty and dishevelled and short of sleep, Laura drove up to the Heights and parked outside her grandmother's bungalow. She glanced in that direction, taking in the boarded-up entrance with a shudder. She had already asked the council to repair the shattered door, but nothing seemed to have happened yet. Until it did, there was no way Joyce could fulfil her now vigorously repeated intention to return home as soon as it could be arranged. Deep down, Laura hoped that the maintenance men would not hurry. The thought of Joyce returning to the Heights filled her with anxiety.

A fine rain was falling and she watched the scene around the flats with her windscreen wipers smearing a film of dust and grease across the glass. She pressed the washer impatiently but nothing happened and the murk merely thickened. There were still two police vans parked outside Bronte and a small crowd of residents standing near the entrance watching the latest police operations in sullen silence.

Up on the walkways uniformed police and civilians seemed to be busy, but she could see no one she knew as she walked slowly over the damp, fouled grass towards Bronte. There was a sense of unease in the air. She knew that she was being watched, both by the knots of bystanders and by officialdom on the walkways above. Closer to the entrance she saw that one of the officers evidently standing guard at the door was the community policeman, Alan Davies.

'I was hoping to see Mrs Tyson,' Laura said. 'There's no news about Nicky, I suppose?'

Davies shook his head grimly. 'Mrs Tyson's not here,' he said. 'She's down at headquarters with CID. They're having a press conference or summat later on and they wanted her there, poor cow.'

'They've not found the child?'

'They've not,' Davies confirmed flatly. 'They've taken the squatted flats apart and they're organising a search of the rest of the block later this morning. Every inch of the place. Much good it's done them so far. As far as I know, they've not found as much as a stray joint of cannabis, much less any sign of the kiddie. How's your gran, by the way? That were a nasty business, an' all.'

181

'She's recovering,' Laura said bleakly, not convinced that it was true. She had left Joyce early that morning propped up in bed, an untouched and possibly unnoticed cup of tea beside her, and no sign that a couple of nights' sleep had erased the faintly puzzled, hurt look from her eyes.

'She's desperate to get back home. You know Joyce,' she added. 'But I want her to stay with me for a bit.'

'That makes sense,' Davies agreed sombrely. 'Can you not get her away from here?'

'My grandmother does as she pleases. She always has and I expect she always will,' Laura said, not sure whether that should be a source of pride or, in present circumstances particularly, regret.

'Keep her out o't'way. This estate's no place to be until they clear this little lot up,' Davies said. 'If then,' he added grimly.

'You think there's going to be more trouble?'

'I know there is. They pay me to know these things. Not that they take a blind bit o'notice when I warn them, but there you go. The kids up here have got nowt to lose, have they? A bit of aggro just breaks the monotony.'

He turned away from Laura towards a young couple, unisex clones in jeans and tee-shirts, pale-faced, hollow-eyed and unkempt. The only indication that one of them might be female was the slight curve of a breast under a tee-shirt where she clutched a baby wrapped in a grubby shawl.

'Now then, what do you want? They've finished with you down at headquarters, have they?' Davies asked, not unkindly.

'All our gear's in there,' the young man said sulkily, nodding upwards at the flats. 'They've no right to keep that.'

'Very true, lad,' Davies said. 'My instructions are to let you in one at a time to collect your belongings, which will be on the walkway in front of the flat where they were found. So look sharp.' He stood aside from the door and let the squatter in.

'There's no harm in them two,' Davies said a little later,

as they watched the young couple drift off across the grass together carrying the bin-liners which apparently contained all their worldly goods. 'And that's more than you can say for most of them they brought out of there this morning. But I don't blame the kids. They've had nowt and they'll never have owt, the way things are. It's the ones living off them I'd like to nail, supplying them with drugs, pimping and the rest.'

He was interrupted again by a small, grey-haired man who burst out of the door behind him and grabbed his arm urgently.

'What are you doing with our Kelly?' Paul Miller demanded angrily. 'Jerry Hurst says your lot took her off with the squatters. What the 'ell did you do that for?'

'I've no idea, Mr Miller,' Davies said. 'As far as I know no one was taken to headquarters who wasn't found in the illegally occupied flats.' A look of doubt flickered across Miller's face at that and Laura wondered if he very often knew where his nubile daughter spent her time.

'You'd no right to take her at all without telling me,' Miller said. 'She's only fourteen.'

'I'll check for you,' Davies said, using his personal radio. 'I shouldn't worry, though. As far as I can see they're letting them all out again now. Like as not she'll be home by dinner-time.'

SIXTEEN

'ZILCH!' DETECTIVE INSPECTOR RAY WILKINS of the drug squad said angrily. 'Absolute zilch. Someone had been through that place with a bloody vacuum cleaner. We didn't find so much as a speck of ash from a spliff. Yet I know for a fact that one of the lads we brought in has been dealing in heroin. And practically every kid on Wuthering is a user of something. So what went wrong, sir? Who told them we were coming?'

Wilkins was leaning against the wall in Chief Inspector Michael Thackeray's office, hands thrust deep into the pockets of his jeans, a look of glowering discontent on his face. CID was reviewing the less than satisfactory results of the morning's operation on the Heights and after this post-mortem, Thackeray knew he faced another with Jack Longley, a prospect he did not look forward to.

'Some of those kids are laughing at us in the interview rooms down there,' Wilkins went on. 'They know bloody well what we're after and that the operation's been a waste of time.'

'For you, maybe,' Thackeray said sharply, with a glint in his eye that told Wilkins that he had gone too far. 'As far as we're concerned, the search isn't over yet. Our top priority is to find the missing child. If we come across anything else, we'll let you know.'

'Right, sir,' Wilkins said grudgingly. 'I'll get back to county then.' He hauled himself upright and nodded to Thackeray without warmth.

'See you, Kevin,' he said as he went out to Sergeant Mower, who was hunched at his desk, trying to make

184

invisible the plaster over the cut on his forehead and the prominent bruise on his left cheek-bone. 'Duck next time, eh?'

'Sir,' Mower muttered resentfully. There was no love lost there, Thackeray observed with a flicker of amusement. He had never fathomed Mower's unproductive spell with the drug squad but suspected that there might have been a woman at the bottom of it. Which only served to remind him that there was justice in Wilkins's complaint about the handling of the evictions. There would inevitably be an inquest at a higher level than his own, and one in which he himself could conceivably be asked some embarrassing questions about a woman. He had not forgotten mentioning the forthcoming operation in an unguarded moment to Laura Ackroyd and felt bound to ask her – sooner rather than later, too – whether she had let it go any further. That was not a prospect that pleased, either.

'Right then,' he said to Mower with an asperity the sergeant did not understand. 'Who knew what was going down?' Mower too had mixed feelings about answering that question but a quick calculation of his best interest came down on the side of frankness, not least because he was sure that under the intense scrutiny that the Heights would attract if Nicky Tyson's disappearance turned into a murder inquiry, his over-enthusiastic involvement with Sue Raban would inevitably surface like some half-submerged log from stagnant water. It was a moment, he reckoned, to get his retaliation in first.

'Who knew? Officials at the town hall,' Mower said consideringly. 'Jerry Hurst probably. And Sue Raban.'

'Sue Raban?' Thackeray's tone was quiet enough, but demanded an answer.

'The woman at the adventure playground, guv. I may have let it slip to her.'

'Pillow talk, Sergeant?'

Mower avoided Thackeray's eyes and gave a barely perceptible shrug.

Thackeray sat silently for a moment, trying to weigh up

the younger man and, as usual, feeling dissatisfied with his measurement of him. There was a sharp intelligence there, he knew, and a driving ambition, to some extent disguised by the good looks which women evidently found so attractive.

He was, in Thackeray's brief experience of working with him, enthusiastic and efficient. Yet he had never completely trusted him, and what trust there was looked like evaporating as the full truth about what had been going on at the Heights over the last few days began to emerge. He was less than convinced that the beating Mower had evidently taken last night was as fortuitous a mugging by unknown assailants as the sergeant had made out when he had reported for duty, still mopping at the blood from the cut on his forehead.

'She found out you were a police officer, did she, or did you let that slip as well?' Thackeray asked, his expression cold enough now to let Mower see quite clearly that he was not playing games.

'It wasn't deliberate, guv,' Mower said resentfully. 'She found my warrant card.'

Thackeray forebore to ask how. He thought he had a good idea.

'Just careless, then. And you compounded that by telling her when the evictions would be?' he said.

'I just wanted to convince her to keep quiet for another day – my last day up there. I thought something might turn up, you know, the way you always do . . .' Mower could see the chasm opening at his feet even before Thackeray spoke again.

'We'd better talk to Miss – or is it Ms with this one? – Sue Raban,' he said. 'And Jerry Hurst. Get them down here, will you? And I'll concentrate on the town hall and see if there was any leak there. There's going to be a few people wanting answers on this one, from Jack Longley right on up.'

'There's the other thing,' Mower said slowly, knowing he had to pre-empt Sue. Thackeray looked at him coldly, waiting.

186

'I told you I followed Nicky when I saw her run off home,' Mower said. He had given Thackeray a sketchy outline the previous evening of what had happened when Nicky Tyson left the playground, but he still felt vulnerable. 'She was out of the playground gate before I could stop her, and when I got to the flats the door had swung shut and I lost her. Obviously she got home safely. We know that now. But I still feel bad about it. It might have made a difference if I'd caught up with her.'

'I doubt it,' Thackeray said. 'This lad's never been seen. He's been keeping out of sight very effectively. I doubt he'd be daft enough to fall into your arms if he saw you following Nicky. And he would have seen you close behind, wouldn't he? If he saw her, he'd have seen you too, trying to catch up with her?'

Mower nodded, relieved at Thackeray's response, but he knew he was not in the clear yet, and he shifted uncomfortably in his chair. Thackeray gazed at him in silence for a moment. There were, he thought, sometimes questions it was better not to ask unless you were prepared to follow them through to the bitter end. And this was not the time to smash the thin ice he suspected Mower had been skating on.

'Get someone to bring Hurst in,' Thackeray said dismissively. 'You can leave your dark lady for the moment. We'll talk to her later. And see what's come of the statements they've taken so far from the squatters. I think that's our best hope of a lead. I'm going to see the super. I've no doubt he's got the chief constable breathing down his neck.'

'Right, guv,' Mower said, a glimmer of his normal confidence returning. 'Thanks,' he added as the door swung shut behind his boss, a sentiment Thackeray neither wanted nor was intended to hear.

Downstairs, Kelly Miller gave Sergeant Mower a hard time and enjoyed every minute of it. She leaned back in her chair, her legs crossed provocatively, her short skirt hitched high, and her loose tee-shirt pulled low off one

187

shoulder, with what could only be described as a superior smile on her knowing young face.

'Coke?' she said. 'Yeah, we had lots of coke. But that's not illegal, is it?'

'Cocaine? Where did that come from?' Mower snapped. The beating he had taken the previous night had made him more tired and edgy than he had realised, he thought. Val Ridley, who was with him in the interview room, merely smiled faintly, guessing what was coming.

'Coca-cola, stupid!' Kelly said, giggling helplessly. 'Lots of coca-cola.'

'Christ,' Mower said in exasperation, annoyed with himself for letting the girl get under his skin. He had spotted Kelly's name on the list of arrested squatters while Thackeray was still closeted with Superintendent Longley and had taken over her interview from the uniformed officers on the off-chance of discovering something useful from a long-time resident of the flats.

'How well do you know John Stansfield, Kelly?' Val Ridley broke in. Just for a moment a flicker of something which could have been alarm flashed across Kelly's pert features but it disappeared as her attention was distracted by Chief Inspector Thackeray who came quietly into the interview room behind Mower and stood against the wall watching.

'He's dishy, is John,' the girl said quickly. 'King John, they call him. But I just see him around, don't I? He says hello.'

'Why King John?'

'Oh, I dunno, that's just what the lads call him,' she said. 'He wears those shirts with a little crown on.'

'He's not interested in you?' Val Ridley pressed and was rewarded with a scowl. 'Or any of the other girls in the flats?'

'He's got a girlfriend,' Kelly said.

'Do you know her?' Mower asked quickly, but the girl's face closed up suddenly and she shook her head.

'How would I?' she said. Mower was sure she was lying but when he glanced at Thackeray, as if to seek permission

188

to press her, the chief inspector shook his head very slightly.

'He's not short of a bob or two, your Mr Stansfield, is he, Kelly?' Thackeray said as Mower hesitated. 'Do you know where he works, by any chance?'

'How should I know,' the girl said sulkily. 'He goes off somewhere. He's lucky to have a friggin' job, isn't he? No one else has.'

Two floors below, Laura Ackroyd waited at the main reception desk of police headquarters with Kelly's father, Paul. Miller had begged a lift into town to try to discover what had happened to Kelly in the police sweep that morning and more out of curiosity than any genuine feeling of sympathy for a father who had not even begun to worry about his absent daughter until he noticed she was missing at breakfast time, Laura had agreed to go with him to tackle the impregnable wall of police officialdom.

They had got little change and less sympathy from the uniformed inspector who eventually emerged to speak to them. There were still at least a dozen people from the flats to be interviewed, he said. No one had been brought to police HQ who had not been in one of the illegally occupied flats. Therefore no one, in his book, was anything other than a squatter. And his instructions were to interview them all before releasing them.

'We're talking about a child of fourteen,' Laura said, summoning up some asperity when Miller's pleas seemed to have been exhausted. A momentary uncertainty flickered in the inspector's eyes at that. 'A lot of them are under-age,' he said eventually. 'At least we think they are. They don't all let on.'

'Then shouldn't they have an adult with them when they make a statement?' Laura asked icily.

'Not just for a witness statement,' he said. 'We're not accusing them of anything. We didn't find any drugs.'

'Didn't you?' Laura said, her interest quickening. 'Can I quote you on that?'

'Quote me?'

'I'm from the Gazette,' Laura said sweetly.

189

'Now look,' the inspector came back quickly, faint alarm in his eyes, 'I'm not authorised to say anything to the Press. You know that. . .'

'But surely you're authorised to let Mr Miller see his daughter, if she's here,' Laura said, not afraid to press her advantage.

'I'll see what I can do,' the inspector said, his jaw clenched tightly, and within a couple of minutes he had returned with Kelly, who gave her father a dismissive wave and Laura a grateful smile.

'It's awful in there,' she said. 'Gaz has been sick all over t'floor. He had ten pints last night. You remember Gaz? You met him on the stairs that day when he were right poorly. It were just lager this time, 'cause there weren't owt else. But they should've let him sleep it off. I told them when they came bashing t'door down, it wouldn't do him no good to be moved.'

'What door? Who's Gaz?' Miller asked angrily.

'Me friend,' Kelly said airily. 'Here,' she said, putting an arm round Laura's waist. 'Do you want to know all about it for your television programme? They were right awful to us in the van, you know. Calling us layabouts and scroungers and that. Take me to Madison's for some chips and a shake and I'll tell you all about it.' Laura looked at the girl's pale, old-young face and her knowing blue eyes and sighed. Kelly would be selling her life-story to the Globe before she was sixteen at this rate, she thought.

It was the patient and time-consuming work of collating all the statements from the Heights that gave Thackeray his next break. Val Ridley spotted it, ran a print-out off the computer and took it to Mower, who glanced at it and felt his pulse quicken.

'The crafty bastard,' he said. 'Come on.' They went to Thackeray's office and waved the statement at him.

'*I didn't think it was wrong to stay there. We paid rent to Jerry Hurst, ten quid a week, and he said that made it official like, the council didn't mind,*' Mower read out triumphantly.

'I had a feeling about Hurst,' DC Ridley said. 'He didn't

smell right – literally or any other way.'

'Did you send someone to pick him up?' Thackeray asked and Mower nodded.

'He's downstairs in an interview room, waiting to help us with our inquiries.'

'Right, well, let him stew there for a bit while I talk to the housing department.'

That was another break. Ken Lawson, the housing manager who had supervised the evictions, was more than willing to discuss his employee Hurst when Thackeray suggested that he had been engaged in a little free enterprise with the council's property. The words almost tumbled out, leaving Thackeray to wonder why, if the suspicion had been lurking in Lawson's mind for years, and he said it had, he had done nothing to catch Hurst out in his dealings.

'That block's been nothing but trouble for years,' Lawson said. 'And I've always suspected Hurst was part of the problem. But it's difficult to prove unless you get a specific complaint, and of course the squatters are the last people who'd complain about what he was doing. They're getting dirt cheap accommodation and a blind eye turned to whatever else they get up to, aren't they?'

'We've still got some of the squatters here,' Thackeray said. 'We'll get details of just what they have been paying Hurst.'

'Great,' Lawson said enthusiastically. 'I'll be able to sack him and that'll save us paying him redundancy when the flats come down.'

'There's one other thing that's been puzzling us,' Thackeray said. 'There's a flat on the top floor that used to be occupied by a Bill Stansfield, an elderly man who apparently died about five years ago. The place is now occupied by someone who claims to be his son, John, but there seems to be some doubt about that.'

Lawson spent a moment or two evidently tapping at his computer keyboard. 'It's still in the name of William Spenser Stansfield,' he said. 'D'you think Hurst has put a mate of his in there?'

191

'Well, it's certainly worth asking him,' Thackeray said. 'Though I suppose if the rent has been paid it's not a significant fraud.' He paused for a moment.

'Do you have a description of this Stansfield?' Lawson asked at length.

Thackeray described the young man with the Alsatian dog he had met briefly on the top walkway at Bronte House. It was a sketchy enough description but Lawson seemed excited by it.

'I bumped into someone I knew this morning up on the top floor, a lad by the name of Sissons, John Sissons. Fits your description. Looked a bit shifty when he saw me. Said he'd spent the night with a lady friend up there and scuttled off with his sports bag as fast as he decently could when I told him what was going on.'

'And where does John Sissons live, do you know?' Thackeray asked.

'No, I don't,' Lawson said. 'But I can easily find out. You see he works here in the housing department. He's one of my employees.' He paused again and again the chatter of a computer terminal was clearly audible. 'Though he's on leave at the moment,' he came back eventually. 'On leave for the whole of this week.'

'And according to our community bobby he's riding around in a very flash car with a very dodgy number plate,' Kevin Mower, who had been listening to the conversation on a second extension, said quietly. Thackeray nodded and made a note of the address Lawson gave him. He passed the note to Mower as he hung up.

'Let's have him in for a chat too,' he said. 'King John they seem to call him and I think a bit of illicit property-letting is just the bargain basement for him and Hurst. I think there's a hell of a lot more to it than that.'

When Mower and Val Ridley had gone about their various tasks, Thackeray reluctantly picked up the phone again and dialled the Gazette. Laura answered brusquely, busy at her computer terminal with a deadline to meet. She was startled to hear Thackeray's voice and annoyed

192

that her heart seemed to jump when she recognised it. Like a bloody teenager, she thought.

'I'm sorry,' she said. 'I'm frantic . . .' He could hear the tension.

'I need to ask you something,' he said. 'I didn't want to do it on the phone. I thought perhaps a quick drink at lunch-time.'

'No chance,' she said. 'Not today. I'm sorry. We're running around in circles to cover your dawn raid at Wuthering.'

'So it'll have to be on the phone then,' he said flatly. 'You remember I mentioned the evictions last night? That they'd be this morning?'

'Mmm,' she said cautiously.

'Did you mention it to anyone else? Anyone at all?'

There was a long silence at the other end and for a moment Thackeray thought the line had gone dead. When she finally answered, her voice seemed to come from a great distance.

'Are you trying to eliminate me from your inquiries, Chief Inspector?' she asked at last. 'Or just covering your back?'

'Something like that,' he said quietly. 'I need to know, Laura. I'm sorry.'

'Then no, I didn't tell anyone. Not even the paper, as it happens. If I had, we'd have been there, wouldn't we, instead of trying to catch up on the story hours later.'

'Good,' he said. The silence lengthened again until Laura ended it by bidding him goodbye and hanging up. With an irritated toss of her head she turned back to her computer screen, while at his end, Thackeray slammed down the silent phone with a quiet curse.

You either went with the job and all its impossible demands, he thought, or you kicked against it and eventually found yourself flat on your face. Either way it was always the innocent who came off worst. He did not think he could risk taking hostages to fortune again. Laura deserved better than that.

SEVENTEEN

WUTHERING EXPLODED THAT NIGHT. THE trouble started with Chief Inspector Thackeray's apparently minor decision to obtain a search warrant for the flat occupied by John Stansfield/Sissons, which the uniformed searchers had found empty and securely locked when they had knocked at the door earlier. Inquiries at the home address the town hall had provided for Sissons had proved fruitless. The address was that of a semi-derelict house in a suburban street where, according to the neighbours, no one had lived for years.

Thackeray was increasingly convinced that Sissons was at the heart of the web of intrigue at Bronte, as much because of the lack of evidence of his involvement than because of any surfeit of clues. When he and Mower eventually interviewed Jerry Hurst he made little attempt to deny what the police now had ample evidence to prove that he had been making hundreds of pounds a week out of the squatters in rent, even more from an informal 'tax' he imposed on the young prostitutes who used the flats and their environs to entertain clients.

'Effing scroungers, the lot of 'em,' he declared in justification. 'I have to work for my brass. Why should kids like that get away with it? Slags, dossers, druggies. What's it matter what I charge 'em? Who the fuck cares?' And when it came to the point, Thackeray thought bleakly, he was probably right. If anyone had cared much about the rootless, jobless, aimless children Hurst had battened onto like a blood-sucking insect, they would not have been washed up on the decaying shore of Wuthering in the first place, human flotsam that came and went on a tide of its own.

But when Thackeray asked Hurst about Sissons, the fat slab of a face closed up and he shook his head.

'He asked me if he could use the flat as a favour,' he said. 'Said he worked for t'council and was short of a place to stay. Paid rent – to t'council, not to me. There didn't seem no harm in it. Apart from that I don't know owt about him. He comes and he goes, keeps himself to himself, no trouble, no trouble at all. Of course he's not old Bill's son. He never said he were.'

And push as Thackeray and Mower might, that was all they could prise out of him about the top-floor tenant. In the end they charged him with the relatively minor offences he had already admitted and let him go. There was little other option.

Nor were Mower's interviews with the remaining squatters to prove any more informative. They had as little information about John Sissons, whom most of them knew as Stansfield in spite of Hurst's claims to the contrary, as they had about drugs or petrol bombs or assaults on children or any of the other criminal activities which the police now knew had been going on inside Bronte and probably in the other blocks of flats as well.

They knew John, yes, of course, they said. A good laugh, John was, and generous with his money if they happened on him in the pub, a king in fact, but apart from the fact that he lived at Bronte, his existence there appeared to be a blank sheet, with only the merest flicker of anxiety here or the inadvertent clenching of a fist there to suggest to Mower that almost all of the youngsters he interviewed were lying through their teeth. Whatever the police could say to scare them was clearly not nearly as effective as someone else had been.

'He's done a runner, guv,' Mower concluded as the frustrating afternoon wore on, the house-to-house search for Nicky Tyson having proved as unrewarding today as it had the previous night. 'He's obviously scarpered. We've got to look at the flat. The kid could be in there, for all we know.'

'Right,' Thackeray said. 'Get a warrant and persuade the duty inspector to give us some back-up. It looks like a sledge-hammer job.'

And so it proved when they arrived on the top floor of Bronte to find the flat as unresponsive to their knocking as it had been for days. With the front door hanging off its hinges, the two detectives stood in the middle of the living-room and looked around in some surprise. Behind the council's cheap wooden door, Sissons, whoever he was, had created a very comfortable haven for himself. Pale fitted carpets covered the floors, the modern furnishings and fittings were tastefully chosen and elegantly arranged, the hi-fi was state of the art, the television and video system extravagant, the tiny kitchen equipped with every convenience, from microwave to food processor, that a single man could possibly require.

'Well, he didn't buy this lot on a housing official's pay, guv,' Mower said, not disguising the hint of envy in his voice. 'That hi-fi system must have set him back a couple of grand.'

'If he paid for it,' Thackeray said. 'Take the serial numbers of anything that could be identified and check them out. Then take the place apart. I want to know a lot more about Mr Sissons before the day's over. I'm going to see Alan Davies down below, to see what he's picked up.'

Thackeray stopped for a moment on the walkway and looked down at the estate. The search for Nicky Tyson had moved on from Bronte and the other blocks back to the streets and open spaces beyond for a second time. Further afield he knew that the river banks, the canal tow-paths, waste land and derelict buildings for miles around were being combed.

From his vantage point he could see a line of uniformed officers again working their way systematically through the sun-browned grass and scrub beyond the adventure playground and the community centre, raising clouds of dust as they went.

There was an unusual number of people on the walkways and he knew that the violent assault on

Stansfield's front door had attracted attention, not all of it friendly. A couple of black youths on the corresponding top walkway of Priestley House gave him a V sign and ran off, laughing and scuffling wildly, towards the lift.

Thackeray took off his jacket and rolled up his shirt-sleeves. It was intensely, stickily hot and he was filled with a deep sense of foreboding. He did not think that his detectives would find Nicky Tyson's body in the immaculate flat they had just broken into and were now systematically taking apart. But neither did he now hold out any hope to anyone, except with perhaps deceitful kindness to Mrs Tyson, that the girl would be found alive.

Too much time had gone by now for it to be a childish disappearing act, too many appeals had been made, too many obvious places where she might have had an accident had been searched, too many other children had already been attacked. Time had run out for Nicky, he was sure. Soon he would have to face what he had feared and had not seen for years, the murdered and probably violated body of a child. The prospect filled him with dread.

Slowly he made his way down the dirty, graffiti-scrawled staircase. It might have been his imagination, he thought, but he was sure that the number of messages inviting the police to indulge in diverse obscenely self-destructive practices had burgeoned in a day or so. So too had the increasingly familiar logo, a J with a crude crown superimposed that he now realised must be the signature of the so-called King John. Whoever he was, and whatever his power, it was evidently pervasive.

On the ground floor the lift seemed to have expired totally, standing with its doors yawning open, unresponsive to a couple of children who were frantically stabbing the buttons. Barely more than eight years old, he guessed, they swore viciously at him as he passed.

The intensity of dislike his presence provoked alarmed him, although after the assault on Mower the previous night it did not surprise him. Bronte House, he thought grimly, was no longer a safe place for a police officer to be alone, even one as confident of his own physical capability as he was.

He went outside, thankful to breathe fresh air. It was evidently the end of the day at the adventure playground, because as he left the main door of Bronte he was confronted by a number of mothers and children making their way back to the flats across the grass. PC Davies was not in sight.

'Have you found her, then?' one of the women asked him belligerently.

Thackeray shook his head.

'I'm sorry,' he said. 'We're still looking.' The circle of hot and sweaty faces accused him silently. Even the children, tow-haired and blue-eyed, hopping from one leg to another as they waited for their mothers, stared like an unsympathetic jury at a prisoner whose defence had just crumbled away.

'We're doing our best,' Thackeray said with finality, forcing a way through the sullen group and walking determinedly away across the grass towards the playground the women had just left.

'Useless bastards,' a single shrill voice screamed after him but when he glanced back over his shoulder the straggle of women and children had gone, swallowed up by the cavernous flats, and the walkways above were empty.

At the playground the chief inspector found Sue Raban alone, packing up bright plastic rings and water wings by the blue paddling pool. She straightened up slowly, wiping beads of sweat from her brow and glanced ironically at the warrant card he flipped in her direction.

'You're the organ grinder, are you?' she said. 'You'd be better served if you let people know when you're inflicting undercover monkeys on them.'

'Wouldn't that rather defeat the object of the exercise?' Thackeray came back mildly. She shrugged.

'I wouldn't vouch for his safety up here any more,' she said. 'These people don't like being made fools of.'

'Is that why he got thumped last night?'

Sue shrugged again. 'Is that what he told you?'

198

'He didn't tell me anything much,' Thackeray said. 'I'm just curious to know whether those who did the thumping found out he was a policeman before or after they laid into him. It makes a difference.'

'Does it?' she said, an edge to her voice. 'How much difference? An extra six months in jail? A year? Because he's one of yours?'

Thackeray looked at her consideringly, taking in the slim hips and legs in cut-off jeans, the firm breasts – no bra, he guessed – under the sleeveless tee-shirt, the long neck and poised, proud head with its close-cropped hair, the dark, angry eyes. He recognised precisely what a challenge Kevin Mower had discovered in Sue Raban.

'You know that's not what I'm interested in, Ms Raban,' he said. 'It's the motive that concerns me. I need to know just how lawless this place has become, just who's protecting whom, whether anyone knows – or just guesses – who's responsible for Nicky's disappearance, whether what happened last night was just a casual mugging or a deliberate assault on a police officer. Whether you set him up?'

Sue flashed him a quick look of dislike at that and then looked away, bending down to pick up an armful of toys and avoiding Thackeray's eyes as she set off across the grass towards the playground hut. He followed her slowly, giving her time to think. Inside the hut, she dumped the pile of damp plastic in a heap on the floor. She picked up a couple of cans of Coke from the table, handed him one and, opening her own and taking a long swig, sat down at the cluttered desk, head bowed. Thackeray stood in the doorway, leaning against the door-frame, apparently relaxed with his drink unopened, but never taking his eyes off her. At length she gave another expressive shrug and looked up at him with a faint smile.

'OK,' she said. 'If it helps to find Nicky, what can I say? They didn't know he was a cop. Not until I came along and told them. They were knocking him about because he'd been seen following Nicky and they thought the worst. When they found out who he was they split.'

'And of course you couldn't identify any of the vigilantes on the staircase, I guess?'

'I guess not. It was very dark,' she said firmly and Thackeray knew he would not budge her on that.

'And I don't suppose you know who made sure they knew Sergeant Mower had followed Nicky?'

'Anyone could have seen him,' she said. 'I saw him myself.'

Thackeray nodded again. Sue Raban was quite composed now, and he knew that he would not persuade her to say any more than she wanted to say.

'The evictions,' he said, changing tack. 'Did Mower let slip when they were going to be?' She shrugged.

'I guessed something was happening,' she said. 'Kevin said he wouldn't be here after yesterday. It was obvious something big was going down.'

'So who did you tell?' Thackeray asked flatly.

'No one. Why should I?' she said and would not be moved from that denial.

'Do you know John Stansfield?' he asked. 'I want to talk to him. Lives on the top floor of Bronte?'

Sue shook her head.

'I know who you mean,' she said. 'He was helpful with some of our committees, when it began to look as though the police couldn't protect the estate.'

Thackeray could think of many reasons apart from altruism why John Stansfield might be willing to undermine local confidence in the police.

'So when did you see him last?' he persisted.

'Two nights ago at a meeting,' she said.

'The night before Nicky went missing?'

'You can't be thinking of John in that connection,' she said, eyes wide, evidently shocked at the suggestion. 'That's crazy.'

'Anyone who goes missing at the same time as a child . . .' Thackeray left the sentence hanging in mid-air but Sue said nothing else.

'You've been talking to the mothers here today. Do they have any idea who might be responsible for her disappearance?' Thackeray asked at length.

Sue shook her head vigorously.

'If they did there'd have been more than a mugging, there'd have been a lynching,' she said. 'No one knows. They're out of their minds with worry.'

'But not worried enough to cooperate with the police?' Thackeray said, half to himself.

'You can't have it both ways, Chief Inspector,' Sue came back, angry now. 'You can't come in here like an occupying army with helicopters and riot shields, killing kids in cars, breaking down doors and throwing people out of the only homes they've got, like you did this morning, and then expect the community to come running to you with information when a child goes missing. They may need you now, but a lot of them won't admit it yet. They don't trust you, Mr Thackeray, and who can blame them?'

By dusk that evening the police had abandoned another day's fruitless search for Nicky Tyson. Every flat on the estate had been searched, every bungalow and back garden along the row of old people's homes, every garage in the two blocks at the ends of the flats, every alleyway leading down the steep hill to the town, every inch of the playground, the community centre and the doctor's surgery and all the waste ground around them, without a single clue as to the child's whereabouts being picked up.

More than a thousand statements had been fed into the computer and were waiting to be analysed the following day. The flat occupied by the man who called himself Stansfield had been particularly minutely searched, to no avail. His description and that of the car Davies had seen him driving had been circulated across the county and beyond, with no sightings reported.

In Thackeray's office the chief inspector and his sergeant were showing every sign of deep frustration as they found a final moment to flick through the Gazette, the front page of which was dominated by the face of Nicky Tyson, pink and white, the blue eyes solemn and

201

accusing. Thackeray turned to an inside page and glanced at the editorial, in which Ted Grant, in excoriating form, castigated the inefficiency of the police in losing control of the Heights. He wondered if Laura shared her paper's sentiments, and if he would ever find either the time or the courage to ask her. He pulled on his jacket with a heavy sigh.

'We might as well have abducted her ourselves, as far as the Gazette's concerned,' Mower said bitterly.

'Your friend Sue Raban thinks it's our fault too,' Thackeray said, hesitating on his way to the door. Mower stiffened. Since they had come back from the Heights he had spent most of his time in front of a computer screen and had hardly exchanged a word with Thackeray, who had been deep in conference with Superintendent Longley for most of the early evening.

'Right,' he said cautiously. 'I didn't know you'd spoken to her, guv.'

'Just a little off-the-record chat,' Thackeray said enigmatically. 'I gather you owe her for extricating you from a nasty situation last night.'

Mower could not disguise the look of surprise which flashed across his face.

'I wouldn't have called it extricating, exactly,' he said.

'I want you to go up there and talk to her yourself tomorrow,' Thackeray said. 'I think we'd get a lot more help, especially from the women, if Sue Raban was seen to be cooperating with us.'

'She's very hostile,' Mower said, uncertainly.

'But she wants Nicky found just as much as the rest of us. See what you can do, Sergeant. Use that fatal charm, whatever. We need her on our side.' Thackeray went out without looking back at Mower, who watched him go with his mouth slackly open in astonishment.

'You devious bastard,' he muttered at last, and then relaxed with a tired smile at the thought that an instruction to mix business with pleasure legitimately, however grim the excuse, might not be so unwelcome after all.

*

At the Heights, PC Alan Davies locked the door of the community police office as the street-lights began to cast an orange glow across the grass in front of the flats. It was still warm enough for him to feel comfortable in his uniform shirt-sleeves. But as he glanced around him before setting off along the pathway parallel to Bronte and Priestley Houses, he was aware of a low noise, which he could not immediately identify, rising and falling in the distance. Up on the walkways above him he could see groups of people moving around.

With a slight feeling of anxiety he went to the main door of Bronte. It was locked and he pressed the caretaker Jerry Hurst's bell-push a couple of times, but without response. Sure now that something was wrong he pressed a few more bells at random and someone above evidently activated the front door, because it suddenly swung open in front of him.

Cautiously he pulled out his personal radio and called his control, but even before they could respond Davies knew that it was too late and that after three years on the Heights he had made what might be his most serious mistake. A tremendous blow from behind struck him at the base of the skull and as he fell forward he felt hands seize the radio from him and smash it onto the concrete floor beside him.

The striking down of Constable Davies could have been fortuitous or it could have been a signal. The police never knew the answer to that. But it was very soon afterwards that the stolen cars began their terrifying circuits of the flats, the streets and walkways filled up with excited crowds, and the community policeman's car exploded in a roar of flames as the first of the night's petrol bombs was lobbed through its smashed windscreen. Not long after that, as the riot vans screamed incautiously up the hill from the centre of town and disgorged their helmeted troops onto the estate, a second petrol bomb was hurled down from the top walkway of Holtby and the disturbance proper began.

When Alan Davies woke up on a hospital trolley several

hours, a riot and dozens of arrests later, it was all over. Screwing up his eyes against the bright light of the casualty department and wishing he hadn't, he gingerly felt the bandage around his head and flexed his arms and legs experimentally. The face of the black nurse who had noticed his return to consciousness swam into focus.

'What . . .?' he managed, in a voice which did not sound as if it were his.

'Concussion, dear,' she said. 'And a couple of cracked ribs. Nothing too serious. We'll keep you in overnight, though, after the knock on the head. You can't be too careful.'

You could be more careful than he had been, he thought bitterly. It was, he decided there and then, the end of it. They could have his resignation tomorrow. As far as he was concerned the day of the community bobby at Wuthering was over.

EIGHTEEN

THE NEXT MORNING HAD NOT been one of Joyce Ackroyd's best starts to the day. She had slept fitfully again in Laura's spare bed and woken early, stiff and in pain. She was not mollified by the irrepressibly vocal blackbird which had taken up a perch in the cherry tree just outside the window and proceeded to greet not just the dawn but the comings and goings of the milkman, the postman and the children tumbling out of doors to play. Then thankfully she heard her granddaughter moving outside the door.

It was Laura's day off and she had resisted all hints and blandishments the previous evening to give it up in the interests of the Gazette's coverage of the ongoing troubles at Wuthering. She needed some time, she had insisted to Ted, time for Joyce, who was not well. In fact she desperately needed some time for herself, just to think and try to sort out her own jumbled emotions. She planned a quiet day at home, apart from tea with Vicky Mendelson and a swim with the boys.

It was not to be. She got up at eight, switched on the local radio station and absorbed the news of the previous night's events with a sinking feeling in her stomach. There seemed to be no end to the violence, she thought, and wondered to what extent detective chief inspectors were normally the targets of the missiles and petrol bombs which had put six officers in hospital overnight and would put dozens of youngsters before the magistrates later that morning.

She took Joyce a cup of tea, carrying the radio with her.

The estate was calm now, the newsreader was reporting, although there was still a heavy police presence there. Joyce sat up in bed, looking frail and painfully thin in her high-necked nightdress as she leaned back, her skin sallow and bruises dark against the plump white pillows. Laura shuddered at the thought of how close she might have come to losing Joyce. Although she often felt trapped in Bradfield she knew she had sprung the trap herself: Joyce neither asked nor expected her to stay. And when her grandmother did finally depart, as inevitably she must, Laura knew that in her new-found freedom she would still be bereft. Joyce was her anchor and she could not imagine life set adrift.

'I want to go up and make sure the house is all right,' Joyce said in a tone which brooked no contradiction.

'The front door's boarded up,' Laura said, prevaricating without much confidence. 'We can't get in.'

'Don't be daft,' Joyce said. 'You know I keep the key to the back door under a stone in the back yard.' Laura did know. In fact she had remonstrated with Joyce a couple of times about the insecurity of the time-hallowed arrangement, to no avail. Joyce had grown up and learned her fierce politics in the close-terraced streets where doors were never locked and community meant solidarity. In spite of what had happened two nights ago she would die, Laura thought ruefully, more trustful of her fellows than anyone of Laura's generation would ever be.

'You'll never learn,' she said fondly. 'I'll take you up before I go to Vicky's for tea, and pick you up on the way back, if you like. Will that suit?'

Within minutes the phone had rung, and Ted Grant had peremptorily demanded some help, day off or no day off, in the teeth of the overnight explosion of violence on the Heights. 'Just do me the one interview, Laura,' he said, as close to saying please as he was ever likely to come. 'The beaten up community copper? Could have been another Broadwater Farm? You remember? Come on, you're the only person who can do it justice.'

206

Wearily she succumbed to the flattery and caught up with Alan Davies at home soon after his discharge from hospital. His wife, a grey, worried-looking woman who had evidently been crying very recently, looked uncertain when Laura rang her suburban doorbell and asked for an interview, but when she checked with her husband inside, he urged Laura in with unexpected good humour.

'It's a load off my mind, now I've taken the decision to pack it in,' he said from the sofa, which had been turned to face the garden. His strapped-up chest was visible under his pyjamas and his face was bruised, but he seemed to be genuinely pleased to have made a decision about which, he admitted, he had been brooding for some time.

Laura perched on the worn armchair to which he waved her, and took out her tape-recorder, accepting Mrs Davies's offer of tea as much to get her anxious, hovering presence out of the room as because she was thirsty.

'To be honest, I've not been happy with the job for a while,' Davies went on eagerly. 'Community policing's fine in theory. But you can't do it for nowt, and that's what they've been trying to do. You never get owt for nowt in this life, do you?'

The problem with this man is going to be persuading him to stop rather than persuading him to start, Laura thought to herself ruefully. There's twenty years of frustration just waiting to pour out.

'Just let me switch on the tape-recorder, Mr Davies,' she said. An hour and several cups of tea later she had accumulated enough material for several background features on the breakdown of law and order on the Heights, which was what she was seeking. The 'Why I quit' headline from the man who had been lucky to be carried out of the previous night's mayhem alive would satisfy Ted Grant, she was sure. Davies's more thoughtful remarks on the plight of the families on the estate were what satisfied her.

'So what will you do now?' she asked, after switching off the tape.

'Oh, there's always jobs in security for ex-coppers,'

Davies said contentedly. 'I hear old Harry Huddleston's looking in that direction. I reckon if he gets a job of that sort, he'd not say no if I applied to join him.'

'Do you remember the Tracy Miller case up at the Heights?' Laura asked. 'That was one of Huddleston's, wasn't it?'

'Aye, that was a nasty one and all,' Davies said. 'I was up there with old Harry at the time. A summer a bit like this one – right hot and muggy.'

'Do you remember a policeman with a beard up there then?'

Davies hesitated for a moment, a wary look in his eyes.

'Why do you ask?'

'Just something someone said to me the other day,' Laura said. Davies's eyes had slipped away from her for a moment and she followed his gaze to a photograph on the sideboard on the other side of the room. She got up slowly and walked over to it. It was a picture of a presentation ceremony, two senior police officers, one on each side of a younger, slimmer Alan Davies holding some sort of award and smiling out at his audience from behind a luxuriant growth of facial hair.

'I shaved it off soon after,' he said. 'My wife went off it, said it tickled.'

'Do you remember a young girl called Linda Smith? Stephen Webster's girlfriend?'

Davies nodded.

'Aye, she were right upset when he was arrested. I told Sergeant Redding about her, but by that time the lad had confessed. I don't think they ever talked to her in the end.'

'No, I don't think they ever did,' Laura said.

Laura went back to the office to write her feature and then took an early lunch-break. But she did not go home, as she had half promised Joyce she would. Instead she turned the car out of town in an easterly direction and pulled up thoughtfully outside a substantial semi-detached house, one of a row set back from the road behind what its neighbours clearly regarded as elegant front gardens, though the occupants of this particular patch had decided theirs should become merely a car park.

There was a red Ford parked untidily across the expanse of tarmac in front of the garage, which gave Laura hope that the person she sought was inside. This, she thought, was it. The local hero's castle, though she feared that in fact the pebble-dashed façade might conceal a dragon rather than St George, and that there would be no one to rescue the damsel if she found herself in distress.

Harry Huddleston opened the door himself and nodded affably enough when she explained who she was.

'I was wondering when you'd turn up,' he said. 'You'd best come in.' A big man, running to fat, but with the watchful eyes Laura was beginning to associate with policemen. He showed her into a sitting-room where a large-screened television was tuned to a cricket scoreboard.

'Rain stopped play at the Oval,' he said dismissively, picking up the glass of beer he was evidently half-way through. 'Else you'd have had to wait until the lunch interval.'

He waved her into a chair and did not offer her any refreshment. There was no sound of anyone else in the house so Laura assumed that his wife was out.

'You're the spitting image of your grandmother, do you know that, Miss Ackroyd? Or do you prefer Miz, like these bumptious bloody lesbians?' Huddleston offered as he settled himself again in an armchair, adjusting his paunch under his blue sports-shirt for maximum comfort.

'Miss will do,' Laura said, unable to conceal a small grin of delight as Huddleston lived up to all her preconceptions.

'Aye, well, I always had a lot of time for your grandmother. Not politically, mind. She'd have had the bloody criminals knitting socks for their victims if she'd had her way. But I like a woman who speaks her mind. So what's on yours, Miss Ackroyd? Tracy Miller, is it?'

'Stephen Webster,' she said, grateful for his bluntness

when it came to the point. 'Or his girlfriend, Linda. Did you know she existed? Were you told?'

'So you've moved off the Huddleston-thumped-a-confession-out-of-the-little-beggar tack, have you?' the former chief inspector said thoughtfully. 'That's summat to be thankful for, I suppose.'

'This is only preliminary research for the programme,' Laura said. 'I won't be making any of the final decisions.'

'Just casting the first stone, is it?' Huddleston said, his tone suddenly more unfriendly. 'Aye, well, these things become a fashion, don't they? They've done the Met, and the West Midlands, undermined public confidence nicely there, so I suppose your telly friends think it's Yorkshire's turn now. Do you ever wonder what their real motives are?'

'Stephen Webster's been in gaol for ten years,' Laura began angrily, ignoring the challenge.

'Aye, and that little lass's been dead for ten years an' all,' Huddleston came back. 'Just think on, Miz Ackroyd, when you go stirring up old tragedies, who's going to get hurt by it all.'

'If Stephen is innocent then the real murderer is still out there,' Laura said.

Huddleston looked at her for a moment before nodding with something like weariness, suddenly looking older and slightly deflated by her refusal to be intimidated.

'You don't just look like your grandmother, do you?' he asked. 'You're just as bloody persistent, an' all. And there's been more attacks on kiddies? I suppose that's what you're saying, is it? And another one missing?'

'That's what I'm saying,' she said quietly, almost unable to believe that she might have won so easily.

'Aye, well,' Huddleston said with a heavy sigh. 'You're right, of course. Alan Davies told Jim Redding and Jim Redding told me. We knew about the girlfriend. But the lad confessed, and there was corroborating evidence. We never interviewed her. Is that what you wanted to know?'

Laura nodded, feeling more deflated than triumphant.

'That's what I wanted to know,' she said.

It was mid-afternoon when she parked the Beetle outside the bungalows and helped Joyce out of the passenger seat. It had been a struggle to get Joyce from her top-floor flat to ground level and she had completed the journey by bumping down the stairs on her bottom. Joyce had not complained but Laura could see from the humiliated look in her eyes that there was a strict limit to the time Joyce could remain with her. She would never consent to being totally housebound, she knew, and three flights of stairs were too much.

The estate seemed quiet now, a single burned-out car and several uniformed policemen patrolling in pairs the only sign of the previous night's disturbances. Joyce stood leaning heavily on her stick outside the garden gate, surveying the scene.

'I know no one learns from history,' she said bitterly, 'but you'd think they'd learn summat from geography. Instead of which they seem to be going out of their way to create another Los Angeles here. They're full of fine words about working with folk, the police are, but when it comes to it they rape and pillage with the best of them.'

'Oh, come on, Nan,' Laura protested. 'From the sound of it they were on a hiding to nothing last night. I don't often agree with Ted Grant, but when he says you can't have no-go areas, he's right.'

'Then you shouldn't tolerate a Third World ghetto in an affluent country,' Joyce said angrily. 'The police are there for the people, not t'other way around. If you can't get consent then there's summat far wrong – which there is, of course.' She turned away to her front gate and made her way painfully round the side of the house to the back door.

'Key's under there,' she said to Laura who stooped down and lifted a stone by the dustbin and retrieved it for her. Laura went in first and held the door open while her grandmother negotiated the step.

'Go and sit down while I make you a cup of tea,' she said. Joyce did not argue. She seemed depressed rather than

211

pleased to be home and shuffled slowly into the living-room without a word.

Laura put the kettle on and arranged two cups on a tray. She wondered now if it had been sensible to agree to leave Joyce here, but she desperately wanted to see Vicky and could think of no alternative now. She took the tray through. Lying in the tiny hall against the remnants of the smashed front door, in a corner made gloomy by the boards across the entrance, she noticed a large black rubbish bag.

'Is that rubbish to go out for the bin-men?' she asked casually. 'What day do they come?'

'What's that, love? They came on Tuesday. I didn't leave any rubbish.' Joyce said. Laura looked at her curiously, a tiny seed of doubt at the back of her mind growing tendrils of fear almost before she could put what she had thought into words. Very slowly she walked back into the hall and reached out for the black shiny plastic with a hand that seemed to be weighed down with lead. Her imagination told her what was inside the black shroud, although she rejected its promptings with a fierce disgust.

The bag was not fastened and when she pulled gently at it, the child's feet, in grubby white ankle socks, were uncovered, one neatly on top of the other as if her body had been arranged for maximum decorum before she was dumped.

'Dear God,' Laura breathed faintly, still having to force her mind to accept what her eyes could now clearly see. She pulled the plastic back carefully to reveal the bright cotton shorts and the still clean white tee-shirt and then the face she recognised well enough from the photograph Nicky's mother had given her and which had been blown up and printed tens of thousands of times on the front page of the Gazette.

'Dear God,' she said again, turning her head as if dazzled by the sightless bright blue eyes which stared at her from the pale, waxen features. She sat back on her heels for a moment and covered her face with her hands. There was no nausea, just a chill which seemed to start at the very centre of her being and spread slowly out to every extremity. She shivered convulsively and covered the child's face again with the loose black plastic. She could not bear the accusation there. Like an automaton, not daring to look at Joyce, she went into the living-room, picked up the phone and called the police.

It was almost an hour later that Michael Thackeray came out of Joyce Ackroyd's back door to find her dozing in a garden chair on the tiny paved area behind the bungalow. Laura was beside her, sitting on the flagstones with her back against the wall. She was in jeans and tee-shirt with her arms round her legs and her chin on her knees, looking pale and dishevelled, long strands of red-gold hair escaping from their clips and falling to her shoulders.

She had not been aware of Thackeray's arrival although she had expected it. Once two uniformed constables had appeared and set the wheels of the murder inquiry in motion, Laura had helped her grandmother out of the house, shielding her from the sight of the body bundled up like so much garbage, and settling her into the chair she found in the tiny storeroom beside the back door. And there they had waited while the police went about their business inside.

Laura glanced up at the tall policeman who loomed blackly between her and the sun, and quickly looked away again, her eyes full of tears.

'I'm sorry,' she said. 'I can't bear it.' He held out a hand and helped her to her feet, glancing at her grandmother who did not stir.

'I need to talk to you,' he said quietly. His face was like stone, only a faint pulse near his jaw giving any hint of the tension within, his concern for Laura lurking far back in his blue eyes. He guided her round the side of the house to the front, where she could see that the police had prized open the boarded-up front door, allowing a portly civilian figure to crouch over the body in the narrow hallway.

'Amos Atherton, the pathologist,' Thackeray said as they passed the doorway. She nodded, still not trusting

213

herself to speak. 'Then the scene-of-crime people will take the place apart – fingerpints, samples of this and that, evidence of how the body came to be there . . .' He was talking for the sake of talking and dried up in mid-sentence, his face bleak and angry. He had already steeled himself to inspect the small body, curled up in a foetal position within its black covering, and had choked back the wave of helpless fury which had threatened to overwhelm him, burying it behind the granite mask with which he now faced Laura and the world. It had been the moment he had dreaded for years and it had passed without embarrassment, though not without pain.

He sat with Laura in the back of one of the police cars which were now lining the road outside the bungalows. They were attracting inquisitive glances from the sullen groups of teenagers who had gathered on the grass outside the flats and the occasional adult making a foray to the shops, the betting shop or the pub.

'We'll need to fingerprint you both to eliminate you and your grandmother from amongst any other prints we find,' he said awkwardly. She nodded her assent to that.

'You touched the plastic bag?'

She nodded again.

'I guessed, but I wasn't sure,' she said. 'I had to open it to see . . .'

'I'm sorry it had to be you,' he said, feeling helpless to reach her through the numb indifference which seemed to have overwhelmed her. All her energy and her natural sparkle, everything in fact that he found so attractive about her, seemed to have drained away, leaving her face pale and almost ethereal, her eyes sunk into violet hollows, overshadowed by the mass of coppery hair.

'We'll need statements,' he said cautiously. 'From you and your grandmother. But it doesn't have to be now. It can wait. Just tell me one thing. How did you get into the house? Did your grandmother have the back-door key with her?' Laura managed an almost imperceptible smile at that.

'It was under a stone,' she said. 'They all do it. You tell

214

them not to but they take no notice.'

'And anyone would have known?'

'Most people who know her,' she said.

'Go home now, Laura,' he said abruptly. Take your grandmother and I'll send someone down to see you later.'

'You won't come yourself?' she asked, trying to keep her tone neutral, but he shook his head.

'I have to see the pathologist now. And then there'll be the post-mortem. There's a routine to be followed to a murder inquiry. It's what keeps us sane.'

They got out of the car in an awkward silence. With an enormous effort of will she stopped herself from reaching out for him and, as if sensing what she wanted, he moved away towards the gaping front door and the cluster of busy technicians crouching there.

'I must find my WDC and go and tell Mrs Tyson what we've found,' he said. She looked at him, horrified.

'There are no words for that,' she said.

'No,' he agreed. 'There are no words. Go home, Laura, you can't do anything to help here. Please go home. I'll see you later, if I can.'

'Why wasn't that house searched earlier?' Superintendent Jack Longley demanded angrily of Chief Inspector Thackeray.

'Somehow it got missed,' Thackeray said. 'They did a house-to-house right along that row of bungalows when she went missing, but didn't go back to do a search yesterday. The place was boarded up before the child vanished, so I suppose they thought it was clean.'

'That's not good enough, Mike. You know it isn't.'

'Sir,' Thackeray said, acknowledging the justice of the complaint. He regretted more personally than Longley could guess that the police had not found Nicky Tyson's body themselves.

'So what's Amos Atherton got to say for himself?' Longley went on abruptly.

'She'd been dead at least thirty-six hours, he thinks, so the chances are she was killed soon after she went missing.

215

She was asphyxiated. There are faint bruises on her neck but he thinks it's more likely that she was suffocated than strangled – possibly by the plastic bag she was found in. There are bruises on her forearms too, which seems to indicate she was grabbed and held tightly by the arms, tied up perhaps. He can't be sure.'

'Raped?' Longley spat the word out with evident distaste.

Thackeray shook his head bleakly. He had steeled himself to attend the post-mortem and had come away feeling drained after watching a second violation of the child follow clinically on the first, legal this time but no less brutal.

'Interfered with, but not raped,' he said. 'There won't be much forensic evidence, apparently, though we've sent off some fibres that were clinging to her socks for examination. They don't appear to match the carpet where she was found or anything at her home.'

'So I suppose you think it's a carbon copy of the Tracy Miller case, do you?' Longley said irritably.

Thackeray gave that question some thought before replying.

'It could be copy-cat rather than carbon copy,' he said. 'It's certainly very similar. And some of the Tracy Miller cast are still around. Jerry Hurst gave evidence at Stephen Webster's trial and we know now he's as bent as the proverbial three-pound note. And there's Miller himself. He could have lied to pin it on the stepson he disliked, or to cover himself. I don't think it's a possibility we can ignore. We'll have to talk to them again.'

'Damnation,' Longley said. 'We'll have every hack from every newspaper in the country on our doorstep if we tell them that. Another bloody miscarriage of justice. Another poor bugger locked up for years for summat he didn't do. Another chance to clobber the police. I don't need that in my division. We've avoided that sort of nonsense so far and I was hoping I'd avoid it till I retired.'

'We don't have to shout it from the roof-tops,' Thackeray said mildly.

216

'The press office at county have arranged a bloody press conference at six. With the Gazette already gunning for us over the state of the Heights, don't you think some clever hack is going to put two and two together?' Longley's normally jovial countenance was clouded with doubt and anger. 'What about the Ackroyd lass, the one who found the body? She's not daft.'

'No she's not,' said Thackeray with feeling. 'She will undoubtedly make the connection. She's not working today and she's very shocked. I might be able to persuade her not to go public for a while . . .' He shrugged, not wanting to pursue that line of thought but knowing that Longley would not let him off the hook.

'She did the inquiries for that bloody TV programme, I hear,' Longley said. 'I did wonder why you didn't tell me about that. Keeping your mind on the job, are you, lad?'

'It's difficult to forget this one,' Thackeray said grimly, his mind slipping back to the white tiles and green aprons of the post-mortem room, and the slight figure under Amos Atherton's scalpel on the slab. 'In the middle of the night, I'll wish to God I could.'

Longley looked at him sharply at that, his pale blue eyes hard.

'Let's see if we can keep any ten-year-old connections under wraps for a bit,' he said at length. 'I'll take the press conference and duck any suggestions of that sort if they come up. You see if you can use a bit of influence with the Ackroyd lass. Public interest, all that baloney. Turn on a bit of the charm, if you have to. I dare say you won't find that too difficult. And then go in hard on Miller and Hurst.'

'Sir,' Thackeray said as he left Longley's office. 'Shit,' he added under his breath as he walked slowly down the corridor to his own room, desperate enough to see Laura again on any pretext but the one Longley had provided. That was one she would be certain to reject out of hand.

Sergeant Mower looked up as Thackeray came back into the office. Thackeray, he thought, looked strained and grey. He must be taking this one to heart, he guessed, in a way which surprised him. He must surely, he thought,

217

have seen it all before.

'I went back to Hurst's flat after we'd finished at the bungalow,' he said. 'There's no answer, and no one seems to have seen him today.'

'Do you think he's done a runner?' Thackeray asked, although the metaphor did not seem very appropriate for the lumbering, overweight caretaker.

'Val Ridley and I had a shufti through his window and she said the place looked much the same as it did when she interviewed him with you, guv.'

'Right,' Thackeray said wearily. 'Ask uniformed to keep an eye on the place and let us know when he puts in an appearance, will you? If he's not turned up by tomorrow morning we'll put out a call for him and search his flat. Any sign of Sissons?'

Mower shook his head.

'Nope,' he said. 'And the gear in his flat appears to be legit. We've checked the stolen property lists.'

'The same for him, then. If he's not turned up by tomorrow, we start looking in earnest. So what did you get at the bungalow?'

'Not a lot, guv. No sign of a break-in. He must have used the back-door key, which means it could have been pretty well anyone in the neighbourhood. They all know some of the old folk hide keys like that. Silly old bats, they should have more sense.'

'And the plastic sack?'

'No distinguishing features. The sort you can buy at any supermarket. A few smudged prints at the bottom edge but they seemed to think they were probably the beautiful Laura's. I sent Val Ridley round with the fingerprint officer to see her and her granny and take their statements. The old lady's not mobile so I thought it was a bit much to bring them down here.'

'Good,' Thackeray said, absently, failing to provide the marks for sensitive policing which Mower thought he deserved.

'So do we dig back ten years on this one, guv?' Mower asked.

Thackeray did not reply, hearing and yet not hearing the sergeant's innocent query, hearing in fact another voice entirely, asking quiet, persistent questions about the death of another child. He sat for a moment drumming his fingers on the desk, gazing out of the open office window at the square below where desultory midsummer crowds were drifting around the waterless fountain or drooping on the wooden benches in the sweltering humidity.

In spite of the heat he shivered as if the chill of the post-mortem room had entered into the very marrow of his bones. Nicky's coffin would be quite small, he thought, although not as small as the one he had carried himself up the aisle of the Sacred Heart on a day of bright sunshine and strong breezes which had sent the reflected light from the stained-glass windows dancing with cruel gaiety across the distraught congregation. He needed to break this case quickly, he thought, or it might break him. He shook himself back to the present to find Mower watching him curiously from his desk.

'Tracy Miller, guv?' Mower said, keeping his thoughts to himself. 'Do you seriously think there's a connection?'

'It's worth looking at,' Thackeray said. 'It's too close for comfort. We'll get a better picture when we see the full post-mortem and forensic reports, but on the face of it, it looks identical. I'll want to talk to Paul Miller tomorrow. In the meantime, read the file. See what you think.'

'Harry Huddleston will be sick as a parrot if he got it wrong.'

'Not half as sick as Stephen Webster is, by all accounts,' Thackeray said grimly. 'He's been inside for ten years, remember? So let's get it sorted once and for all, shall we?'

NINETEEN

CHIEF INSPECTOR THACKERAY LEFT POLICE headquarters late, tired and depressed. He let himself into his car and sat at the wheel with the windows wide open for a moment before starting the engine. It was slightly cooler now, although he was still in shirt-sleeves, and felt soiled in a way he knew no amount of washing would cure.

No one, he knew, was immune from the anger that the murder of a child provoked. It drove police officers to frenzied feats of stamina and long hours of overtime about which they would normally complain bitterly. But the feeling that had wrenched at his guts ever since he had peered over Amos Atherton's shoulder as he made his preliminary examination of Nicky's small body was more than righteous indignation. It had a personal dimension which he feared might be as destructive as it was motivating, tending to distract rather than focus his attention on the problem in hand.

He had driven Mower and the other detectives in the incident room mercilessly all afternoon and evening as they checked and cross-checked the statements and reports which had been accumulating in the computer data-base since the child disappeared. Mower had also sat for an hour reading the Tracy Miller case file with a lengthening face.

'They got it wrong, guv,' he said flatly, when he had finished. 'The forensic evidence is too similar. It can't be coincidence. I'd put money on it.' And for Mower there was no greater vote of confidence than that. Thackeray had nodded non-committally, recalling Longley's perturbation at the possibility of a mistaken conviction and its inevitably bruising consequences for them all.

'We'll check it out,' he had said. 'I'll talk to Harry Huddleston.'

'Rather you than me,' Mower had said with feeling.

Reluctantly Thackeray started the engine and drove out of the police yard into the late evening traffic, unwilling to take the road west towards his own bleak and unwelcoming flat and unsure where else to go. He stopped briefly outside an off-licence and watched the groups of young men coming out with their six-packs of lager, laughing girlfriends hanging on their arms. He could easily buy oblivion there, he thought, terminal oblivion if he chose. He put his arms on the steering wheel and his head on his arms and groaned.

High above the town, Laura Ackroyd wandered moodily around her flat in a pair of loose silky pyjamas, her eyes heavy with tiredness but unable to sleep. After the police had finished taking their statements and dirtying their fingers with fingerprint ink, she and Joyce had picked at a meal, and Joyce, unusually silent, had eventually hobbled to her bedroom with all the light gone out of her eyes.

Laura stayed up, unable to settle to anything. She watched the television news with half an eye, concentrating only on the two- or three-sentence report on the finding of Nicky Tyson's body. She picked up a book and hurled it down again after five minutes, and thought with dissatisfaction about the next day's work which she was committed to start at eight the next morning.

Ted Grant had not been pleased to discover from the police press conference that one of his own staff had found the body of Nicky Tyson and had not troubled to tell him. He rang Laura to let her know of his displeasure and she had not even bothered to try to find excuses for her evident lack of journalistic zeal.

'I couldn't talk about it,' she had said flatly. 'Tomorrow, maybe, but not now.' Unexpectedly the unvarnished truth had seemed to satisfy Ted, whose last edition had gone to press almost before the news of the discovery of the body had reached the Gazette, and long before the police announced formally that they were treating the case as murder. He therefore had nowhere to publish Laura's revelations until the next day.

But he expected her in the office at eight, he had said, in a tone which left her in little doubt that if she prevaricated any longer she might not have a job to go back to. 'And don't talk to anyone else about it, either,' he concluded. 'If I find an eye-witness account on the front page of the bloody Globe in the morning, I'll swing for you, girl, I promise.'

A couple of restless hours later she was sitting with her feet up, gazing at her bare toes, still trying to work out, not for the first time, whether she was in the right job. Most of the time she loved the work, but she knew she lacked a certain ruthlessness – had been told so, in fact, by her former lover who had moved on to the Globe with scant regard for the human misery he caused on the way. She would never get to the top with her sentimental scruples, he had said, and she was inclined to believe it. What she could never decide was whether she cared.

Her reverie was disturbed by the doorbell. Wearily she went to the entryphone and was surprised to hear Michael Thackeray's voice.

'I'm not dressed,' she said with uncharacteristic uncertainty, and if he had come back with the flippant comment she would have provoked from most men she might not have let him in. But there was silence and after a moment's hesitation she pressed the button to open the front door and unlatched her own.

They stood for a moment on the threshold looking at each other. Thackeray appeared tired and crumpled, his shirt-sleeves rolled up and his tie hanging loose at the neck, while she, for all that the cream silk revealed more than it concealed of the curves underneath, was pale and dark-eyed beneath the cloud of copper hair.

'I'm sorry,' Thackeray said awkwardly. 'It's late. I needed to see you.'

'I think I needed to see you too,' she said simply. She hesitated for a moment and then cast caution aside and put her arms round him, comforted by the warmth and solidity of his body. He hesitated too before he touched her, instantly conscious when he did of the thin silk which slid beneath his fingers against the bare skin beneath. Determinedly restrained, he bent his head to kiss her on the cheek.

She pulled away after a moment and led him into the living-room where he slumped wearily into the corner of the sofa and ran a hand through his hair. He did not know where to begin and opted in the end for the impersonal, cursing himself for his own cowardice.

'My boss,' he began, 'Superintendent Longley asked me to ask you, to ask the Gazette in fact, if you could not make the connection between Nicky Tyson and Tracy Miller – not for a while, anyway. It would help us if the killer didn't know – if it's the same person. And we think now it is.'

'I'll talk to my editor,' she said, a slight distance opening up between them again. 'I dare say he'll cooperate. So this is a business visit, is it?'

'Not really,' he admitted with a ghost of a smile. 'It gave me an excuse, that's all.'

She stood gazing at him with cool greeny-grey eyes, unsure whether he needed an excuse for himself or some third party, until he looked away, discomforted.

'I needed to tell you something too,' she said awkwardly. 'I found out that Stephen Webster had a girlfriend, Linda Smith. She doesn't give him an alibi exactly, but casts a little doubt, maybe. Enough to interest "Case Re-opened".'

Thackeray nodded, alert again.

'I'll talk to her,' he said.

'There's more . . .'

'And I won't like it?' he prompted.

Laura shrugged uncertainly.

'Your colleague Harry Huddleston,' she said. 'He knew about her, and did nothing about it. Didn't want inconvenient facts to interfere with a good case.'

'And never told the defence lawyers, I suppose? Wonderful!'

223

'I'm sorry,' Laura said.

'I'm sorry, too,' he said again, wearily this time. 'You've had a miserable day. I shouldn't have come round to burden you with my problems.' He glanced at the bottle of vodka on the coffee table and Laura's empty glass.

'You've been drowning your sorrows,' he said, carefully neutral. Laura picked up the bottle defensively.

'Not really,' she said.

'Is your grandmother all right?'

'As well as can be expected,' Laura said with a wry smile. 'I suppose that's the best you can say for both of us. It's easy enough to write about these things, isn't it, from a safe distance? Different to see it in the flesh.' She put the bottle carefully on the side-table which housed her drinks, and glanced at herself in the mirror above. She was wearing no make-up and felt uneasy and slightly vulnerable in her nightwear. She turned back to Thackeray and sat opposite him in a chair on the other side of the coffee-table instead of beside him. He smiled faintly at that but said nothing.

'You went to see Mrs Tyson?'

'I took DC Ridley with me. I thought a woman would make it easier.' He shrugged dispiritedly. 'The usual cop-out. Nothing makes it easier.'

'I suppose it's naive to think you get used to it,' she said.

'You never get used to it. And children are the worst thing.'

'But you must have seen it before, in your job . . .'

'Not really. I suppose I've been lucky. This is the first child murder I've had to handle since . . .' He stopped, his determination to tell Laura about his son faltering as he stood at the threshold of the confessional.

'Since?' she said softly, and he knew that if they were to go any further he must commit himself now or not at all.

'Since my son, Ian, died,' he said. 'He was eight months old.' She looked at him, appalled and moved that he should have told her what evidently cost him so much to tell.

'That must be the cruellest thing.'

He shrugged slightly.

'I sometimes go whole days now without thinking about

224

him, but seeing Nicky Tyson today brought it back. Seeing her just filled me with anger, disgust, the sort of revulsion I shouldn't be feeling if I'm to make sense of this thing.'

'You stopped concentrating on the bastard who did it?'

'I should know better,' he said.

'Can't you hand over to someone else?' she asked tentatively, but he shook his head at that.

'I can't pick and choose my cases because I'm too fragile to handle some of them, any more than I guess you can pick and choose your stories. You're in this business for better, for worse, like marriage, I suppose. And this is definitely for worse.'

'You had a wife,' Laura said very quietly again. It was a statement, not a question. 'Your son had a mother – but there's no help there?'

'We're not together any more,' he said, not looking at Laura.

Laura watched him for a moment in silence, trying to weigh up the previously elusive man who had unexpectedly opened himself up to her in a way she guessed was very rare. But in search of what, she wondered? Comfort certainly, although whether of the physical or the emotional kind she was not sure. She could at this moment, she was certain, end it and simply send him away, and he would go without complaint, locking up his distress again, grateful for whatever it was he had briefly sought from her but not likely to ever insist that she should share his burdens. She was equally sure that was not what she wanted. Very deliberately she got up and sat on the arm of the settee beside him, leaning down from above to kiss him on the lips.

'Stay here tonight,' she said. He looked up at her. The front of her pyjama top had slipped open to reveal a breast that he could have touched without effort. Instead he cupped his hand round her face and pulled her close to return the kiss.

'My mother would call you a brazen hussy,' he said. She laughed at that, suddenly releasing the tension between them.

'Your mother would probably be right, but it's a bit late for me to change my wicked ways now,' she said.

'And what about your grandmother? Will she approve?' he said, glancing at the closed bedroom door with a hint of relieved amusement returning to his eyes.

'Totally,' she said, kissing him again.

The alarm went off too soon the next morning and Laura irritably reached out a hand and turned it off before she realised that she was not alone. She recalled now just why she was so unusually reluctant to face the day and smiled at the recollection. Michael Thackeray had not reacted to the insistent buzzer and very carefully Laura eased herself into a sitting position so as not to disturb him. They had fallen asleep in each other's arms after making love urgently and without much sophistication, but he had turned away from her in the night and was sleeping now with his face half hidden in the pillows, broad back bare and one hand clenched above his head.

She watched the steady rise and fall of his shoulders as he slept and felt the same sense of tenderness and triumph with which she had slipped into his arms the previous night. What she did not feel was any confidence that having won him she would keep him. She knew very well that he had come to her as the lesser temptation in the dark night of his depression and that when he had found his balance again he might no longer feel the need for her he had so passionately expressed last night. That she would still need him she had no doubt.

Gently she leaned over and kissed the soft hair at the nape of his neck. There were, she noticed, a few grey strands amongst the dark.

'Michael, it's time to wake up,' she said. He turned towards her sleepily, looking at her for a moment with puzzled eyes before he smiled.

'Laura,' he said in mock astonishment, and she felt renewed desire flood her body. He evidently felt the same because he pulled her towards him and kissed her hungrily, pulling off her silky pyjama top as he did so.

226

She glanced at the clock and pulled away regretfully.

'I can't be late after taking yesterday off,' she said trying to convince herself as much as him. He let her go, his hands following her as she slid slowly from beneath the quilt to stand looking down at him, half naked and flushed with excitement.

'Ted Grant will probably sack me if I don't turn up on time,' she said. Thackeray groaned as the reality of the previous day crowded in on him again in all its gothic horror.

'And the not-so-good folk of Wuthering will probably lynch me if I don't lay hands on their child-killer sharpish,' he said. 'And if they don't the chief constable will probably oblige. I've a meeting with Jack Longley at nine and I need Kevin Mower to brief me before that.'

He hesitated, as if about to continue but thinking better of it. She gave him a mischievous grin, evidently restored to normality herself by the night's events, and shook her head.

'We didn't, if that's what you're wondering,' she said.

'Nothing was further from my mind,' he exclaimed innocently. 'I'm sure it takes more than a Chinese meal . . .'

She picked up his clothes from the floor where he had dropped them and threw them at him.

'You're evidently a pig by nature as well as by profession,' she said. 'But I never did fancy your Kevin half as much as I fancied you.'

'I'm pleased to hear it,' he said lightly, though his eyes were sombre and she recognised, if she had not before, that this was not a man who could be trifled with.

'I'll be ten minutes in the bathroom,' she said, leaning over and kissing his cheek. 'Then it's all yours.'

The newsroom was already busy when Laura arrived at the Gazette. Ted Grant looked up briefly from his consultation over page lay-out with Fred Powers, the chief sub-editor, as Laura walked in.

'In my office in five minutes,' he said and Laura nodded

without enthusiasm. She switched on her computer terminal, checked through what other reporters had filed on the murder at the Heights and headed her own contribution DEATH with angry stabbing fingers. Before she had finished the first paragraph she heard Ted's rasping smoker's cough just behind her as he read the screen over her shoulder.

'Right,' he said. 'That's more like it. But I still want a word.' 'A word' was the only understatement in Grant's vocabulary and generally meant a fierce and abusive bollocking which had left tougher nuts than Laura in pieces before now. But this morning Laura was floating on a cloud of contentment and Grant had no means of bringing her to earth. She followed him into his office and pre-empted his first strike by passing on the police request not to explore the similarities between the new murder and the death of Tracy Miller. Grant listened stony-faced and then harrumphed in some displeasure, his colour rising dangerously. 'If Jack Longley wants to ask me owt, he should ask himself, not employ monkeys to send messages,' he said.

'I wouldn't underestimate Chief Inspector Thackeray,' Laura said sweetly. 'I think the request was his as much as Longley's.'

'Aye, well, it's Longley as runs CID, and it's Longley who'll have to do the asking, as far as I'm concerned,' Grant snapped. 'I'll give him a bell later on. We'll have to see about keeping things from our readers, won't we? It's not summat I'll do lightly, isn't that. There'll have to be bloody good cause. So now, let's hear about this murder you stumbled into then, shall we? Better late than never, I suppose.'

Sergeant Mower drove up to the Heights in a state of subdued fury and parked outside the adventure playground with a squeal of brakes. He was breathing heavily and for a moment he sat clutching the steering wheel, trickles of sweat running down his back which were not caused entirely by the heat.

228

He had been going about his business in the incident room half an hour earlier when Chief Inspector Thackeray had appeared at his shoulder with a look in his eyes that Mower knew instantly meant trouble. In his office Thackeray had closed the door deliberately and handed Mower a file.

'You, my lad, have been conned,' he said quietly, his anger confined to his eyes. 'The Raban woman has been leading you by the nose. No wonder you wasted your time on the Heights.'

'Sir?' Mower said, opening the file with deep foreboding. It contained standard fingerprint forms from the forensic team, two of them juxtaposed and identical. Thackeray leaned over his shoulder and jabbed at each image in turn.

'That,' he said, 'came from a can of Coke Sue Raban had just handled. That was an unidentified print from Sissons' flat, one of dozens like it. She may not have actually lived there, but she certainly spent a lot of time there. Her prints are everywhere – kitchen, living-room, bedroom.'

'His girlfriend,' Mower said faintly, remembering Kelly Miller's suggestion that there was a girlfriend and her refusal to identify her.

'I wondered,' Thackeray said. 'I saw her up on that top walkway the night Nicky Tyson went missing and it didn't register until later. I picked up the can at the playground when I saw her yesterday, just on the off-chance.'

Mower looked at him, uncharacteristically lost for words as the implications of what Thackeray had discovered sank in.

'Guv,' he began hesitantly, but Thackeray did not give him the chance to continue.

'If you ever let personal involvement get in the way of an investigation again,' he said coldly, 'you'll be back down the M1 so fast you won't draw breath before you hit the Edgware Road. What is it they say in the Met? I'll do your legs? In fact if your friend Miss Raban has disappered already I wouldn't bother to report back in. You might as well go home and pack your bags. Bring her in, and if she won't come voluntarily, arrest her.'

By the time he reached the playground, Mower's own anger and anxiety had stretched him taut. He opened the high playground gate and scanned the familiar scene. A game of football was in progress, small children splashed in the paddling pool under the watchful eye of their mothers. At first he could not see Sue, and panic grabbed momentarily at his stomach. Then he spotted her, in a bright yellow tee-shirt, kneeling in the dust at the side of a small girl who had evidently fallen and scraped her knee. She met his eyes and nodded impassively as she got up and led the child to the hut, where she proceeded to wash the wound and put a plaster on it while Mower stood in the doorway watching, his fierce anger gradually ebbing away to be replaced by something akin to pity.

When she had finished she stood up and gave the child an affectionate push out of the door.

'I thought you'd come back,' she said. 'You or your boss. I knew he didn't believe me.'

'You were covering for Sissons,' Mower said. 'Stansfield, King John, whatever he calls himself? You knew what he was up to?'

'Not really,' she said. 'I knew he was a bastard, just like I knew you were. I just put that down to your both being men. I fancied him just the same. And I thought he was the sort of man these people need – someone local and tough, someone to stand up for them.'

'And me?' Mower asked bitterly.

'You?' she gave him a ghost of a smile. 'I just thought you were snooping, a bit nosy – John thought it was a good idea to keep an eye on you . . .' She shrugged.

'A close eye,' Mower said angrily.

'Sorry,' she said. 'I thought you enjoyed it. I didn't know you were a cop until that day I found your ID.'

'And you told Stansfield everything?'

'I had no reason not to,' she said. 'I thought he was probably involved in the car crime, but he never said much. He was very secretive.'

'Thackeray wants you at the police station,' Mower said. Sue smiled faintly again.

'He sent you to prove you're still a good boy, did he?' she mocked.

'You realise if you're charged you could be deported?'

'I guess I'd better tell him what he wants to know then, hadn't I?' she said.

By midday Laura had committed her story to the first edition and was leaning over Fred Powers' proof to see how it looked in print. Nicky's photograph was prominently displayed again beside a picture of her mother, red-eyed and distraught as she had left her home the previous day to take refuge with the friends who were supporting her on either side.

Laura's eyewitness account of how she had discovered Nicky's body was displayed in bold type down one side of the page alongside the crime reporter's latest update on the police operation. Ted was even now composing his latest editorial broadside on crime and punishment in his office, from which the occasional expletive could be heard as he pounded his ancient typewriter as if it too deserved the sort of painful physical chastisement he was confidently recommending.

'It looks good,' she said, and as a piece of tabloid display it did look good. Fred knew his job and melded pictures with text and headlines to impressive effect. But Laura felt no satisfaction at the contribution she had made to the finished paper today. On this story she had penetrated too far beneath the sanitised version of reality which was all the Gazette ever saw fit to print to feel comfortable with what she had written. She knew it would not make her readers weep as it ought to make them weep and as she knew the best of her profession could make them weep. The Gazette did not want life too raw or too upsetting, and Laura knew that she was conniving in a lie.

She went back to her desk and logged off her computer terminal, intending to go to lunch, but before she could leave her desk the phone rang. The voice at the other end did not identify itself immediately, but she recognised Stephen Webster's mother, a little uncertain, a little

231

breathless, though whether with hope or fear it was impossible to tell.

'This little girl?' June Baker said. 'Do you reckon it's the same man who killed our Tracy? Was it the same sort of attack? Does it mean Stephen's in the clear after all?'

Laura thought of Thackeray's strictures and of the apparently acrimonious conversation Ted Grant had had with Superintendent Longley before he had reluctantly agreed to hold off making that particular connection in print. She felt that she had to prevaricate.

'That's very difficult to say at this stage, Mrs Baker,' she said carefully. 'But I'm sure it's something the police will consider.'

There was a long silence at the other end before June Baker spoke again and when she did she sounded even more breathless.

'I went to see Paul the other day, you see. I thought maybe I could persuade him to remember a bit more clearly about the times, what he said in court and that. He went all funny on me. He was very angry with Kelly about something, said she'd been arrested and she was a little tart. And then he said if I wanted to get at the truth about Stephen I should talk to Jerry the caretaker. He said he'd backed Jerry up because he said he'd seen Steve going out and because – well, really, because he wanted to believe Steve had done it.'

'Are you saying he's not sure any more?' Laura asked, trying to keep the excitement out of her voice.

'He. didn't seem sure about anything any more. He was ranting and raving about Kelly and the little girl who was attacked – what was her name, Josie? – and the squatters. He'd got himself into a right state.'

'This was before Nicky disappeared?'

'Oh, yes,' Mrs Baker said. 'I should think he'll be even more upset now.'

'Did you talk to Jerry Hurst?' Laura persisted.

'No, he wasn't around when I left. I hadn't told my husband I was going up to Wuthering. I had to get home to get his tea or he'd have thought there was something funny going on. Can you get your television people to talk to him? Or the police?'

'Yes,' Laura said. 'I'm sure I can.'

When Mrs Baker had hung up, she sat staring at her phone for a moment before shaking her head. She would tackle Paul Miller herself one more time, she thought, before bothering the police. If he really was changing his story after all this time she wanted an interview with him before the forces of law and order moved in and made him inaccessible to the Press.

Even if there was a quick arrest it would still be a useful background interview for the Gazette to use when the trial was over, particularly if Stephen Webster was cleared of any involvement in Tracy Miller's murder. The release of another innocent man after a long period in jail would hit the headlines in a big way and Ted Grant would want all the details he could get. She slipped a tape into her recorder, put it into her bag and left the office with a tingle of excitement driving her on.

TWENTY

HARRY HUDDLESTON PACED UP AND down Superintendent Jack Longley's office like a much provoked caged
animal. His bright green Aertex sports-shirt was strained
into creases across his chest and belly. His beige slacks
slipped dangerously low at front and rear. But it was his
florid complexion that held the attention of the other
two men in the room.

Huddleston had caught the sun: or perhaps it would be
fairer to say that the sun had caught Huddleston as he had
sat an hour or two too long on the Headingley terraces
with no more than a knotted handkerchief for protection,
regarding anything as practical as a hat as a southern
affectation that no real man would contemplate. The sun
had stripped the skin from his nose and forehead and
abraded his temper to match. On top of that, Yorkshire
had lost to Middlesex by four wickets. The pale blue eyes
glittered like chips of ice unexpectedly flung into the
molten heart of a volcano. Harry Huddleston was very
angry indeed.

'I don't care if the lad turns out to be the bloody Angel
Gabriel himself,' he said. 'He confessed to that bloody
murder and we did not bully him into it. I repeat, we did
not bully him. I didn't. Sergeant Redding didn't. And no
other bugger got close enough to get a chance, I promise
you that. And then there was corroboration. Not one
witness. Two of them! What more did we need? He never
claimed he had an alibi. Why should we go looking for an
alibi when we'd got a bloody confession, answer me that?'

'If the lad is cleared at this late stage there's bound to be

234

an inquiry,' Longley said coldly. 'You know there's nowt we can do about that, Harry. It'll be out of my hands. I don't like it any more than you do. It reflects on the whole division, not just on you.'

'So what do you think about it, lad?' Huddleston said objectionably, turning to Michael Thackeray who had been watching the two older men impassively, quite convinced that if either Huddleston or Redding had beaten Stephen Webster to within an inch of his life, or ignored a whole platoon of inconvenient witnesses, neither of them would ever admit it. Their code, the old code of loyalty to the job, would never allow it.

'You're standing there as if the cat's got your tongue. Do you reckon it's the same bugger, or not?' Huddleston asked.

'It's too early to tell,' Thackeray said carefully, keeping his own temper well under control. 'But there are similarities. She had no shoes on when she was found. Just socks, and they'd picked up some dark fibres from somewhere else, according to the SOCO report. They don't match anything in the bungalow. I've got a search on for her trainers, pink and white, her mother says, almost new. My guess is she wasn't killed there, she was dumped after she died. But the most significant factor from your point of view is that black plastic bag. She went into that before she died, Amos Atherton says. She'd caught the plastic between her teeth, just like Tracy Miller did.'

'Aye, I remember that from his report on the Miller child,' Huddleston said sombrely, his attention caught now by the problem, his own predicament forgotten, temporarily at least. He gave Thackeray a look of calculated appraisal, and nodded, as if concluding that perhaps his successor might make the grade yet.

'I tell you what,' he said grudgingly. 'If you give me the file I'll go through it and see if there's owt significant I can recall that's not in there. Would that help?' Thackeray glanced at Longley for guidance and the superintendent nodded.

'I'd be grateful,' Thackeray said formally. 'You can use

my office – your old office – if you like. I've some other matters I need to talk to the super about and then I'm going up to the Heights.'

'I'll buy you a pint in the Woolpack about twelve-thirty, Harry,' Longley said as the ex-chief inspector took the buff file from his desk and made to leave.

'Aye, you owe me one,' Huddleston said grimly as he closed the door.

Longley leaned back in his chair, pale blue eyes half closed, as they listened to Huddleston's heavy footfalls receding down the corridor.

'So you think he got it wrong, do you?' he said.

Thackeray shrugged.

'I'm sorry,' he said, knowing how much Longley would dislike his conclusion. 'Whatever you say about tape-recorded interviews at least it gives you some idea what's going on behind those closed doors. Then . . .?' He shrugged again. 'A young lad, frightened, confused, upset, maybe, if he was fond of the child. It wouldn't necessarily take much pressure. Harry Huddleston could put the fear of God into me if he put his mind to it, so what chance would Stephen Webster have?'

He knew himself the pressure senior officers could exert in the privacy of an interview room. At the point where his life had been running out of control towards a precipice it was just such pressure which had been used on him. In his case it had dragged him back from the edge. In others, he guessed, it could just as easily administer the fatal push.

'And he should have talked to the girl,' Thackeray went on. 'Or given the defence the chance to talk to the girl. However certain you are, there's always that chance you might be wrong. No one's infallible.'

'Ten years,' Longley said grimly and Thackeray knew that he had come to his own conclusion and that it was not so different from his own. 'Ten years, God help us. The media'll have us for bloody breakfast, dinner and tea.'

Thackeray nodded wryly, thinking of one reporter in particular who would be anxious to put the record straight on Tracy Miller as soon as the chance presented itself. The longer Longley remained in ignorance of what he would probably regard as consorting with the enemy the better, he thought. He pushed the insistently seductive image of Laura Ackroyd slipping out of her silky pyjama top out of his mind with difficulty.

'I've put out calls for Jerry Hurst and for John Sissons,' he said. 'Neither of them has been seen for two days, and I want to talk to them both.'

'Two suspects?'

'Too soon to tell,' Thackeray said. 'There's the father too. You can never rule fathers out. But we need to eliminate the other two, at least. And there's other matters to take up with Sissons – what he's been doing in that flat, for instance, and where he got his very desirable wheels and the rest of his gear on a housing clerk's salary. I've caught up with his girlfriend and should get something useful out of her, I think.'

'Right,' Longley said gloomily, hunched up in his chair, his fleshy face collapsing over his collar and militarily striped tie. 'I can't see there's going to be much satisfaction at the end of this one, Michael, however it turns out. There'll be mud flying our way whatever happens. It'll be a public relations disaster. It's not what I was looking forward to at this stage in my career, I can tell you.'

'Well, I can live with public relations disasters if I get the bastard who did it,' Thackeray said flatly, provoked by Longley's taking what he felt was a wider view too far.

'Aye, well, you'd best get on with it then,' Longley said, irritated. 'Les Dobson will thank you, for one, because there's no way he and the uniformed lads are going to calm that bloody estate down until this bugger's found, you can bank on that. And until it's calmed down this division's name'll be mud at county.'

'Sir,' Thackeray said, turning to the door to hide his annoyance. 'I'll keep you in touch.'

Paul Miller squirmed in his seat, pressing himself into the corner of the well-worn sofa and wringing his hands, under Laura's uncompromising gaze.

'It were obvious the little bastard 'ad done it,' he said again, his pale eyes pleading with her for sympathy. 'Jerry saw him going out when he said he were here. It were obvious. And there were them magazines in his room. The police found them when they searched. He must have done it.'

'But you told June the other day that Jerry pressured you,' Laura said sharply.

'It were her doing the pressuring,' Miller said. 'Cow! She's still crackers about that lad. She always were. They both were. I came nowhere in their little set-up.'

'Both?' Laura said softly.

'June and Tracy,' he mumbled. 'Thought the sun shone out of Stephen's bum. Fish from t'chippie for tea because that were Stevie's favourite, this programme or that programme on t'telly because that were what Stevie liked so they liked it too.' He mimicked June Baker's slightly refined tones savagely and gave a gesture of disgust at the memory.

'You really hated Stephen?'

'I never wanted him here,' Miller said. 'Tracy were my little lass till he moved in, my treasure. She loved her dad, did Tracy. Then it were Stevie this and Stevie that.' The bitterness of that old jealousy was still raw on his pinched face and Laura realised that even if he had not been sure that the boy was guilty he would have been pleased to help convict him.

'Tell me about Jerry Hurst, then?' she said, checking to make sure that her tape-recorder was running. This was an interview she did not want to lose.

'He came up for a bit of a chat after Stephen had been interviewed a couple of times. He said it'd be a right pity if he got away with it for lack of evidence. He'd seen him going out, he said, and if I said I'd come home with Kelly and found the flat empty just after, then that would clinch it.'

'And it did?'

'Aye. When I told them that, they arrested him straight

off,' Miller said. 'Good bloody riddance, as far as I was concerned. I told them that, an' all.'

'But it was a lie? You didn't find the flat empty when you said you did, when Stephen said he was here watching television?'

Miller shook his head.

'I didn't come back till much later,' he said. 'But so what? I knew he'd done it. If he'd got away with it I'd have killed him any road.' Laura looked at the slight grey figure opposite her and wondered at the curdled emotions which had soured within for so long, reducing Miller to a husk who had found not an ounce of love or affection for the daughter who was left.

'You were never tempted to tell the truth later? At the trial? You stuck with that story right to the bitter end?'

'Jerry made sure of that,' he said. 'I were drawing benefit while June were working. He threatened to shop me to the Social if I let him down.'

'So the two of you had Stephen put away?'

Miller nodded, his eyes shifting around the room, looking anywhere but at Laura, who could not keep the contempt from her voice.

'And now?' she said at length. 'What do you think now that there's been another murder that looks so similar?'

'I don't know, do I?' Miller shouted angrily. 'It's not my bloody fault. It were t'police who put Stephen away. They thought he'd done it all right. That Inspector Huddleston thought he'd done it. And the jury. It weren't just what I said, you know. He confessed.'

'Will you go to the police now and tell them the truth?' she asked, glancing at the tape still turning slowly in the recorder so that he would have no doubt that if he did not, she would.

'Aye, all right,' he muttered reluctantly.

'Doesn't it bother you that you've wrecked that boy's life?' she asked angrily. Miller did not reply and she switched off the recorder in disgust, put it in her bag, and got up to leave. As they moved to the door of the living-room they heard the front door slam.

'I thought she were out,' Miller said, and Laura wondered if Kelly had been listening at the door and if so for how long. Miller, she thought, had lost not one daughter but two, the second loss following inevitably on the first as the bitterness of Tracy's death corroded his soul. She suddenly felt suffocated by the stale air of the cramped flat and moved quickly to the front door.

Outside on the walkway she took a deep breath of the still humid summer air and walked slowly back towards the stairs deep in thought. She would have to tell the police what she had just discovered. She had no confidence that Miller would take the initiative himself. Nor did she expect much thanks for the service, she thought wryly. June Baker would be delighted to see her son free, but elsewhere there would be anger and embarrassment as the full horror of the injustice became clear.

She pushed open the heavy door onto the landing unaware that her progress along the walkway had been observed. At the lift doors she hesitated, wondering whether it was worth pressing the call button or whether it would be just as quick to walk down the five flights of concrete stairs.

She never took that simple decision. Even as she hesitated, she heard a sudden scuffling noise away to her left and a low moan as if someone were in pain. Startled she hauled open the door onto the other walkway, but caught no more than a glimpse of a figure disappearing into a recessed doorway to one side of the lift-shaft. A door thudded closed behind whoever had been on the landing.

Suddenly alarmed, she eased open the solid wooden door. According to a much abused notice hanging askew from a single screw, warning against entry, it led to the roof and was strictly out of bounds to tenants of the block. She held the door open slightly with her foot and listened before very slowly and quietly beginning to climb the steep stairway at the top of which she could see absolutely nothing. The steps led to another door which was very slightly ajar, offering the merest sliver of daylight, through which Laura could hear movements and the mumble of voices.

'Interfering bitch,' a voice said suddenly, quite clearly, a voice she knew and feared, the voice from the swimming pool, and she thought for a heart-stopping moment that she had been seen. But the sounds on the roof receded slightly and, peering cautiously through the crack between the door and the wall of the lift-shaft, she realised that the invective had been aimed not at her but at another figure who was being bundled unceremoniously across the roof with head and arms swathed in a black plastic bin-bag by two men.

Suddenly breathless, Laura leaned back against the wall and tried to think clearly, the roof-top tableau imprinted on her mind in all its horror. The heavier of the two men she recognised. It was the caretaker Jerry Hurst. The muffled figure between them she could not identify for certain, except that it was young and female and could quite possibly be Paul Miller's younger daughter Kelly. The other men was tall, young and powerful and, she knew from her own brushes with him, very frightening indeed.

We're on the top floor, she thought frantically, trying to stave off the panic that threatened to engulf her as the implications of the girl's plight sank in. She glanced through the door again as Kelly, if it was Kelly, was dumped roughly on the floor on the far side of the roof. If the girl was conscious, or even alive, she gave no sign of it. She lay limply near the parapet, the black plastic pulled tight across her face, and Laura thought desperately of how easy it must be to suffocate within that clammy embrace, as Nicky must have suffocated.

She had almost decided to push open the door and fling herself across the open roof-space in an effort to save the girl, when the hairs on the back of her neck prickled as she realised that someone had crept up the stairs and was standing just behind her in the gloom.

'Christ, you gave me a shock,' she breathed as she turned and recognised Carl Tyson, thin and gawky and clenching and unclenching his hands in frustration as he peered over her shoulder.

'Who is it?' he asked.

241

'Never mind,' Laura said. 'You go and find the police, quickly. I'll stay here and try to distract them somehow. Go on – quick!' She pushed the boy back down the stairs and, to her relief, he went, just as silently in his soft trainers as he had arrived.

Easing the door open a fraction more she could see, if she craned her neck, the backs of the two men who now appeared to be leaning into a large galvanised tank adjacent to the head of the lift-shaft. As she watched Hurst gave a muffled grunt of satisfaction and withdrew a dripping holdall. Apparently satisfied, they dropped the bag and walked deliberately back towards where the girl had been dumped.

'Is she dead? It doesn't take long to suffocate in one of them things,' she heard Hurst ask and the other man crouched down and lifted the girl's wrist where it protruded from the plastic and felt for a pulse.

'You should know,' the other voice said with a chilling acceptance of Jerry's experience in the matter. 'But not this time. She's still alive.' He dropped her limp wrist onto the ground. 'Just unconscious. She'll never know what hit her.'

It took Laura a moment to absorb the horrific implication of that remark, by which time Hurst had unfastened the bond around the girl's arms and pulled the plastic bag away. She lay sprawled on the tarmac, her face pale, her head lolling to one side, so limp that Laura found it hard to believe the other man's conviction that she was still alive.

'Right then,' the tall man said, close enough for Laura to smell him – not the stale odour that Jerry Hurst carried with him but the fresh tang of some expensive aftershave she half recognised. 'Over the edge with her, and then we're away. It's the perfect distraction. They'll all be running round the back so no one will even notice us nipping out the front way. You can see the Escort from here, look, on the other side of the road, next to the white VW. The blue one. That's mine. Come on. Let's do it.'

Hurst took hold of the girl under the armpits and began to drag her across the roof towards the parapet. Almost mesmerised by horror Laura knew that she must do something but just as she pushed the door fully open and took a deep breath she was knocked to one side by Carl Tyson, who had come silently up the stairs behind her again. Behind him she could hear the blessed sound of heavy running footfalls.

'The pigs are here,' Carl said, but did not wait for an answer. As the two men hesitated with Kelly's body suspended between them the boy hurled himself at them with an eldritch shriek of rage. Head down, he took Jerry Hurst in the midriff, knocking him off balance, and for a long moment of slow motion clarity the two of them teetered on the edge of the roof before Carl broke free and gave Hurst a final shove. They briefly glimpsed the big man's face contorted with fear before he disappeared, with a despairing scream, arms flailing, the black plastic bag, which had been caught up in the struggle, swooping behind him like a vengeful crow.

The other man, even in shock, was more controlled, and now much more circumspect. Pushing the unconscious girl aside and ignoring Carl, who was now kneeling against the parapet looking down at his victim a hundred feet below, his shoulders shaking uncontrollably, he turned swiftly, picked up the holdall and headed towards the top of the stairs to meet Laura face to face and behind her the half dozen uniformed police officers who had pounded up the stairs some way behind the boy and now spilled out onto the roof. They were closely followed by Thackeray and Sergeant Mower. The scuffle was brief and one-sided before Laura heard the handcuffs close.

Thackeray put a hand on Laura's shoulder.

'Are you all right?' he asked. He was breathing heavily and a nerve throbbed at the side of his jaw. She managed a reassuring smile.

'I'm fine,' she said a shade uncertainly. 'You got here very quickly with the cavalry.'

'I was already on my way when the boy waylaid us. Sue Raban had given us a pretty good idea of what's been going on.'

'Well, good for Sue,' Laura said faintly. She glanced at Carl Tyson, who slowly turned away from the edge, his face drained, his eyes staring and his lower lip unsteady.

'It's all right now, Carl,' Laura said. 'It's over now.'

'He were the bugger who killed my little sister,' the boy said as if he still could not take in what had happened so quickly on the roof's edge. He slumped down on the floor beside Kelly, whose eyes were already flickering open in response to the ministrations of a couple of the police officers. This thing had begun with the death of a little sister, Laura thought, and looked as though it would end the same way.

'Hurst?' Thackeray asked, scanning the windswept roof. Laura glanced at the parapet and shuddered.

'You didn't realise?' she asked, swallowing hard. 'He went over the edge. Which was what they had in mind for Kelly.' As the full enormity of events began to sink in she buried her head in her hands, not wanting Thackeray to see the belated panic which threatened to overwhelm her.

Thackeray's face hardened and he turned towards the prisoner who stood watching impassively, his hands handcuffed behind his back. For a moment the two men faced each other in silence and Laura saw Thackeray's fists clench and unclench at his sides.

'Don't, Michael,' she said so softly that she was not even sure he could hear her, and the moment passed so quickly that she thought later she might have imagined it. Mower came up to them with the holdall, now open. He lifted out several small packets, carefully wrapped in plastic to keep out the water.

'Enough of the hard stuff to keep him in Sierras for a lifetime, guv,' he said. 'Cocaine, E's . . . Could that be why we found damn all when we searched the squatted flats? He'd collected it all up and hidden it up here. Plus . . .' He rooted around in the bag again. 'Plus car keys . . .' Mower jangled them at the prisoner. 'A couple of portable phones, a couple of balaclavas . . . you name it. Everything he didn't want us to find when we searched down below.'

The prisoner watched in silence as Mower carefully laid

out the evidence on the floor at his feet. Only when the sergeant pulled out the very last exhibit did he show any sign of emotion and then it was to give a low murmur of anger as a pair of pink and white training shoes emerged.

'Nicky's?' Mower asked, unable to keep the satisfaction from his voice. Carl gave an audible moan of distress at that, and Laura moved closer to him and put an arm round his bony shoulders, feeling the uncontrollable trembling beneath the thin tee-shirt.

'That's down to Jerry,' Sissons said. 'You can't hang that on me.'

'We'll see,' Thackeray said, his voice under control now. Sissons stared impassively at Thackeray, as he was cautioned, only the glittering eyes indicating his fury.

'Get him out of here quickly, Sergeant. If the locals find out about the connection with Nicky Tyson, they'll have him. I'll follow you down.'

Thackeray turned back to the boy and Laura as ambulancemen put Kelly on a stretcher and carried her away.

'You'll have to come to the station with us,' he said to Carl gently. He beckoned to one of the uniformed officers at the far side of the roof. 'Take the lad down to his mother and then see they both get down to the nick,' he said. Carl offered no objection and walked dispiritedly to the staircase, shoulders slumped and long thin arms dangling, with the constable close behind him.

'Was it deliberate?' Thackeray asked. 'Did he push him?' Laura shrugged.

'I'm not sure,' she said.

'And if you were, would you tell me?' he asked, trying to read her pale, closed face.

'It all happened too quickly,' she said, avoiding the question. 'If I were you I wouldn't strive too officiously with Carl. You might get a conviction but you wouldn't get justice.'

Thackeray put a hand lightly against her cheek and looked at her sombrely for a moment.

'You have a genius for finding trouble,' he said. 'It frightens me.'

'I only came to do an interview,' she said, trying to look as innocent as she decently could. 'I've got a tape of Paul Miller that you'll find very interesting. Jerry Hurst blackmailed him into giving evidence against Stephen Webster.'

'We were going to issue a picture of Hurst to the media,' Thackeray said. 'The fibres on Nicky Tyson's clothes match the carpet in his flat. Plus a single hair from a ginger cat. We had him.'

'So it was him, not the other man – Sissons, did you call him?'

'Oh, yes, I think so. Sissons was covering up for him, but I doubt if he was actually involved in Nicky's murder. Darren Sullivan, of course, is another matter. He'll have questions to answer on that one.'

'And Tracy Miller?'

'I imagine Tracy was the first child Hurst attacked,' Thackeray said. 'Long before Sissons came on the scene. If Miller is withdrawing his statement, that just makes it more certain. They found animal hairs on Tracy's body too, but of course the place is over-run with dogs and cats so no one thought too much of it at the time. Something else which wasn't regarded as particularly significant. Huddleston was happy with Stephen's confession. Didn't think it worth pursuing the girlfriend or looking hard at the forensic evidence. Sloppy, but not criminal. We'll have to live with that.'

'And do you think Huddleston pressured him?' Laura persisted, knowing that was the question Thackeray would not want to answer.

'I shouldn't think we'll ever be able to prove that one way or the other. He'll never admit it and none of his lads will shop him. In Sicily they call it "omerta". Here it's just The Job.'

Thackeray glanced over the parapet at the crowd which surrounded the spot where Hurst had landed, close to the rubbish chute and the dustbins where he had dumped Tracy Miller's body all those years before, and there was no compassion in his eyes.

'I'd be lying if I said I was sorry he was dead,' he said.

'You'd like to have seen him hang?'

Thackeray shrugged.

'No, of course not,' he said. 'If they'd hung Stephen Webster where would we be? Even so . . .'

'You got the bastard who did it,' she said. 'Isn't that enough?'

'Maybe,' he said.

He watched as another ambulance arrived and made its way through the crowd below towards Hurst's sprawled, crumpled body before he turned away from the parapet, looking drained rather than triumphant, and put his arm round her.

'Come on, I want a statement from you as well, and then I suppose you'd better get back to your office as you seem to have got yourself another story.'

'With a bit of luck Ted Grant will buy me a vodka and tonic tonight,' she said, without much satisfaction. 'I'll be hackette of the month after this.'

The message from David Mendelson had been on her desk when she eventually returned to the Gazette. Vicky had gone into premature labour, it said. She called police headquarters to let Michael Thackeray know. It had been at the Mendelsons' that she had first met him, and she knew he would be concerned.

As soon as she was free she drove to the maternity wing of the Infirmary in a state of high anxiety, only to be met in reception by Vicky's father-in-law Victor, his eyes bright with tears that were evidently provoked by good news not bad.

'It's a girl,' he said cheerfully. 'Six pounds and three weeks early. Go up, go up, they're both fine. Gave us all a fright, but they're both fine. I'm going home to tell Mama all about it.'

Laura raced up the stairs and found David Mendelson, the two small Mendelson boys and Michael Thackeray in attendance on a smiling Vicky, who was sitting up in bed holding her new-born daughter in her arms. Her face, already radiant, lit up even more when she saw Laura.

'Take her,' she said, handing the tightly wrapped bundle to her friend. 'This is Naomi Laura and just to make it quite perfect it looks as though she might have red hair.'

Laura held the child close. Her tiny face was screwed up, as if she was concentrating on the serious business of sleep, the almost transparent eyelids flickering in the bright sunshine from the window as though she had not yet quite got used to the light of the world. Laura bent her head, her hair falling in copper strands around the paler copper down on the baby's head, and she kissed her very gently.

'That's a wonderful present,' she said to Vicky. Bright with happiness, she turned to look for Thackeray, but as he had watched her take the child in her arms he had turned away and walked out of the ward without a word.